M31

A FAMILY ROMANCE

Also by Stephen Wright

MEDITATIONS IN GREEN

STEPHEN WRIGHT

M31

A FAMILY ROMANCE

HARMONY BOOKS
New York

Publisher's Note: This is a work of fiction. The characters, incidents, and dialogues are products of the author's imagination and are not to be construed as real. Any resemblance to actual events or persons, living or dead, is entirely coincidental.

Copyright © 1988 by Stephen Wright

All rights reserved. No part of this book may be reproduced or transmitted in any form or by any means, electronic or mechanical, including photocopying, recording, or by any information storage and retrieval system, without permission in writing from the publisher.
Published by Harmony Books, a division of Crown Publishers, Inc., 225 Park Avenue South, New York, New York 10003, and represented in Canada by the Canadian MANDA Group.
HARMONY and colophon are trademarks of Crown Publishers, Inc.
Manufactured in the United States of America

Library of Congress Cataloging-in-Publication Data
Wright, Stephen, 1946–
    M31, a family romance.
    I. Title.
PS3573.R5433M18   1988   813'.54   88-900
ISBN 0-517-56869-1
10 9 8 7 6 5 4 3 2 1

First Edition

To Nort and Andy

M31

A FAMILY ROMANCE

"IS THIS SOMETHING?"

"What?"

"That."

"That? That there?"

Their green faces hovered balloonlike over the warm radar screen. The antique equipment popped and fizzed.

"The big blobby thing."

"Move your finger."

"Look, it's moving."

"Where?"

"It's getting bigger."

"This?"

"It's miles and miles."

"This here?"

"What is that?"

"You tell me."

"I don't know."

"Say it."

"The mother ship?"

"Come to carry us home, yeah, and all the people who ever died, and all their luggage, too, are there smiling and waving and chewing on cotton candy."

Edsel's mouth clapped shut as suddenly as a ventriloquist's dummy's and he swung around in his seat, propped his skinny elbows in front of the screen, and leaned forward with exaggerated intent, hands clamped over his ears, scuffed sneakers dangling above the sloping floor, I hate you, I hate you, I hate you.

"Thunderstorms, herbert, remember? Fucking thunderstorms."

Tiny arms turned in the shining ovals of his eyes.

Dallas moved his lips in close, hissing wet obscenities into the back of his brother's small freckled hand. Then he pushed himself away from the table, the folding wooden chair scraping across bare boards, collapsing in an explosive slap as he stood up. His profile, the broken nose, the ECT hair, was silhouetted against a stained-glass scene of quaint kneeling figures in Friar Tuck robes lifting flat, badly proportioned eyes to a burning in a violet sky. Dallas stared down at the back of Edsel's skull, an ostrich egg pasted with dry pale hair. "Okay," he said. He stared down at the thin bunched shoulders. "Knock yourself out. I'm going to see about Poly." The screen was making a sound like tires on fresh asphalt.

Silently his bare feet descended the narrow spiral staircase from the choir loft to a floor pockmarked by clusters of screwholes and worn into a pattern distinct and gridlike. In the center of this long open room, between the facing rows of high uncurtained windows, sat an ellipsoidal metallic construction bigger than a diving bell and obviously bolted together over time by various hands employing available material, zinc plate, roof tin, brass sheeting, and other junkyard scrap. From its patchwork interior came the rustle of female voices:

"The light?"

"Yes."

"Bright and heavy, it's been like that a lot lately."

"So when my eyes came open I could see him clearly standing there bare-assed and gripping the windowsill and gaping up at the moon like he was about to turn into something awful. Scared the shit out of me. His skin was so weird.

It looked like the moon and his body were made out of the same stuff."

"He used to sleepwalk almost every night when he was a kid. Sometimes Father would tie him down to the bed."

"I don't think he was asleep."

"Yeah?"

"His tube was on."

Dallas stepped behind a plasterboard partition where something was bubbling in a pot on the stove. He got a can of beer from the wheezing refrigerator and padded quietly back into the other room, his attention ambushed for a moment by the soundless television set in the corner where a woman's angry face alternated with a man's angry face in an apartment full of plants and designer furniture. He popped the tab on the beer can. "I heard that," said one of the female voices. Maryse. Her head was stuffed with kapok. He slipped quickly out the open door into the failing afternoon. A wind was beginning to stir the stalks of corn in the fields falling away under the anvil of a summer thunderhead. The sun, already buried beneath the advancing storm, continued to rise out of the stone steps under his feet in soft steady waves; it pulsed in the iron railing under his hand. He looked down. Feet. Funny word, funny parts: they were too narrow or too long or too far away. Veins slithered over them like squiggly blue worms. Everything either stayed the same too long or turned into something else too fast. A place was many places all at once. This corn was also pink and the sky a polyurethane glitter above the flashing steel wires stretched taut and parallel out into the plastic bridge horizon and his feet? . . . his feet were fins. He was already there: where they all wanted to be.

He shuffled out into the middle of a scraggly patch of lawn, blades of spiky crabgrass tickling his ankles, and stood there, scratching at his navel and drinking in the dramatic atmospherics, the long drafts of cold beer. Moving in from the west was a plow of high clouds as dark as the earth it seemed to be overturning. Fissures of white opened and closed across its shifting surface. The wind made him aware of the shape of his face and drove the savory smell of warm shit deep into his nostrils. God, he loved the country. Off to the east, where plows run up against concrete, Dash and Dot were walking the same streets, eating the same food, breathing the same air! as Vic and the Vectors. He was here. Here. He tilted his head and let the beer drain down his throat, then, rearing back, heaved the empty can clattering down the gray gravel road. Behind him loomed the church, solid black from foundation to steeple where revolved the small dish antenna, a black angular shape as flat in appearance as a shadow cast from something unseen in the distant sky.

Around back in the old cemetery he found Poly, as he knew he would, munching on her favorite delicacy—graveyard grass. "C'mon Poly, let's go," his hand raising puffs of dust on her bony rump. The goat edged away, wide eyes, busy mouth. Headstones, tilted, chipped, and broken, were strewn about like loose teeth, names and dates blurring away into the discolored mossy stone. All Dallas knew was these people had all been dead a long time. Overhead the thick heavy branches of the cemetery tree began to sway, the leaves to flick back and forth like magician's cards. Around the base of the trunk he found an aerosol can of red paint. He shook it noisily, tested the nozzle in the air, and, bending over, wrote across

ALPHEUS PAGE

1821–1872

On April 3rd His Sun Did Set

Where Oh Where Is Pa Now At?

the letters BOF. Similar scrawls decorated other graves: BULLOCKS, OI, RHINO. "Hey"—he aimed the can at the goat—"wanna be an Irish setter?" Poly chewed on, oblivious. Dallas bounced the can off the tree. He hooked his fingers under the dog collar on Poly's neck and tugged her resisting bleating body around to the front door—the air now charged with ozone—and up the steps and into the church, brittle hooves exploding across the floor like firecrackers.

[4]

A woman's head popped like a jack-in-the-box out of the top of the metal egg, "What the hell!" in a shriek known to younger brothers everywhere. Trinity. His sister. Once when she was four and a beautiful Princess living in a Magic Tower, a nasty goblin left outside the castle door a basket of tears and bad smells that Mommy and Daddy actually believed was cute, and for many more nights than there were fingers and toes to count to she had wished on the star outside her window that in the morning when she awoke baby would still be sleeping and would go on sleeping forever and ever. She had no memory of this at all. She had black hair and gray eyes and wore fire-engine-red lipstick day and night, a slash of color as unexpected out here as a Porsche in a beanfield.

"It's gonna rain," Dallas said. On the television set the same pair of faces was now pressed together in an action clearly involving the use of both tongues.

"I don't care if it's gonna shit bricks."

He was fascinated by her beetle lips preparing to fly away home.

"What have you been told about that animal in the house?" It was not a question.

"Blah-blah-blah. Maryse," he called. "Hey, Maryse." Anger was a cloud twisting up.

Out popped a second head too wasted to pass for a puppet of any kind, the only coloring on her face the velvety bruise-tinged half-moon under each eye.

"Hey, Maryse, I remembered that dream."

"I don't want to hear about it." Lanky hair was tucked behind protruding ears.

"You and I, see, were on this street—no, it was this bare room, only I wasn't there, I was on night shift at the pork plant and—"

"I really don't want to hear this, Dallas."

"There were other bodies in there with you in the dark, but you were the only one who wasn't—"

"Get that goddamn beast out of here!" Trinity shouted.

Poly was eating one of the photographs off the wall, me-

[5]

thodically pulling into her mouth a glossy image of an unfo-
cused hubcap sailing out over the scraggly tips of a couple
pine.

"And then somehow I was there and we found a broken
light bulb and squatted in a corner, sharing, first you bit, then
me, you, me, you, me."

Trinity's head sank from sight, leaving Maryse and her
eight white fingers gripping the rim of the hatch like something growing out of a jar. She emerged from around back,
moving briskly and brandishing a plastic fly swatter. Dallas
reached out an arm. "Leave her alone." The swatter slapped
against the side of his head. At the sound Poly darted through
the space between the partitioning boards and into the
kitchen, hooves clicking on the linoleum. "Stay here," Trinity
ordered, going in after her. Dallas heard a shout, a crack, a
brief interlude of frantic tap dancing, a bang, a crash, a curse,
before an accelerating mass of fur and legs exited the kitchen
at a velocity and an angle too late for him to do anything but
try to protect his head with his arms as the force of a rolled-
up rug whacked into his ribs, dropping his dead weight to the
boards behind the stubby tail of a frightened goat flying
through the open doorway like a gazelle.

"You okay?" asked Trinity, bending down over Dallas's
fish-on-dry-land routine.

"Knocked," he gasped, cheeks going in and out, "the wind
. . . out . . . of me." In between his own sounds he thought he
could hear laughter from inside the egg.

"I think you might have been unconscious there for a second or two," said Trinity. She was wiping at a huge blotch of
spaghetti sauce on her shirt with a blue sponge.

"It's as big as a house," announced Edsel, short tanned
arms dangling over the railing above their heads. "What's
going on? Dallas was saying bad words before."

"Jesus." Of course, the stain kept growing the harder she
rubbed, that was a law. "Might as well be running a full-time
daycare in here, too, try to turn a profit on all this damn brat
tending. Tell you this, next time Mother and Father hit the

road they can take you two along, help polish Zoe's football helmet or something. Because if I liked policework, I would have become a nun. How many beers have you had today, anyway?"

The stars overhead still refused to make sense. If his father had had any specific constellations in mind when he painted them up there on the ceiling, he hadn't told anyone. Upside down the silent mouths on TV opened and closed like cyclopes' eyes with teeth. "Fuck you," Dallas mumbled.

"See," proclaimed Edsel, disappearing behind the rail.

"Babies." Squatting, Trinity began to pick up the chewed bits of photograph. "This family should be driven around in a van and displayed at pro-abortion rallies."

Dallas rolled onto his side, searching along the floor for something loose to throw when his eyes flicked instinctively toward the door. Two white faces hung there like lanterns between the frame, watching. The man's smile gleamed from a tentative beardlike growth resembling stringy black mold, the woman's was metallic and fixed by rubber bands. Behind them the sky slid by thick as molten rock.

"I should number the cans," Trinity was saying, her back to the room, "and start rationing it out one can at a time like they did on the USS Dewey Dell or the Rat Fink or whatever the hell it was that Father"—and turning—"oh."

"Hi," said the man in an affable radio voice, arm half-lifted in shy greeting. "I'm Beale. This is Gwen." Gwen's smile broadened on a glitter of orthodontia and extended rubber bands that seemed to connect her jaw to the rest of her head. "She's a five-time contactee." Her dimples were deep enough to stick raisins into.

"Hi," said Trinity, cupped hand held stiffly at her waist. She caught Dallas's eye, and in an instant: These are goofs.

Grade A Prime.

Let's run 'em out.

Let's play.

Beale poked his shaggy head in and surveyed the interior with a paying tourist's avid curiosity. "Ohmigod," he ex-

[7]

pack of cards. Gwen's legs were poised in a crouch before the
faded map of Sharpsburg, Maryland, tacked to the opposite
wall amid a riot of newspaper clippings, magazine pages,
Crayola renditions of Hollywood spaceships and carrot-
shaped monsters, and dozens of amateur photographs depicting the miracle of flight. Blue veins crawled over the backs of
Dallas's hands. On television everyone ran around in gauze
masks.

"These pictures," declared Beale. "Some of them are the
actual originals."

"From the actual actuality," explained Trinity.

The wind began turning the door on its hinges, then
abruptly hurled it shut. "Let's get these windows closed,"
said Trinity. Dallas looked at his sister and belched. "Get the
herbert to do it." Methodically he laid out a game of solitaire.

Gwen ran her fingers through her unwashed hair, and it
stood up just like Dallas's after he had fussed with it for about
an hour. "Is there a john?"

"In back." Trinity pointed to a wooden door. She watched
her brother watching Gwen walk.

"I guess Dash and Dot aren't here at the moment," said
Beale, tilting his head toward the walled-off altar end of the
room.

"No," said Trinity.

"They out speaking or something?" thoughtfully stroking
the clump of black moss hanging off the end of his chin.

"Yes."

"Well, do you by any chance happen to know—"

"Tomorrow."

"Tomorrow," he repeated, bony fingers busily stroking.

Dallas rapped the side of the deck sharply against the edge
of the table.

"Well, we'd sure like to meet them if you wouldn't mind."

"Thought you already did," said Dallas, engrossed in the
lengthening columns of alternating black and red.

"No, no, we were just in the audience, in Yellow Springs,
big audience, just listening."

In the john, which was a cramped stall with an elevated water tank and a stained toilet bolted to a wooden platform, Gwen splashed some funny-tasting water on her face and looked into her eyes in the speckled mirror, her eyes, the ones she looked out of, and then it was too late, the questions started their routine, and, hands riveted to the electrified sink, she went into the black holes: who is this guy? where are we? why are we here? who's that boy? when will he try to rape me? how do I get out? why did I come? who am I when I say who? She finally managed to pull herself off the mirror, the part that goes before you and clings to things, peeled it off the glass and slumped on the stool, studying some hands, and feeling for several long minutes presences other than her own using her eyes.

"You can throw your sleeping bags on the floor," said Trinity.

"Long as it's no imposition." Beale pulled his beard into a stiff point. "Gwen'll be thrilled. We've followed your parents all over the country, Buffalo, Albuquerque, Fort Smith, like a couple of groupies actually, but of course they're more important than any rock star, as I'm sure their own daughter knows, look here." He knelt down, unfastened the straps, and lifted the flap on a backpack stuffed, jammed, bursting with paper. "I've read all their work. Everything still extant, that is." He began filling his long arms—inches longer than the frayed sleeves of his unseasonably warm shirt—with books, magazines, pamphlets, newsletters, handbills, her parents having appropriated every print medium except cocktail napkins and matchbook covers. "The load gets heavy now and then, but sometimes words are more important than food."

In celebration of the thirst for knowledge, Dallas wandered back out to the kitchen. Pop!

"I don't believe I've ever seen this one," said Trinity, reaching for an off-center two-tone cover proclaiming *News From Etheria*.

"I've read it three times," offered Beale enthusiastically. "Everything's invisible and going on in perfect freedom right among us and the sky is all the time filled with these gigantic creatures shaped like amoebas that are floating around propelled by this weird energy and beaming down instructions."

"Yeah, we've seen 'em," interrupted Dallas, coming through the door, the open can held brazenly in his fist.

"You have?"

"More than once. First time Dad tried to communicate with them, second time he started taking shots."

"Wasn't that the other way around?" said Trinity. This book was a mess.

"No, the mirrors were in Circleville."

"The tubes and pipes up on that little hill?" The printing job was typical; lines of fat overinked blotches thinned into readable words that usually managed to keep their shape for a couple paragraphs before wasting away into pale, barely visible suggestions of legibility. A column of jagged type slanting left leaned up against a column slanting right.

"Benton, right. That was later."

"Who cares? I was gone a lot then." Published just two years previously, the volume was not aging well; light had already established around the edges of each page that ugly brown border that crept irredeemably—the clock was always ticking—toward the shrinking white nebula at the center of every cheap book. Everywhere the fire Father raved about.

Gwen emerged from the john, the pink of her scrubbed face now matching her eyes.

"It's cool," Beale assured her. "We can stay until Dash and Dot get back."

"This felt like a good place," Gwen declared.

"We were talking about Etheria. They've actually seen The Occupants."

"A glimpse," admitted Trinity.

"I rode in one," said Gwen calmly, as if announcing the time of day.

In between the sheets of static rested the woman from the beginning of the show with tubes up her nose and after she said something to the man a smiling nurse came in and gave her an injection on the television set.

"It's covering the whole screen!" shouted Edsel in a breathless soprano.

The windows had darkened dramatically. Clouds boiled behind the glass like chemicals in solution. Cool air poured in around the warped frames. The tasseled corn dipped and tossed. Outside everything was streaming, and as they watched, it was as though they were moving, too, passengers at the rail, slipping away from the last solid pier. Then lightning broke the flow into pieces, and all their faces went dead, featureless moons of calcified white, silenced in a moment echoing with thunder, beaded with fear.

"Imagine us," said Beale brightly, "lost out there in that."

"Wet," commented Trinity, and led their visitors away from these exposed windows back into the kitchen and the dinner to be mopped up and the dinner to be prepared.

Dallas stayed behind, watching the gray hull of the storm pass majestically overhead, waiting for the spiral hoses to come dangling down and vacuum up specimens off the planet floor. But swiftly the sky smoothed its threatening ridges and suspicious bumps into a low flat innocuous ceiling, and he turned away, agile fins sneaking soundlessly across the empty room, to the musty bundle of Beale's pack, stealthy fingers at the insides: the collected heap of Dash and Dot, a dark green T-shirt wadded about a cracked transistor radio, a crushed blue baseball cap missing its insignia, several aluminum packets of freeze-dried hiking snacks, a small vial of either perfume or vanilla extract, another plaid shirt, a pair of weathered bib overalls, and then a quick look over his shoulder and in plunged the arm up past the elbow into this cozy private darkness and a ball of roughness probably wool, probably socks; elastic bands of . . . underwear no doubt; the pliant coil of a leather belt; a round metal can of shoe polish? of chewing tobacco? something in cellophane; something long and plastic; something, something . . . up sprang his arm into astonished air, the trembling hand attached—custom-fitted, actually—to the trite reality, the phallic heft, the lethal delight of a chrome-plated Saturday Night Special.

When the hail hit the roof it was like a chattering of insects.

THAT NIGHT BEDS WERE TOO hard, beds were too soft, sheets scratched, covers oppressed, and the dark grew luminous with possibility. Sleep, when it came at last, settled over them like a thin rag.

Dallas was stretched out on top of his mattress, arms locked at his sides, as stiff as a patient posing for X-rays. Wind from a cracked window streamed over his body, toes to scalp. He was thinking of rubber gloves with hands inside. The moon, full, clear, freshly scrubbed, dwindled to a dim bulb, weak on batteries, behind the robed figures of colored glass he had named Larry, Moe, and Curly. Black water slid down the wall, dripped from the plugged eaves outside. The round eye of the radar screen was shut. Suddenly he sat up, the gun gripped in both hands, fanning the air in the general direction of the wheezes and snorts that were his brother dreaming of puddles and bricks and shadows with claws. Bam! Bam, bam, bam. The crickets made sounds like screws twisting into dry wood. He fell back into a sleeper's pose, trusting, vulnerable; he jerked upright, fully armed. Practice: the sign of the professional. He wanted to glide, to be mechanical, he wanted to be *it*. He pressed the gun up under his nostrils, breathed in the dark, secret aroma. He worked his little finger up the barrel and let the weapon dangle off his hand, a strange growth he wouldn't allow any doctor to touch, the coming of the new. Later, he tiptoed down the spiral staircase and crept naked among the slumbering bodies, white as a bone. He hovered over a pair sheltering in the rounded shadow of The Object. A bunch of frizzy hair stuck out of the top of one of the down bags. He moved in closer, blood booming in his ears. His hand went out in front of him, the automatic deployment of a reaching device. The approaching surface, sleek in the lunar light, was all humps and folds, a material of uniform texture. Weightless, he dropped dreamily through warm space as the planets sighed, a forest of fiberglass trembled. "Under the table," mumbled Beale, shifting in his sleep and unknowingly aborting a nearby docking procedure. Dallas disappeared into the kitchen, grabbed a couple beers, and, clutching a can in each fist, a balanced set of weights, stepped out the back door into wet grass and patches of mud that squeezed up cool and sticky between his toes. In the deserted cemetery he found a low benchsized stone and sat down, the cold raised letters HANNAH printing themselves in mirror image across one cheek of his pimply butt. He popped a beer, drained all twelve ounces in one long chug, head tilted back to that tremendous night sky, his father's sky, where the stars burned like lights in a grand hotel and every light was a window and every window a room and every room a VACANCY, twinkle, twinkle. He finished the second beer as the cemetery tree deposited something raw and liquid down his knobby spine. The stars were swarming now inside a gentle expansion that was always like a costume to him. He assumed a soldier's stance upon the convexity of earth marking HANNAH POTTER's exit from the space-time continuum, cocked his arm, and heaved the imaginary grenade off into the gray corn. He hunted through the weeds along the iron fence until he found some Krylon Red. Then, settling back onto the monument, TOꟼ impressing itself into the other cheek, and humming the theme from the old *Bonanza* television show, he began carefully spraying first one foot, then the other, with successive layers of cool, tickling paint. When he was finished he hopped up on top of the marble, squatted there motionless under the night's fluorescence, an alien toad.

In the morning everyone woke up and knew at once exactly who they were.

In the kitchen in the daylight everything seemed projected on a screen. Three of them sat at a wobbly linoleum table over cups and bowls of amazingly bright plastic. Cold noodles dangled in squiggles and loops from the dishes stacked in architecturally unsound piles on the counter beside the sink. The white enamel was stained and chipped. On the wall opposite the stove and the scorched pot hung a random arrangement of fish-shaped Jell-O molds and a large black-and-white chart showing the commercial and retail cuts of beef, veal, lamb, and pork. Bottle-green flies as big as bees patrolled the air corridors between the table and the counter and the empty 9-Lives cans scattered around the sticky floor. The refrigerator was decorated with a colorful array of little magnets designed to look like pieces of real food. Gwen accepted each disquieting detail with an oddly composed eye. This was a room concocted of images masquerading as objects, and it induced in her a not unpleasant reverie, simultaneously familiar and unreal, the expectation of something "remembered." She could wait with whatever patience was required. A black-encrusted ketchup bottle the size of a water jug occupied the center of the table with the ludicrously apt authority of a piece of pop art.

"You don't have to eat any of this," said Trinity, pushing away her bowl. "I never do." The oatmeal resembled shredded cardboard.

"But I like it," Beale declared enthusiastically, raising a dripping spoonful mouthward. "I grew up on this stuff."

Trinity glanced at him and lit a cigarette. Her knuckles were large and red as a maid's. Blue arabesques of smoke drifted against her expressionless face.

Gwen shifted in her chair. The fumes made her as queasy

as the wall clock, a black ceramic cat with a dangling tail that switched in time with the second hand. She had hardly uttered a syllable to anyone since rolling up her sleeping bag and locking herself in the bathroom with the faucets roaring and her head swooning over the splattered stool as bits of undigested spaghetti were flushed briskly away. Then she went out to crouch on the steps, chin on her knees, studying the damp earth and the freshly baptized pebbles and the astonishingly wide spectrum of green generated along a single blade of grass, ignoring Beale and his fussiness until Trinity called them in. Now all she wanted to do was face the open window and the sweet air and the fluttering corn and the distance; had she ever before been confronted at a greasy breakfast table by so much distance? Or so much flatness? Or so much strangeness? The freak quotient here was exceptionally high. Sensations were beginning to align themselves in ways that suggested a ship might be drawing near and extensive travel was imminent. And, of course, a ship was near, a rather obvious one sitting on the floor in the next room. Outside the window the goat was gnawing vigorously on the rind of an old golf ball. The little boy came into view, pedaling a silver dirt bike down the gravel road, tiny rump bobbing furiously from side to side. "This is a far place," she said at last, turning around. She could see blue pieces of fallen sky in the flooded landscape of her oatmeal. "I feel . . . bubbular."

"Bubbular?" asked Beale, lifting his eyebrows and holding the smirk for Trinity to see.

"Like a goddamn bubble, you know what I mean." You rotten creep. "Where's that kid going?"

"I think," said Beale, spacing the words like separate bricks, "the road has flattened all of us out."

Smoke jetted from Trinity's nostrils in audible irritation. She wished the road didn't always run by her house. These early morning conversations with her parents' groupies made her feel as if she'd been inhaling her own exhaust for hours. She tossed the cigarette hissing into a cobalt-blue cup of cold tea. She guessed it was her turn to speak. "Travel can be tedious," she said.

"But not for The Occupants, of course," replied Beale.

"No, of course not."

"It's practically instantaneous."

"Yes."

"Biomorphosis, you know." Droplets of milk clung to the spidery hairs on his upper lip. Trinity lit a second cigarette. Gwen hunched over in a spasm of theatrical coughing. Fuck you.

Maryse came through the door, a log-sized bundle of gray towels hugged to her chest. "Hi, hi." She put the towels on the counter and felt the teapot with her finger before twisting on the gas. Overnight the mouse under each eye seemed to have sprouted fur. Her wrists weren't any wider than two of Beale's fingers. She looked at Trinity and took a deep breath. "So," she said.

"We're tired," said Trinity.

"Of course. When you move around it takes a while for the dreams to find you again."

Beale watched Trinity smoke. He tried not to stare, but she performed the act with such languid flair he thought for the first time about taking it up himself. When she exhaled, a cloud of secrets from the dank interior hung shifting and turning in the light, a living organism. Lipstick clung to the filter like flakes of dried blood.

The bundle of towels began to stir. Gwen wasn't actually seeing this. It twitched again. "What is that?"

Maryse laughed, exposing an enormous number of big gray teeth. "Mignon," she said.

"Mignon? As in filet?"

"As in my kid." She picked up the bundle and placed it in Gwen's lap.

"Oh," said Gwen, folding back the towels. It *was* a baby, an infant of unexpected qualities. Its head appeared to have been shaped by clumsy hands from a ball of soft cheese, asymmetrical, lumpy, and hairless but for a cap of moldy white fuzz at the crown. The dull black eyes were as animated as a pair of marbles. Tiny transparent fingers were glued into tiny fragile fists. Gwen tickled it under the chin, and it made a sudden sharp sound like the squawk of a bird. "How old is this child?" she asked.

"Ten months."

"Kinda runty for ten months, isn't she?"

"She is a he."

"Oh, I'm sorry."

"All of mine have been small."

"You have more?"

"They aren't here."

"Oh."

Maryse took a can of Weightlesse from a shelf stocked with similar cans. She opened it and poured half the chalky tan liquid into a jelly glass and half into a baby bottle. She screwed on the bottle cap, pulled up a chair next to Gwen, and held out her arms for the child.

"You feed him that?"

"Same thing I eat." She inserted the rubber nipple between the baby's colorless lips. After a prolonged pause the tiny jaw muscles commenced a faint nursing action that reminded Gwen of looming close-ups in educational films about the private lives of insects. The movement faltered and stopped.

"You think there's enough nourishment in that for a baby?" asked Gwen.

"Here"—thrusting the label under her face—"it's got everything you need."

Gwen read slowly, trying not to mispronounce: "Cupric sulphate . . . pyridoxine hydrochloride . . ."

"Those are just the scientific names for vitamins and other stuff that's good for you."

"You're not even a little bit fat."

"Of course not, I drink this." Maryse smiled, held up the

glass, and tossed back the sludgelike contents with stylish gusto. It was a commercial moment.

"But that's why your baby is so small."

"Maybe she doesn't want it to grow up," said Trinity.

"Oh," said Gwen. She looked at her oatmeal. The milk had turned brown. Overhead the light was dark with flyspecks.

"All right," Maryse declared in a peremptory voice. She deposited the baby in the empty sink and began to pour steaming water into a mustard yellow cup. "Who can remember last night's dreams?"

"Somebody die?" asked Dallas, sauntering through the door in a pair of fashionably torn jeans. He yanked open the refrigerator and a watermelon magnet flew off the door and bounced against the wall. "Bingo," he said. He rooted around inside the cluttered refrigerator and finally emerged with the last of the Rolling Rock.

"I like your feet," Trinity commented.

"Thanks." He shuffled off into the other room. On the television set a pleasant farmer in a smart blue cap was dumping a jug of chalky solution into a spray tank mounted behind a tractor. Cartoon cutworms burst into vanishing exclamation marks. Dallas went upstairs and slumped in front of the radar screen. He drank the beer and flicked the toggle switch back and forth. He liked watching the sudden glow, the slow fade, as the alcohol wound through his head. The blip he wanted to see had already been picked up by the state police moving at a commendably legal pace it couldn't exceed if it wanted to and, having putt-putted past the three two-storied blocks of Albert, was at this moment bearing down in a more-or-less straight line right at the nougat of the buzzy cocoon in which he sat, ball joints rattling, transmission rumbling, air screaming through the cracked vents, the football helmet bouncing around the backseat, the child's arm stretched out the rear window and lifting into the wall of wind like a wing.

"There is an ocean of dreams," Maryse was explaining, "that our sleeping heads dip back into late at night. The tides go in and out, cleansing the shore. Who we are is whatever silhouettes against that great sea. It is deep and vast and strong, and even in the clearest moment of the brightest day something is leaking in, a permanent trickle in the plumbing. Sometimes, in some of us, things collapse, but now the moment is approaching when the wave will break to carry us all away. This will happen. Consider the signs. Learn how to float."

"But what's all this got to do with UFOs?" asked Beale.

"They're the openings the dreams come through." The flesh of her face, no thicker than the skin on a pot of boiled milk, had become temporarily vitalized by the ardor of her argument. A gaudy dot of color appeared on the point of each cheek like a pasted-on decal. She resembled a terminal case in brief remission.

During the lecture, Trinity played with her food. Wielding a spoon as delicately as a surgical instrument, she hunched over her bowl, carving out of oatmeal an elaborate spiral trench.

Brooding Gwen had refused to offer up a sample of her nightwork for Maryse's presumptuous inspection. Quiet presences framed by the window continued to occupy her attention, the big leafy tree, the small shaggy graveyard, the serried heads bobbing in unseen decay on the turning tide.

"It's a gift," added Maryse, sipping from her cup. Her hands were long and thin; there was a gold band on the ring finger. "I try to share it as best I can."

Trinity braced her palms against the edge of the table, leaned over, lips pursed, and allowed a gob of spit to fall into the bowl, a mound of bubbles foaming at the milky center of an oatmeal spiral. She smiled all around. "I think it's just what it needed," she said.

The blue Bug came off the road in fourth gear, gravel spewing, muffler banging, bounced across the uneven lawn, and jerked to a halt atop a grassless patch of oil and cinders outside the kitchen window. There was a pause, the anticipation of a comic interval, a sudden geyser of radiator steam, popping headlights, exploding tires, the disgorgement of a hundred clowns. But nothing happened, the car sat there, engine continuing to tap out its uncertain, arrhythmic beat. The robin's-egg-blue body was pitted with rust, from angry freckles to thick fuzzy scabs; the rear fender was crushed; the hubcaps lost, stolen, misplaced by careless mechanics; the antenna bent; one window replaced by a wrinkled sheet of plastic; and inside, the heat was jammed in the on position. The dented door on the passenger side swung open, and a child of indeterminate gender, wearing a silver football helmet, squeezed out of the backseat and bolted for the corner of the house, hands flapping erratically from outstretched arms, adult-sized mouth emitting an avian shriek that seemed to tear a jagged diagonal across the pastoral fabric. The child's name was Zoe. The wipers flipped on, the lights flashed, the horn honked, the engine died. Movement carried on within the car, half-glimpsed shapes plotting behind the windshield glare where the sky burned clear as ice and a toy plane in the form of a cross etched a white furrow across the curved glass.

At last the driver's door creaked open, and out climbed a man to pose for a moment against the corroded metal, broad hand resting atop the dimpled roof, a pair of black sunglasses turned toward the house, scanning brick and board, window and door, on up to the pyramid of a steeple and the motionless dish at its tip, then glancing off the sharply defined roof edge and into the blinding blue. A tall man in a black turtleneck and black pants, a black figure contemplating a black structure. When the woman got out she was wearing a hospital gown and turquoise cowboy boots.

Trinity hurried out to greet her parents.

The football helmet dashed past the kitchen window, the scream peaking and echoing away as it began its second revolution of the house.

"I guess she's glad to be home," mumbled Beale.

Gwen chewed on the raw pink nub of her thumbnail. The car, the kid, the man, the woman. Even the light was momentous this morning, startlingly three-dimensional, solid as a column plunged slantwise through the wall. Out of the sink, like the pale wavering tendril of a sun-starved plant, a human limb lifted itself tentatively into view, fluttered for an instant in the vertiginous air, and dropped abruptly from sight. Warm fur moved against Gwen's leg and she leaped, yelping, from her chair as an orange cat scurried away, claws clicking on the tile, to the snug sanctuary of its hairball collection beneath the leaky refrigerator.

"How do you do, sir?" exclaimed Beale in the whiny adenoidal manner he affected before whatever authority he hadn't yet cajoled a favor out of: a dull observation once absorbed osmotically and only now passing into Gwen's melancholy awareness. "It's been a great honor for both of us." He wound stray wisps of beard about his nervous fingers.

Shaking Dash's hand was like squeezing a sponge. A disconcerting impression. Gwen waited for him to ask a personal question she wouldn't seem to know. Quick now, how many times had she vaulted the stars in the hollow of a golden ball? He peered at her over the tops of his glasses as though there were a piece of orange pulp stuck in her braces. Yes, this was what it was like when The Occupants threw down a beam, your helpless nerves surfaced in an indecent frenzy of embarrassment and confusion. Of course, he was smaller than she'd remembered. Off the podium everyone shrank. Then she was noticing all kinds of fascinating details memory had never had a chance to know, magnified specifics particularly about the eyes, in a glimpse she saw that they were exceptionally large and a complicated gray, the color of old driftwood, grainy and varnished; there were wrinkles around them, nothing serious, a shallow grid lightly traced in time's permanent cosmetic, and under them, maturity's sad pouches set among a broad scattering of youthful freckles, and in them, deep and clear and distant, what size was she? She smiled and muttered something dumb. The Object blazed like a bell in the bright raking light. The room smelled of attic dust and cracked hymnals baking in an early summer sun.

"The kids been treating you square?" Dash asked. Unamplified, the voice was barely recognizable, so flat, so disembodied. Gwen watched the mouth move and heard the words arrive after a slight delay as if the man had been poorly dubbed. With his military bearing, his uniform, his dark glasses, he looked like the director of a school for assassins.

Beale was beaming, unashamedly, all liquid eyes and sleek teeth. "It's been a positive delight. Spending the night, I mean, in this house, under The Object. We are in awe."

Each being was a point and each point pulsed and there were these concentric waves piling up in the corners because where there is not enough space there is only noise. Everyone was made of blood. Bodies shifted into predestined orbits in accordance with the laws of gravitation. The room reeled. Gwen sidled over behind Beale. Black ovals tracked her every move. She was going to faint, she wasn't going to faint, she was, she wasn't. Echoes, ghost images, surges in voltage, was something approaching, something actually growing near, a real moving object to contend with, a "working" ship?

"Newton, Tennessee," Dash was repeating, head inclined in a thoughtful attitude, master to pupil, "don't believe I know that one."

Beale eagerly explained the origins, the convoluted and pathetic geography of their trek. Dash's hair was short and brown and graying on the edges as it thinned out from the middle.

"The Kenneth Arnold Symposium, too?"

"All five days. We were in the third row, over to the right, between the ex–Air Force guys and the druids."

"That *was* fun, wasn't it?"

"I have a tape."

Under the hospital gown Dot was dressed in her famous white outfit. She had a rural face, angular hardworking features, ruddy outdoorsy complexion, and when she spoke the occasional stranger was sometimes surprised by the expensive caps and the careful, dramatically modulated tones of a commentator at a fashion show. "All our people journey such vast distances," she said, and hurried out to the kitchen.

"So how was the trip?" asked Trinity, who had welcomed her father with a kiss on the mouth that persisted several beats past the allotted time for daughterly devotion.

"Psychopaths and pornographers," boomed the father. "Who left the goddamn set on?" The television was throwing jittery light across his dark chest. Ray decided to risk half his fourteen hundred dollars on the next spin of the wheel. The category was Famous Mining Disasters. Dash switched the channel.

Drawers slammed, cupboards banged, dishes clinked, utensils rattled. Dot returned from the kitchen displaying a mason jar full of either ammonia or soapy water in which floated blobs of a leafy wrinkled gray. "Maryse tells me you're pregnant," she stated breezily. "Dash, honey, would you mind?"

Dash took the jar between his large hands and twisted. Jason and Jennifer were lingering over their fettucine as they discussed in urgent stilted voices Harold's emotional constipation and what Melanie could possibly have done with the missing inheritance money.

"Why, no," said Gwen, searching the disorganized features of Beale's face for signs of support, "no, I'm not at all, I really don't know where she got that idea."

The lid came open with a wet pop.

"It's nothing to be ashamed of." Dot held the jar under her twitching nostrils.

"But I'm not ashamed." Her face pleaded with Beale; he wore the goofy smile that indicated he was no longer in attendance.

"That's all right, dear," said Dot. She turned to her daughter. "Where's Edsel?"

"Over at the MacGuffin twins'." Trinity was bouncing a

piece of tektite from palm to palm with a deft self-satisfied coordination.

"Well, call them up and tell him we're home."

"He's probably not there anymore."

"Why not?"

"They might have gone someplace else after."

"I don't suppose you bothered to find out where that someplace might be."

"Where the hell you think they went, the choices being so multitudinous and all?"

"I'm your mother, remember."

"They're at the stupid mall, where else they gonna be?"

Maryse crossed the room, stepping gingerly as a fawn among the brambles and the flames. She crawled into The Object without a word, her progress monitored by big black glasses.

"I know no one else in this family but me is going to take the trouble to find out," declared Dot. "God knows where Edsel's been and what he's seen and what he's done."

"I didn't notice anyone chaining him to a tree when you guys pulled out of here two weeks ago."

"All right," said Dash. Jason and Jennifer decided to attend Jeff's wedding. Glenn's cancer began to eat his stomach.

"This is what I came home to?" Drops of suspicious gray liquid fell from the gesturing jar in starburst patterns across the floor.

"Apparently so."

"Why doesn't someone get me a drink?" asked Dash. "Trinity, honey, why don't you fetch your dad a nice cold beer?" Gwen and Beale, silent as children, pretended to look out the tall windows that reminded Gwen of distant classrooms. A light wind dizzy with pollen and manure was pushing huge clumps of cloud across an empty blue stage. Raggedy shadows swooped in over the rolling fields. Inside, the room went from light to dark and back again as if the equipment were being tested for a performance later that night. "She loves to wait on her old man."

[27]

"There isn't any."

"Isn't any what?"

"There isn't any beer to get."

"What about the cases under the sink and the six-pack in the refrigerator?"

"See for yourself."

"Why is it every time I step out the door all the alcohol in the house instantly evaporates?"

"Beats me, maybe some kind of mysterious chemical reaction."

"Where's Dallas?"

Trinity shrugged her shoulders. Her mother dipped a finger into the swirling murk and tasted the contents of the jar with a bland thoughtful expression. Dash turned to face the choir loft. "Dallas, you up there? Dallas!"

There was no response.

"Maybe he went to work," said Trinity.

"Does he work today?"

"I don't know, what day is it?"

"Jesus Christ."

"Shouldn't someone check on Zoe?" said Dot. "I don't hear her anymore."

They paused and listened to the silence.

"She's probably crawled under the house again," said Trinity.

"Well, why don't you go drag her out," suggested Dash.

Dot screwed the lid back on and, sloshing jar in hand, headed for the closed door in the wall where the communion rail must have been. "I'll be in our room."

"How many of us does it take to screw in a light bulb?" Trinity asked the guests. "I'll be back in a moment with the answer." She exited through the front door.

Dash eased himself down onto a rickety piece of aluminum tubing and synthetic webbing. He leaned back, the impenetrable lenses of his glasses filling with cloud and streaming sky. "Chicago," he said. All eyes turned. "Chicago was u-foria." Yellow animal excrement was wedged into the tread

[28]

of his nylon-cord soles. "Look at those lips." Distorted TV faces slid around each other like globules of oil in vinegar. "I saw that pair in the same clinch ten years ago in the dayroom at Allendale. Ten years. There's fire for you." His laughter was dry and artificial, something frozen in a lab for future consumption.

Up in the loft Dallas poured the last drops from the last can onto his extended tongue and wondered if the gun in his hand was the same make his father packed with spit-shined boots and a whistle when he was an MP in Berlin back in the first great end-of-the-world days. The Germans shot defectors with stubby machine guns and pulled the corpses off the wire like deer carcasses with thick lengths of canvas rope. They were Communists. He rolled onto his side, pointed the barrel at the floor.

In the mechanical method of immobilization, the pistol is placed against the forehead of the hog and the charge of a blank cartridge propels the captive bolt into the skull.

"OF COURSE, YOU'RE STAYING for dinner."

Dallas's solitaire table had been pulled from the wall, lengthened, tableclothed, and carelessly set for eight, the afternoon light collected in points and puddles on the hard glaze of things, the mismatched china, the dented silver. In the center of the table was a pile of papery leaves and a damp twig skewering the ivory ring of an old hambone—treasures Zoe had rescued from the dank crawl space underneath the house. Zoe had black frantic eyes that avoided contact, and when Trinity tried to drag her over to meet the nice company she growled and scratched at her sister with the soft nubs of her bitten nails. Now she sat on the hardwood floor, wrapped in a fraying blanket, gaze inturned, rocking back and forth in ceaseless desperate rhythm as if the body were a hinge on a swinging door to nowhere. Gwen felt like a monster.

The boy, Edsel, returned from the mall alone, cheeks flushed, sweat running out of his hair, one nostril crusted with blood from which a brown trickle disappeared down into his mouth.

"I got 28,210 on Cosmic Creatures," he cried. He was wearing a black T-shirt with a silver motto: LIFE'S A BEACH.

Dot seized his shoulder and drew him toward her. "Were

you riding on that elevator again?" she demanded, tilting his chin. "After all the times I've told you."

He shook off her grip and headed back out the door. "Where's Poly?" he asked. No one knew.

In the crabgrass outside Dash and Beale sat elbow to elbow on identical web loungers behind scepters of iced tea, chatting away like deck passengers on a liner bound to ports of coconuts and ease. But it was only their minds that voyaged as the lengthening shadow line of the house turned toward them certain as a minute hand and the stone dice of the cemetery locked in midtumble under the sieved shelter of the old tree. They talked and talked, and their conversation was of matters primal and architectonic, astral and eschatological.

"Look at a piece of wood," offered Dash. "What do you see?"

"Knots?"

"There's a galaxy in the whorl of the grain."

"Why, of course," piped Beale immediately in junior scientist dawn-of-wonder tones.

"Seashells and wood screws, water spouts and pinecones. Spinning maple seeds. The secret is in the shape."

Gwen slipped back inside where Maryse asked her how old she was and apparently finding the answer unsatisfactory turned away without a word and crawled back into The Object, banging the hatch behind her.

Voices from the kitchen kept going in and out of hearing all afternoon like soap opera dialogue on a too distant channel, so when the line "Wipe away the smirk, young lady, I won't have that in this house" arrived loud and clear, answered by "You'll have it any way I give it to you," Gwen peeked around the open doorway to glimpse mother and daughter facing each other over a table heaped with sliced peppers and diced onions, paring knives poised.

Gwen retreated to stand before a wall of high windows. She looked out, she counted the panes, she looked out at the road. A dust as fine and white as spilled pesticide powdered the summer weeds along the shoulder and the folded leaves of corn behind the wire in the adjoining field. The crowded tassels drooped like jesters' caps, and the stainless sky in the plunging fall of its descent was as sheer and pure as the face of a freshly split gem. All she could see was road, corn, and sky, and none of it had an end. Behind her the floor creaked on under Zoe's relentless rocking. Gwen had her hand on the bathroom door when Beale came up from behind, hissing insanely at her ear, "What's wrong with you? You're screwing up everything royal."

She stood there with the door angled between them. "Let's go."

"Go?"

"I want to leave."

"We just got here."

"His eyes. They're like black holes."

"You're jealous."

She stepped inside, locked the door, and paused, hand at the latch, head cocked like a wary bird's. When she could no longer hear the distinctive shuffle of Beale's boots, she turned, and out of this cramped space lunged a form, dark and nameless, and she choked back a scream. It was her own startled reflection. She covered the mirror with a musty towel and sat down on the cracked stool. She could cry at any moment now if she wanted to. The wood under her feet was warped and spongy and emitting a harsh stablelike reek. A fat fly bumped along up the wall, a furious buzz searching for a way out. Under the sink was a wicker basket stuffed with old wrinkled magazines she had never heard of. It was twilight in here, hidden from the sun and all its commotion, her only company the cave movement of unseen things dripping, gurgling, sighing away in long cool subterranean rushes. In any home this always seemed to be her special room. Someone came and rattled the door.

"You still in there?" It was Beale's voice.

She refused to answer.

"If you're not out by the time I get back, I'm coming in

anyway." He paused. "Dash says I know more about his work than his own kids do." He paused. "Gwen?"

After he left she filled the sink with cold water and plunged in her face. She counted methodically to ten and straightened up, gasping, water snaking in transparent veins down her neck—a ritual performed whenever she happened to begin worrying about her worry lines. She dried herself off, and as she stepped out of the bathroom she heard Beale's laugh, loud as sunlight, erupting through the open windows, lancing through the solid walls. It sounded like someone twisting a balloon.

So when Dallas reappeared from wherever he skulked she said yes to going for beer, yes to his smile and the danger at the corners of it. The interior of the car smelled of rotten fruit, and the floor was deep in empty soda bottles and fast-food wrappers. She arranged herself quietly on the sprung seat with a formal deliberation. "Bye," called Beale from his lawn chair. At this distance he resembled Charlie Brown. Gwen watched whatever presented itself in her half of the windshield without expression or gesture in the manner of famous felons being escorted to the state pen, even as the spinning tires slapped grass divots off the side of the house and the creaking car veered a corner, mounted a bank of crackling weeds, and burst, fishtailing, onto a narrow county road of potholes and loose gravel. Stones banged against the bottom of the frame. Her head bumped into the roof. Dallas turned toward her a display of smirking lips. She ignored him, watching the white inverted V of the road opening endlessly on. Dust coiled out behind like a tail of chemical smoke. Goodbye, she said to the receding scene, a passenger again on another machine careening through space. They exchanged no more than a few syllables all the way in to Albert. Spokes of corn strobed past in hypnotic green succession. The sky was a clear bowl a million miles deep. She counted off the utility poles and imagined them tumbling behind like matchsticks as the wire dipped and climbed, dipped and climbed, over ground as flat as a table on out to the edges where voices drown, the familiar rhythms reasserting themselves all too easily now and everything had already been seen and felt and the road merged into The Road: truck exhaust and sticky clothes and pavement glare and humid nights and cramped seats and perverts with b.o. and clogged toilets and greasy milk and piles of metal and glass buckled and splintered from sea to shining sea, temporary roadside shrines spontaneously erected in daily numbers duly noted and recorded as sacrifice to the spirit of good motoring that kept America on wheels. At night the revolving lights of red, white, and blue clustered about these sites like the fires of ancient Indian encampments where human flesh in unexpected poses seemed to leap out of the dark, naked and monstrous as those blind sea creatures who exist at levels beyond the reach of light. Gwen remembered the Blue Man who came to earth between a runaway Mustang and a wet oak somewhere west of Columbus when an eddy of time caught up and juggled some muscles and neurons, some tires and pistons, into a pattern too intricate to endure. As the Mustang left the rain-slick road, bouncing between an out-of-control Pontiac, a skidding Mayflower van, and a stubbornly immobile bridge abutment, the door snapped open and the driver, already unconscious, started to fall, slipping sideways out of the car until the tree stepped forward, slamming the door shut across his waist, where he remained to be pinned in the glare of the ambulance lights, head the size of a pumpkin, hair stiffened into bloody clumps, an upper torso glued to the side of a Ford. If she wasn't blown up first, Gwen was convinced she'd die in a car crash, her dreams had told her so. What had the Blue Man's dreams told him? His skin was the color of the interior of The Occupants' ship.

The road was running through her now, filling her insides with outside, warping inner distance so that all points recognizable and safe expanded away from one another, deforming her sense of self into something strange, as alien and rampant as the country outside. Like the corn, for instance. The corn was winking at her, a bright spangling of light. It had stood out here for so long the paint was wearing away, revealing the shiny metal underneath. There were no shadows any- where. She needed a pair of those wraparound sunglasses with the mirrored lenses.

Dallas steered with one elbow poking out the window, the other arm, tanned and muscular, draped over the wheel. He grunted constantly, shifting restlessly in his seat as if the car were an organic thing susceptible to urgings of the flesh. Gwen almost said something to him, but she changed her mind. Suddenly the VW hopped a bump, and for no apparent reason the road changed into a length of smooth asphalt over which the sloping blue snout of the car glided like the head of a vacuum cleaner. Gwen turned her face into the cooling wind. A white farmhouse floated by, big and clean, on a big clean patch of lawn, its porch wide and deeply shaded, the big picture window opening, she imagined, into refrigerated rooms of mahogany furniture and porcelain animals as the reflected image of the car zipped across the glass. Off in the distance a large green spidery machine under no apparent human supervision trundled over a plowed field, doing some- thing funny to the dirt. She hadn't seen another person out- side her window since leaving the house. It was an abandoned landscape out here in the heart of the country where all the food came from, and disquieting events seemed about to transpire on their own—the sort of place one sped through without stopping. The road went abruptly back to gravel, and the frame began to chatter. Gwen had counted eighty-six poles.

"This scenery hurts my eyes," she said to the window.

"Yeah," said Dallas to the back of her head, "wait 'til you see what it does when you've been out here long as us."

At the corner of her eye his arm on the rattling wheel was scored by a crosshatching of cuts, random, razor thin, that excited her in a troubling way. A yellow butterfly exploded against the windshield, one shredded wing struggling to rise from a gooey star. A black 61 inside a white circle rushed at her and was gone—a highway marker planted in a clump of

[35]

thistle. A little bearded man was peering inquisitively out of the top of each ear of corn. She wasn't even sure what state she was in.

At the first intersection with stop signs there were the first trees, the cement blockhouse of a 7-Eleven, and a Shell station without any pumps. Dallas screeched into the lot at an angle, cutting across two parking spaces. Gwen waited in the car, reading the misspelled sale signs in the store window. She felt like a runaway delinquent on a cross-country crime spree with her sociopathic boyfriend. A thin man in a zippered jumpsuit stepped from the shadows of the Shell garage to stand bow-legged, staring at her as he wiped his smudged fists on an oily rag. Then he began a series of maneuvers too strangely fascinating to ignore. He opened the zipper on his right thigh, tucked the rag in the pocket, and closed it. He opened the zipper on his left arm, removed what appeared to be a pocket calculator. He punched some buttons, examined the result, replaced the calculator, and closed the zipper. He was still staring at her. He opened the zipper on his chest, extracted a black box the size of a cigarette pack, held it to his mouth as his lips moved in a furtive whisper, replaced the box, closed his zippers, and ambled back into the garage. She couldn't see Dallas anywhere inside the store. She leaned over, tried the horn, but nothing happened. A hard-used pickup banged mufflerless into the sun-scorched lot, its cab crammed with an impossible number of adolescent boys in knee-high black rubber boots and bloodstained pants, who paraded past her, key rings jingling at every waist, eyes roving boldly over hers, their very skin seemingly about to burst from the pressure of its fermented contents. Gwen knew the type: strands of pubic hair caught in every fly. One of them with head hair combed sleek and black as the wing of a crow, half a cigarette tucked behind a freckled ear, came to pose in the window, punching at a video game machine with his hips. Dallas backed out the door with four cases of beer. He was smiling.

"Who were those guys?"

"More saucer people." He jerked the stick into reverse and skidded out backwards at high speed. "Hell, you've probably already met 'em on your various travels."

Gravel spat out behind them. Gwen said nothing. At the stop sign he popped open a can of beer and turned off onto a different road, recently resurfaced and bisecting infinite fields of the same monotonous corn. He chugged the can, wiped his mouth on the back of a hand, and flipped the empty over his shoulder onto the rear seat. Ahead of them the road ran straight and flat and empty, a runway to nowhere. He drove with one hand, sipped his second beer with the other. There was a blue bandanna knotted around his sunburned neck, and when he drank his eyes rolled up off the road and his Adam's apple hopped as if a creature crouched there in the warm well of his throat. She started counting the animal pancakes frying on the hot pavement. A big dark bird symbolic of something or other swooped in low over the stalks. Dallas leaned over, bare arm brushing the surface of her denimed thigh, and fiddled briefly with the radio knobs.

The sound hit her in the cheekbones. The tiny car speakers were buzzing like mutant wasps.

An iron ball on a long chain sailed into a wall of bricks— the moment as plain as if it were happening before her—and everything began to fall and fell continuously over intonations grave and German punctuated by hammers on anvils, shattering tubes, the held amplified note of a boys' choir, files on guitar strings, the voice of the president on a loop repeating, "Well . . . well . . . well . . . " in a long dead chime, bottles clattering over concrete, a quartet of chain saws, and the screeching of pterodactyls in a riotous stampede along a broken pulse to an unexpected precipice of silence in which one clear English voice recited harshly, "Twist my lemon, eat my head, crawl down the pipe, dead dead dead," and then the noise of collapse resumed.

"All right!" shouted Dallas. "Vic and the Vectors! They're great!"

It wasn't too bad, actually, it gave her head a tooled quality, of something clanky and inorganic, clumsily affixed to her body, and the sensation of momentarily straddling disparate kingdoms was not altogether unpleasant; she experienced a beat, a life, where logic claimed there was none: in the fracture, in the rust, in the crash, and all her control towers were quickly and thoroughly stormed. She shook her head (this new oxidized one) and slapped her hands in time against the dash.

Beneath Dallas's foot the accelerator pedal sank squeaking into the floor and they rocked and they rolled all the way down this long lonesome runway and the fields blurred into walls and the road was a wild thing loose as a snake and she was a sound and a force and she had no name and the world was a window and a mirror and the light was in the window and she was the rock hurling toward the pane. Then the tape stopped and the air went out of the car and the flatness out of the world.

"Vicious," declared Dallas. His hands with difficulty were maneuvering the vehicle back into the proper lane.

"Oh," she said. "Yeah." This was that vague area between now and not.

"It's the only way to really get into these guys. After their last concert at the Amphidome, they found black gunk oozing out of cracks in the foundation. The first two rows tore up their seats. A rent-a-cop had a heart attack."

"I wish I had been there."

"Me too."

She had lost some moments back there, scraps of time blown backward down the road like highway litter, and here she was simultaneously conducting a perfectly coherent conversation (wasn't it?) in the light and a bewildered search in the dark for something only she could find or even miss.

"Look," she said. Clouds from nowhere were getting up on top of one another in a mad pile-on out there at the end of the road. The blue had come hopelessly apart, spilling the stuffing white and suffocating down upon them. They'd be gagging on it in a few minutes.

"Yeah, we get that shit all the time around here."

"Amazing. Amazing skies."

"Thanks."

He lobbed another can over the seat where it joined the clanking chorus in back.

She looked out the window and suddenly all the corn was gone and they were running along an open field of cut grass behind coils of barbed wire and a double row of high chain-link fence hung with big red signs in important capital letters. Dallas switched off the key and they coasted over onto the shoulder, pebbles and sand crunching under the tires. When they finally stopped, a sheet of dust settled evenly over the car. Exhaust drifted forward through the open windows. Gwen could smell the shiny blacktop cooking in the after-noon heat. They sat there in the quiet, staring out stupidly like tourists on a bus. The sun was white. Dallas hooked his fingers through the cardboard beer case and glanced over at her. "Here we are."

"Where?"

He got out of the car.

Her door wouldn't work, the handle seemed smeared with butter. A long arm bristling with hair came through the win-dow. "You do it like this." The door popped open, she had no idea what he had done. The road was as sticky as freshly chewed gum. She followed him over to the opposite shoul-der, their bunched shadows slinking behind like strange mongrel dogs, down through a ditch of prickly weeds and up a low grassy bank, driving before them a swarm of gray grass-hoppers on papery wings. At the crest was a small circular space where the brush had been flattened by the weight of a large animal.

"Okay," said Dallas, pulling her down next to him. Only the tops of their heads were visible from the road where the VW sat abandoned and strangely foreign now, as though it belonged to someone else and was property of the fence. Gnats swirled over them like soot. The stems of brome sawed gently before their eyes. The back of Gwen's head felt

[39]

cupped by the sun, like a basketball palmed in a giant hand. Dallas opened another can.

"They're watching us," he announced.

She looked up into the steep empty sky.

He laughed, a contemptuous barking sound that entered her hearing like a knife.

"Who's 'they'?"

"Where the fuck you think we are?"

She shielded her eyes with one hand. "Where? What am I supposed to see? I've never been this close to farms in my life."

"Don't they grow shit in Tennessee?"

"I don't know. Ask Beale. I'm from San Jose."

"So what do they grow there?"

"Nothing."

His arm described a vague arc. "Welcome to something."

"There is a lot of it, isn't there?"

"Don't see much of anything else."

"So what are they growing behind the fence?"

"Mushrooms."

"In those little sheds?"

"Under 'em. Uncle likes to farm deep."

"Your uncle owns that?"

"Everybody's Uncle."

"Oh." She scanned the enclosure for signs of secrecy and menace. There were some telephone poles, some white storage tanks maybe, there was a blue truck. The silos bulged with warheads under the living camouflage of the gentle grass. The toy buildings reminded her of outdoor latrines at summer camp.

Dallas sat up and peeled off his sweaty T-shirt. There were long thin cuts across his chest, too.

"I come out here a lot," he said. "It's quiet, it's a good place to think."

"Gives me the creeps."

"Isn't that the point?"

"About what?"

"Thinking."

He popped open a can. "I hope it goes when I'm sitting here. No one would ever have seen that before."

She thought of the geysers at Yellowstone.

He finished that can and immediately opened another.

The road was a piece that connected to all other pieces. The keys were in his pocket.

"It's a strange country," he said, the beer beginning to muse through him.

"Yes," she replied. The light seemed to be getting brighter as the day died.

"Things shift."

"Yes," she agreed, not really sure what he meant.

"You can sit out here for hours looking at nothing in particular, zoning out, and suddenly fffft! everything shifts."

"Shifts?"

"Like driving a stick and shifting to another gear, colors, shapes, stuff like that, like two pieces of film are stuck in the projector at the same time."

"Oh."

"Yeah, I don't remember anything like this when we lived in the city, but out here it happens all the time." He sent a gob of spittle flying out into space where it broke apart into a glistening necklace of tiny translucent eggs clinging to the swaying columns of a few grass stems. "Fact is, this is an alien planet. Don't no one know it yet."

A rush of fear passed over her quick as a wind. But if he was one of them, would he be talking to her like this, occupying this form?

Then, as if he had read her mind, he said, "Shapes, you know, are just a different kind of music."

"Yes. That's fascinating. What does your father think about these interesting ideas?"

"My father is an asshole."

He studied the dark triangular opening in his beer can. When he looked up, there was more shine in his eyes than she wanted to see in the average rogue male.

[41]

"I like being drunk, know why? 'Cause it's like licking metal, and that's a radical feel."

"Give me one."

He moved the dripping cardboard case between them. "You ever go to work drunk?"

"I suppose I must have once or twice in my long career."

"All the knives going at once, that's all you see, and all the flashing like hypnotizes you or something and someone tells you to get moving and it's like you got to get across this room without getting cut."

"Is that what happened to your arms?"

"You ever go to school drunk? Puke in your locker, pass out in history. Everyone a zombie. I fell down the stairs once, eight stitches right here behind my ear."

His arm jerked out in front of her, and he opened his fist on a couple broken stems and one beige grasshopper drooling brown fluid on his fingers.

"Tobacco juice," said Dallas.

He held the insect by the abdomen and squeezed. The insides popped out the tail like pus from a pimple.

"Shouldn't we be getting back?" asked Gwen. The beer was tepid and backing up her throat.

"That herbert you came with."

"Beale?"

"He's a pud."

"What's that?"

"Something you don't need. What storm did he come in out of?"

"We met at a space show."

"Yeah, I know all about those. Like, show me some space."

"We're not exactly handcuffed together."

"Yeah, see his eyes crawling on my sister like nasty fingers."

"I like how clean clothes smell on his body."

"Screwing him must be like getting it on with The Occupants."

"Hardly. He's only got one tube."

Dallas barked. "Hey, not bad for a diskhead."

"Beale's much funnier than I am."

He pressed a fist to his stomach and forced a belch. All the beer he had drunk was condensing on his forehead and trickling down his cheeks. He turned to look at her. "On other planets," he said, "atomic explosions are a natural occurrence, and all the people eat chrome." The light burned. He unzipped his jeans and shoved them quickly to his knees. He wore no underwear. "Hey?" cried Gwen, scuttling away backwards on her hands. But it wasn't her he was reaching for. She looked and looked away. The band of bright flesh, untanned and prickly with hair. The beating of his blood in the naked sun. He eased himself back onto the ground. "Go ahead," he urged. "I won't look." "No," she declined softly, "that's . . ." Her voice faded away. And even when she wasn't watching, she was still aware of the unmistakable exertions of hand in lap as of someone attempting with mighty effort and limited success to catch a floppy fish without a net. She realized now why the fly on his shoulder hadn't moved. It was a tattoo. The loosened shadows of the advancing clouds came on in hectic silence, slipping seamlessly over their sprawled bodies, the black road, the dull roof of the car, the grass browning beyond the fence, and the invisible young men beneath it with their zippered uniforms and their earnest little keys. His legs stiffened and the air turned pink around her. He wiped himself off on the grass. "Looks like rain," she said.

They rode back in silence, unaccompanied by pterodactyls.

THE TABLE HAD ALL BUT DIS-
appeared beneath a Thanksgiving-sized spread of green food,
yellow food, white food, and brown—all the colors unnatu-
rally bright—in heaped and steaming platters and bowls
seemingly suspended together on an invisible plane, and still
Dot kept bustling in from the warm kitchen, mittened hands
full, and somehow, magically, a space was opened for yet one
more bubbling dish. When the jellied herring salad went
quivering by, Gwen experienced a dip in the room and settled gratefully onto the nearest firm chair. The boy, Edsel,
appeared before her, the corners of his thin mouth stained a
pale cherry red, sticky fingers curled possessively around the
plastic body of a man-shaped lizard in cape and jackboots. He
aimed a tiny reptilian fist at her face.

"She's in my seat."

"She's company," responded Dot, wiping her hands on the
spotted hospital gown. "Sit over here for today."

"No."

"For one day."

"I can't see TV from there." He pressed a button on the
toy's back and the fist sailed over Gwen's head.

"I'm sorry." Gwen pushed back her chair. "I didn't know."

"Don't you budge another inch. We'll just move the set."
Dot dragged the squeaking video trolley out into the center

[44]

of the room, angled it toward her son, and crouched over the knobs. "It's his favorite show." The picture bloomed and held. A dapper mustachioed man in a smoking jacket was declaiming in a broad theatrical manner. A thin long-haired woman stood listening before him, her evening gown too tight to accommodate sitting. A pair of strange-looking children ran up out of the basement. A monster perched on a bench playing a harpsicord. A disembodied hand emerged from a box with the day's mail. Lines of dialogue were shunted in and out between crashes of mirth from the laugh track. Maybe Gwen had seen the show once or twice; she couldn't recall the name.

"This is good, huh?" asked Edsel seriously.

Gwen smiled, nodding. She always agreed with children. The clear late afternoon light was of a quality that transformed the earlier day into something glimpsed behind smudged glass. Across the room The Object glowed with the warm good humor of a burnished distillery vat. Gwen could hear the pronounced reassuring tick of a large unseen clock. She closed her eyes and allowed herself to be drugged by the gentle weight of the light on her face. She could feel the movement of her insides, popping and trickling in total darkness. Secret recipes were being prepared in there.

Dash came in and stood at the head of the table, staring down without expression at either her or the comical woman shrieking out the door on television, she couldn't tell because of the sunglasses. She smiled and nodded. The skin of his face was drawn tight and thin as a surgeon's glove over the bone, and the top of his steely flat-cropped hair resembled the business end of a brush whose bristles, Gwen imagined, must be coarse and sharp.

Dot announced dinner, and Trinity led in Zoe by the hand, blinking and looking about like an imprisoned creature let briefly into the light while the cage was being cleaned. Dallas took the seat directly opposite Gwen, furtively adjusting himself under his clothes where the gun was tucked in his waistband. He saw how Gwen was looking at him, but he gave nothing back. Beale left the bathroom without washing his hands and squeezed in around the table to the empty chair beside Gwen. "This young man," said Dash, patting his shoulder as he went by, "once majored in physics and, not only that, claims he can play the trumpet, too."

"So what," said Dallas.

Dash looked at his son and waited. Seconds passed like drops from a slow leak. Dallas removed the cigarette dangling off his lip and flipped it backwards out the open window.

"Well, actually, to tell the truth, I never really finished," explained amiable Beale. "I dropped out my junior year."

"Some never even bother to drop in." Dot handed a package of paper napkins to Trinity. "Here, everybody take one and pass it on."

"He got a girl pregnant," said Gwen, as surprised as Beale to hear the words coming out of her mouth, "and had to leave town in the middle of the semester."

"But I came right back, yeah, I came back and everything was worked out okay."

"That kid," declared Maryse. She emerged from the interior of The Object wearing a dirty white turban on her head and a mass of handmade ceramic necklaces. "He's so quiet I spend half my time just checking to see if he's still alive."

"Wonder why," muttered Dallas, eying the tall glass of Weightlesse centered on her otherwise empty plate.

"Fuck you."

"All right," said Dot. "You know I won't stand for that sort of thing at the table."

"Or on it," added Trinity.

"A little company shows up, everybody gets excited and thinks they have to perform."

Gwen leaned her arm against the wobbly table and circles of milk went pitching and yawing inside the glasses and she laughed out loud. "I'm sorry," she said. "It's just that this reminds me so much of home." It was a Sunday afternoon, and she was a daughter again.

Zoe rocked back and forth in her chair, crooning softly over

[46]

her plate as if to raise the painted lilies there. The cords in her neck were as thin and taut as telephone cable.

"Shall we begin?" asked Dash. He bowed his head, folded his hands. So did the family. Gwen and Beale traded looks. Then everyone huddled together in silence, listening to television noise and the dozens of flies already swarming over every edible surface. Finally, Dash spoke: "From crab nebula to finny fishes, we thank You Whoever for these swell dishes."

Dallas snickered.

"A family joke," explained Trinity.

"What's the joke?" asked Dash.

Edsel began banging knife and fork on the table. "Let's eat!" he cried. Zoe dug into the mashed potatoes with her hands.

"I hope there's enough." Dot lifted a salad bowl heaped with green beans.

"Oh Mother," said Trinity. "She's so worried you're not going to get the complete Midwestern dining experience. Whatever that is."

There were traces of dried egg between the tines of Gwen's fork.

"There's enough here for all of Buchanan County," said Maryse. She was rationing out her meal in brief sips. The dark half-moons under each eye resembled the marks rubber soles make on a linoleum floor.

"It's good to be able to feed your guests," said Dash. Whenever he looked at Gwen she felt as if she were being scrutinized by the wrong end of a telescope.

Poly stuck her head through the window and made a sound like a squealing brake.

"The whole family together again," said Trinity.

"She looks sick," said Dot. "What's the matter with her eyes?"

Dallas bounced a muffin off the goat's nose and she disappeared.

"What's that?" asked Edsel, pointing.

[47]

"Swiss steak," answered his mother.

"I hate that."

"No, you don't."

"Yes, I do."

"Last time you cleaned your plate and begged for more."

"Is Swiss the same as Midwestern?"

"No, of course it isn't, what are you talking about?"

"I'm not eating any."

"Yes you are."

"No because you said."

"Yes, what did I say?"

"You said we were having Midwestern and this is Swiss and I'm not eating any."

"No, no, they just call it that, dear, Swiss steak, it doesn't mean the meat comes from there."

"We all know where the meat comes from," said Trinity in a stage whisper directed at her brother.

"Oh God," Maryse groaned, "if we have to endure this juvenile conversation one more time . . . Really, people are trying to eat."

"I wouldn't call what you do eating," said Dallas.

"Don't you tell me you—"

"Pass the gravy," said Dash, and everyone shut up. They stared at him in surprise, then turned to their plates as if discovering only now there was actual food in front of them to be eaten. The sound of the television sitcom was joined by the scraping of utensils, the creaking of chairs, the clinking of china. Gwen became uncomfortably aware of her own chewing, the physical act of it, the muscles, the juices, the warm inner night of animal life.

Zoe sucked gobs of chocolate pudding from her fingers.

"I think the potatoes might be a bit overdone," suggested Dot.

"Nonsense," replied her husband. "The potatoes are perfect."

"Jesus Christ," muttered Dallas.

"Load up on legumes, everyone." Dash displayed a steaming white chunk on the end of his fork. "Holy eggs of light tenderly laid in the nesting darkness of the earth." He plopped the piece into his mouth.

"You're supposed to eat one a day," Trinity explained. "Like apples."

"Ask any doctor," offered Dash, cheeks bulging.

Under the table Beale scribbled surreptitious notes in a pad he kept in his back pocket. There were words that should not be lost. "We haven't eaten this well in months," he said.

"Yes." Gwen dipped her head shyly as if to stoop beneath a low door. "Delicious." She had tried everything that was leaf or root or pod and had carefully carved the meat into ragged fragments she was arranging about her plate to suggest enthusiastic consumption. Even the vegetables seemed to have been fried in animal fat.

"You've outdone yourself, dear," said Dash. He still had not removed his sunglasses.

"Yeah, Mom, real good," chirped Trinity.

"Yeah, Mom, real good," repeated Zoe in tone-perfect mimicry. There were bits of chicken skin hanging in her hair. She let out a whoop and, leaning forward, overturned her Donald Duck drinking cup, splashing milk over half the table, one pearly drop clinging to her forehead like a caste mark. Without a word Dot picked up the curtain rod beside her chair and reached over and cracked the backs of her daughter's hands. Zoe's howl lasted about a minute, and then she subsided into an entranced silence, watching the particles of dust drift across the bar of light above the food like a heaven of stars.

On television a chubby bald man in a fur-collared gown inserted a bulb in his mouth and it went on. "Look at that, Dad," said Edsel.

Dash lifted the lid on the Styrofoam cooler he kept at his feet. "Who needs a beer?" He handed the dripping red-and-white cans around the table.

"Hey," protested Dallas. "What about me?"

"Yes, what about you?"

[49]

"I'm the one who made the run to Seven-Eleven."

"Yes. And you're the one who was the reason for said run."

"He's too young, anyway," Maryse declared. "Drinking the way he does. If Mignon ever grows up to carry on like that, I'll slap his face."

"Mignon," said Dallas, "will be lucky if he's ever able to sit up."

"Did it rain here?" asked Dot brightly. "It rained the whole time in Chicago."

"Did you have watches and warnings?" said Trinity. "We had watches and warnings all night."

"Cold front," said Dash, scooping up some lima beans. "Supposed to start getting hot again tomorrow."

"Yeah? I heard more rain."

"All right," cried Maryse. "Could we please for once talk about something other than the weather?"

"It's an interesting topic."

"If you're a farmer."

Edsel jumped in his seat. "Dallas kicked me under the table," he yelled.

"I did not."

"You did too."

"Did not."

"I don't care if that steak grows fur," said Dash. "You're going to sit there until it's gone. And turn down that damn television."

There were eyes of grease, clear as a cat's, lying flat and still on the surface of the gravy.

"I had a dream while you were gone," said Maryse.

"We don't want to hear it," said Dot, stirring her iced tea as if ringing a bell.

"Pass the ketchup," demanded Edsel.

"I saw your hotel room on fire."

Edsel spanked the bottom of the bottle, once, twice, and a red plug shot out onto his plate, releasing a flood that swiftly submerged one small outpost of Switzerland.

"There was a painting of a windmill over the bed. It was in flames."

Employing a butter knife, Edsel sawed away with clumsy intensity, the steak darting from him as if alive, pushing before it a thick tomatoey tide that broke over the rim of the plate in a long dripping arc across the tablecloth.

"Do you remember?" Dot asked.

"Sure," said Dash, "I always take careful note of every example of motel art."

"Then there was just a rectangle of fire, burning up into space."

Edsel managed to stay the meat long enough to detach a wieldy chunk that he was carefully maneuvering, trapped between fork and finger, toward his open mouth, when his mother seized his arm, twisting it over his protests to expose on the hairless underside of the elbow a weeping patch of raw skin cloved with grit.

"What happened here?" she demanded.

"I fell." The meat plopped back into the red sea.

"What do you mean you fell? Are you all right?"

"Sure, Mom." Now his spoon took up the chase, unsuccessfully pursuing the quarry about an obstacle course of untouched cauliflower.

"No one is listening to me," Maryse complained.

"That's right," agreed Dallas.

Edsel switched back to a fork and almost immediately speared his prey.

"Why didn't you clean this out? Do you want an infection? Where's your bicycle? How did this happen?"

He pulled the slippery lump off the fork with the ends of his teeth and began to chew, long, slow, thoughtful chews. "I don't know," he said.

Outside the windows, the land was as flat, as interesting, as the head of an anvil, and the shadows of the corn advanced like the rifle barrels of an approaching army. Something touched Gwen under the table. It was not the cat.

"Were you fooling around with those MacGuffins again?"

"I don't want to talk about it," he mumbled through a full mouth.

"He has a whole other life," commented Trinity.

He had already assumed his habitual pose, back to the living, face to the radiant screen—Dot more familiar with the hairs on his head than the freckles on his cheeks—when the points of his thin shoulders shot upward and his body convulsed for a moment in the exaggerated grip of the gag reflex. He raised his hand to his mouth and placed with deliberate neatness to the side of his plate a wet wad of gray, tooth-marked fiber. Calmly he turned to his mother. "I told you I didn't like it."

"My God," cried Maryse, "cover it with a napkin, please."

"I had a dream," said Dallas.

"You did not." She was arranging a wall of bowls between herself and the "thing" on the table.

"We were living in one of those big old houses with black turrets and funny curlicues hanging off the gutters and it was out in the woods someplace and it was always dark and outside behind all these jungle bushes were strange humanoid shapes with hoses for faces and big railroad gloves and I was the only one who knew but I couldn't tell whether they were trying to get in or trying to keep us from getting out."

Maryse made an elaborate show of lighting her cigarette. "Better luck next time, kid." The match dropped hissing into her chalky glass.

"Why does she get to smoke at the table?" asked Dallas.

Dash ignored his son. "Chicago," he said to Maryse. "The Great Fire. That's what you were seeing."

"Of course."

"Our adventures were not so dramatic."

"We were bumped," said Dot.

"Again?" asked Trinity.

"By Blascoe Gadgett."

"I've heard of him," said Beale, putting down his beer. "Isn't he the one—"

[52]

"Yes," said Dash. "Who impersonates famous men so he can go to bed with famous women and write famous books to be made into profitable movies starring these same famous women."

"He thought we were evangelists from Arkansas," said Dot. "Then Zoe tried to bite the lady with the clipboard."

"The place was crawling with dero," said Dash. "Everyone with Hollywood hair and button shark eyes."

"Dero?" Edsel's child's forehead crinkled up into adult worry lines. "Did they have guns?"

"No self-respecting robot could be fully detrimental without one," said Trinity.

"It's the echo they can't stand," said Dash. "Once she cranks up her echo we might as well edge toward the door. You know how television despises repetition."

"We should stick to radio," said Dot. "Where our friends are."

"Sure. And our ninety seconds in between processed cheese commercials. Like the baloney in the bun."

"That's terrible," said Gwen, genuinely shocked. She thought anyone who wanted to should be allowed on TV. She had been on once herself.

"We dwell in the shadow of the electronic sun."

At that moment the real sun, spent and ailing in its long passage, dropped into the slot of the middle window on the western wall, turning faces to jaundice all along the opposite side of the table. Figures on the television screen were bleached a dim protoplasmic gray. Beale shielded his eyes with an uplifted hand. Gwen squinted down into her beets. Trinity yanked a cord, and a tremendous curtain of black cloth fell with dramatic suddenness, cutting off the light like a blade. The room seemed to go from color to black and white.

"Can I light the candles?" asked Edsel.

"Eat your Swiss," said Dot.

As soon as Maryse got the first wick going, Zoe's hand moved out across the table. Dot tapped her rod against a chair leg and the hand withdrew.

[53]

"Okay," said Dash, rubbing his palms briskly together, cornbread crumbs sprinkling down on his sauerkraut, "now let's hear what everyone learned while we were away."

"Me," cried Edsel. "Me, me."

"He's been waiting all week for this," said Trinity.

"Okay, go."

"I learned about light."

"Yes?"

"It's fast, faster than anything, faster than bullets. If you turn on a light in a dark room and you're standing in the way, it could kill you. And time couldn't work without it or clocks, either. If you had twins and put one in a dark room the second it was born and kept it there where there wasn't even the tiniest crack, after a while the one outside would be an old man and the one in the room would still be a baby."

"It's true," said Trinity. "A fact of science."

"Who told you this?" Dash asked.

"Arnold did. He knows everything. He's in the sixth grade."

"Who the hell is Arnold?"

"One of the MacGuffin twins," said Dot.

"The one they kept in the dark?"

Edsel was the only one who didn't laugh. "Isn't that true about light?"

"Yes," said his father. "It's true."

"I have some facts," said Maryse. "Ever hear of the Iveys, the Ivey family of Mercator, Kansas? Ma and Pa and all the young 'uns and the cousins quote unquote and the animals in and out and on top of the little sod house in windy prairie nowhere. A wagon trail ran by the front door and today that's part of I-80. Travellers disappeared a lot in those days and nobody wondered much about it, hazards of the road and all. The last Ivey, a shriveled-up aunt who claimed to have slept with Buffalo Bill and said he had two navels, lived well into her nineties and died about the time of the stock market crash. They tore down the house for a gas station and found a root cellar full of human bones. Stacked up like firewood for a long winter. Neighbors weren't surprised, they'd been seeing things for years, certain members of the family they weren't supposed to see, mongoloids, dwarves, hairless monkeys, toads with fingers, lizards with pink skin. Inbred worse than royalty. Seems the Iveys lived by the philosophy 'Fuck one another and kill the strangers.' "

"How the West was won," said Trinity.

"The women stood behind parlor curtains and strangled visitors in their chairs with strips of braided rawhide. Strong women with strong arms from churning butter all day. They melted everything down in a shed out back."

"What's this goop?" asked Edsel.

"Cottage cheese," said Dot. "You like that."

"No, I don't."

"I learned," said Trinity, "the importance of consecrating my life anew to the principles of stringent contraception."

"Good thing I didn't believe that," said Dot.

"And what about you?" asked Dash, turning to his eldest son. "What did you learn?"

Dallas was picking his teeth with his fingernail. "Nothing," he said.

"Of course, nothing." Dash addressed the table. "Your major field of study for the last five years."

"Let's not start," said Dot.

"But I want to hear about the Lost Order, Dunker church, the Burnside Bridge, blood on the corn. I was looking forward to it."

Dallas sat silent.

"How about those weeds?" He might have been inquiring about a favorite football team.

"Yeah." Dallas poked at his mashed potatoes as if there were something dangerous under them.

"They finished yet, is what I want to know."

"Some."

"And how many exactly is that?"

"What it sounds like, I guess."

"In half a month you can't yank out a couple dozen sick weeds?"

"It ain't like that's all I got to do."

"No, no, of course not, I understand that, when you're not considering 'nothing' you might have to put down a beer can long enough for your hand to risk heat stroke."

"Let's try to enjoy our dinner," said Dot.

"Good luck," said Trinity.

The telephone began to ring and everyone froze in place. Dash glanced at his watch. "Are they still calling?"

"Every day," said Trinity.

"They know when you're at home eating dinner."

The phone made an old-fashioned clacking sound like a metal ball being shaken vigorously inside a wooden box.

"They're threatening to place a blemish on your permanent record."

"Hah. Debt is the engine that powers this country. We should be commended on the depth of our patriotism."

"I said you certainly did appreciate the gravity of the situation and would be getting back to them at your earliest convenience. They said you were shirking a moral obligation. They're trying to appeal to your ethical centers."

"Yes, well, did you also inform them that the hours at our centers have been drastically reduced?"

"Are we going to have to move again?" asked Edsel.

"No." Dash's voice was huge and firm. "Nobody's moving anywhere." He was cutting ham into boneless slivers he dropped one at a time to the complaining cat at his feet.

"But I like moving," said Dallas.

"But I like moving," said Zoe.

Gwen watched the sun struggling against the dark curtain and thought, This is the second dusk I've seen here, I don't want to see a third.

Finally the ringing stopped, a series of diminishing ghost echoes left hanging in the gray air.

"Gwen, dear," said Dot. "You've hardly touched your dinner."

Gwen stared wistfully down at her rearranged plate. "No, I'm sorry, I guess I wasn't very hungry."

"Hardly a surprise now, is it," said Dot. Gwen avoided her eye.

"But look how rude we've been," Dash exclaimed. "All this bickering has reduced our guests to silence."

"Not at all," said Beale. "This has been quite an education." The beer had begun to interfere with his note taking.

Dash was looking steadily at Gwen, smiling in a manner that seemed foreign to his facial muscles. "We'd like to hear your story," he said.

"My story?" She was suddenly aware of her voice as others must hear it, a thin tentative sound. She wanted to flee to the sanctity of the john, but Dot was watching her, too. "I don't have anything interesting to say."

"There's no such thing as an uninteresting contact," said Dot.

"It'll do you good," Beale urged. "You know that." He turned to Dash. "She keeps all this bottled up too tight."

"We understand," said Dash softly, and the black lenses of his glasses seemed to be pressing in against her. "Trinity, honey, would you please get the machine now."

"This is silly," protested Gwen. "It's just going to put you all to sleep."

A portable tape recorder appeared to the right of her plate. Trinity's thumb depressed the red button. Dash gave her an encouraging nod. Gwen stared at the little holes in the recorder's leather case. They waited. She took a breath. "Okay," she said, "it was like this."

Even Zoe sat motionless, as if to listen, her hard churning body gone into idle, its stupendous force humming on quietly, spinning gears, momentarily disengaged.

"The first time was two years ago, the summer I worked the booth at Cinema West. I liked that job, I felt safe in there behind the glass on my vinyl stool, punching the ticket buttons, watching the faces come and go, the light already in their eyes. It was kids mostly, we showed a lot of space war stuff, but I never bothered, I never even looked at the sky. I used to pretend I was a guard in a box at the border, processing happy refugees. In between shows I read fashion magazines or talked to Tommy, he was one of the ushers, and sometimes, when the movie was loud, you could hear crashes and explosions through the closed doors, and my clothes and my hair always smelled of popcorn.

"Usually I'd get off somewhere between ten and eleven, about an hour after the last show started, and I'd clean out my drawer and Mr. Newman, the manager, would come and lock the money bag in the safe. We kidded him a lot about his name, he was this porky guy without much hair, no relation, but he said it was being born with that name that had driven him into the movie business. And every night, whenever I left, he always waved and called, 'Ciao.' Then I'd walk through the empty mall and out to my car in back. All the display windows would be dark, and all the merchandise, things that were never even alive to begin with, just looked dead. That was why I always wore tennis shoes to work, I couldn't stand to hear that horrible click-click behind me, gave me the creeps.

"Anyway, I always tried to park as close to the exit as possible, but by the time I got out most of the other cars would be gone and I'd have to walk across an empty lot with the wind blowing and the moon shining and shadows everywhere and the month before the girl at the glove counter at Sears had been attacked and murdered in the same lot and of course no one had been found and everyone was just waiting for it to happen again. Sometimes I'd dream it, my face lying in a puddle of black rainwater and I'd wake up and my hands would be cold and wet. So the minute I pushed open the door I knew something was wrong, it was darker than usual, there were more shadows. I walked straight toward the car, not too fast and not looking around because I thought if I didn't see anything, there wouldn't be anything there. I could feel things scurrying up behind me but I wouldn't turn around, they couldn't get me if I didn't see them. I reached the car and touched the door handle and it was like ice and there were twice as many keys on the ring as usual and when I finally found the right one it wouldn't work, it wouldn't turn in the lock, and I started cursing my mother, it was her car, and I started thinking it was her fault, she had taken my keys even though my keys were right there in my hand yanking and twisting and I kept seeing her apron hanging on the refrigerator door handle and I think I might have been crying a little by then. Then I really did hear something, a quick swooshing sound like maybe the wing of a big bird passing over or a big blade flashing down and my heart was going and it was like arms were already around me because I couldn't get my breath and every time I blinked my lids went click when they touched and my hand wiggled and the keys fell and the sound was like a couple of trash cans rolling over 'cause my whole body, all the skin of it, was tight and focused as one ear and when I stooped down to pick them up something bright jerked at the corner of my eye and I jumped up and started to run over the blacktop toward what I don't know, chased by my own screams—at least I thought I was running, I didn't know what was happening then, I still don't know what happened now—and that's when the gaps started. I can see myself at different moments but there are holes in between like there's this stage and the lights go off and everything is rearranged and the lights come on again.

"The first light hit me in the eyes and I must have fallen in the parking lot because I could feel the rough pavement against my back and smell the oil around my head but my eyes hurt and I couldn't see and of course I'm thinking it must be a flashlight with a cop behind it so 'Who is it?' I say and there's no answer but I can feel the shadows moving around behind the light and I must have thought I was still near the car because my hands went searching around for the keys to put between my fingers to cut like jagged claws when suddenly, without really understanding, I did know what was happening like in school when you're taking a test and come to a problem you don't know and then you do and you have no idea where the answer came from. I knew the answer then and it wasn't a cop or a psycho killer or a crazy dream. It had come out of the sky and it wasn't a bird or a star or a piece of space junk. It was something from off the screen at work. And I thought how it was supposed to be like one thing but it was like something else instead because somehow the light from outside went straight inside with nothing to stop it like if a doctor was looking at your eye with a bulb and suddenly it's shining up on the walls of your skull only you haven't felt a thing and now you aren't you anymore but something empty and full like a sponge. I think there was a gap and I felt and then I heard this awful tearing sound like adhesive being ripped, only in my brain, in my consciousness, and I think it was then that some sort of station or terminal was opened in my head for these 'things,' whatever they are, to come and go, whenever they please, wherever they like. And I tell myself no, this isn't true because this can't happen to people but I know it did because sometimes I can hear them in there and that's when I know I'm crazy.

"So finally I told my mother and she made me see a doctor who said it was hormones and bad periods and he gave me pills that changed nothing, they keep on coming whether I take the medicine or not, whether I have a period or not, and now I'm thinking maybe they even fixed it so I'd take the pills because they need something that's in them and that's why I came to you because it's not stopping and I'm afraid and sometimes I'm afraid because I think maybe I like it and I think about how thoughts are like scabs on top of something else and what it would be like to have that tearing go all the way through, your thoughts picked clean away, who would you be then? and please, I'm sorry, I haven't told all this to anyone except Beale."

She stopped, the tears fell without a sound. The room was

all blobs and streaks of light. Trinity leaned over and popped the Off button. Dot fiddled with the silverware.

"We know," said Dash, and there was a new tenderness in his voice. She looked up through salty prisms at his bulbous head and glittering insect eyes. "You are not alone," he said.

"What was playing?" asked Dallas.

"Huh?" She wiped her face with a napkin.

"At the theater where you worked. What was playing that night?"

"I don't know. It was a multiplex."

"You were abducted, my dear," proclaimed Dot. "There's little question of that. Why, we've got cases in those filing cabinets that would—"

"Sssssh." Dash had raised a hand.

Zoe was twisted around in her seat, burning eyes aimed between the bars of the chair she gripped with bony paws, staring through the open window as if the night were staring back. A soft wind dark with dust and decay pushed in over the sill, teasing the candles and rattling like husks the curling photographs pinned to the opposite wall, the whole armada of hubcaps and pie tins fluttering together on the verge of spectacular launch. The window framed a field of deep black, intermittently broken by the nervous light of a handful of fireflies. Or were they fireflies? Snip, snip, snip went the shears of the unseen clock. Zoe apparently possessed the ability of certain game animals, deer, rabbits, to hold her body immobile for incredible lengths of time. Dallas, bored, turned away, a carrot stick cracking between his teeth with the sound of splintering wood. Zoe slipped from her chair and crept trancelike to the window, soiled dress unbuttoned halfway down her back, round head balanced on her small square shoulders like a stone. She stood motionless as her watchers waited and the wax trembled and dropped in hot quick tears down the thick candle stems. Then her arms went up as if to still a crowd and held there, reaching skyward, a midget preacher prepared to bring down the brimstone on an audience of "normals." Moths flapped in confused orbits around the flames. Her breathing came wet and labored. Beale lifted a beer can to his mouth. It's happening again, thought Gwen, it's happening again. There must have been a signal, some cue pitched off the end of the spectrum or a soundburst silent as a dog whistle, for a shudder rippled across Zoe's back and her arms twitched and lifted in a conductor's pause and then, round-toed Keds rooted to the floor, went jerking about her body in a mesmerizing sequence of cryptic gestures, each move performed with such electric concentration the possibility of meaning hovered around her like the aurora borealis, shifting, dancing, flirting, but never quite present, never quite within reach. She seemed to wave to a friend, she seemed to sketch a figure in the air, she seemed to twist a tool, but were the metaphors real or was this commotion nothing more than what initial appearance suggested so strongly —a mad semaphoring of the night? After a while, perhaps because of fatigue, her elbows dropped to her sides, hands faced one another and began executing their own group of nimble signs, each hand representing a little head engaged in animated conversation or merely demonstrating the physical equivalent of speaking in tongues. For if an intelligence guided these nerves, it was one apart and unrecognizable, having chosen to exhibit the structure of chaos in the frantic pantomime of this troubled little girl. Like a volcano or a geyser or any act of nature, Zoe had to expend herself before her arms would cease and a haunting stillness descend over her for the length of several unhurried breaths, and then she turned and stumbled into a flat-footed run around the dinner table, pink sneakers hitting the bare floor like a drill sergeant's jump boots. On the second revolution she started to scream.

"Zoe!" Her mother rapped on the table with a heavy soup spoon. "Zoe!" Dot tried to grab her, but she dodged her arm, veering across the room, and, still wailing, hurled her small unprotected body as if it were some separate inorganic object flat against the screen door and was gone.

Edsel took his hands off his ears.

Maryse lit a cigarette.

Dash sipped from his beer and carefully replaced the can in its own wet ring on the table.

Beale's eyes were as large as saucers. "Was that . . . was she in communication just then, was she actually talking to The Occupants?"

Gwen could feel her pulse in her teeth.

"Hand jive," said Maryse.

Inside The Object Mignon began to cry.

"Look, she's woke the baby again." She stabbed her cigarette into her glass and pushed back her chair. "I want to know when somebody's going to do something about this."

The howl waxed and waned as Zoe circumnavigated the house, and the wind from her passage entered the window like air blown across the mouth of an empty bottle, and in the convulsions of the candle flames huge shadows writhed and leaped against the walls. The television picture, having lost the horizontal, rolled endlessly from top to bottom.

"She knew," said Dot. "She always knows."

"I think they were drawn by Gwen's story," said Dash.

Edsel crawled under the table.

Dot scooped out the meat from half an acorn squash. "And she'd never seen frame one of any of those movies, either. Not even *Twilight Zone* on TV. So you know where it's got to be coming from."

"Our telephone to the stars," said Trinity.

"Has she ever seen a doctor?" inquired Gwen. Again something living touched her leg, she hoped it was Edsel.

"What do they know?" asked Dash. "Look at you."

"Lightning," claimed Dot. "Simple as that."

"Cosmic rays," said Dallas.

The news had come on and a very important head kept jumping from the bottom of the screen to the top, from the bottom to the top, from the bottom to the top. Gwen didn't feel so well. The Soviets, announced the head, the Soviets.

[63]

"What a strange day," said Dash. "All that thunder and not a cloud in the sky, those rainbows and not a drop of rain."

"I was four months along," remembered Dot, "carrying in groceries from the car, we were in Circleville then, and I never saw or heard a thing."

"The lights went out in the house," said Trinity.

"It sounded like a bomb," said Dallas.

"I remember how hard the driveway was and the cans all over me and I had a pounding head as big as the Liberty Bell. My skin smelled like Edsel's train set."

"What did the doctors say?" Gwen could hear the child rounding the house like a ravening wolf.

"What could they say? Of course, she seemed normal at first, but once all this business started up it was pretty obvious to everyone. Lightning."

"Well, either that," said Dash, "or just plain bad chromosomes. I mean, look for Christ's sake at the rest of 'em."

"Hah, hah," said Dallas. Gwen didn't like the way he looked at her. She didn't like the way the father looked at her, either. "What's that?" she asked.

There was a banging coming from beneath the house.

Trinity groaned.

Dash looked at his son. "Go get her."

Dallas leaned back, stretching out his legs. "She'll get tired."

"I'm going to count to three."

"Don't look at me," said Dot to her son, busy herding her peas into a neat pile. "I'm just the mother here."

"One."

Dallas's hand slipped under his shirt. Edsel climbed back up into his chair, never missing an opportunity to see his brother in trouble.

"Two."

Dallas's finger rubbed the metal surface of the revolver in long contemplative circles.

It was Trinity's turn to scrape back her chair. "I'll go," she said.

[64]

Dash watched his son. His face was orange in the warm candlelight, and the flames reflecting up across his sunglasses seemed to be burning inside so that his head resembled a Halloween pumpkin.

Dallas was looking at Gwen. "Don't you like my mom's cooking?" he asked. "Looks like you're gonna be keeping Edsel company at the table here."

"We know why she's not eating," said Dot.

"Yeah, why?"

Now there was banging and scratching under the floor, some desperate creature attempting to claw its way in.

Arms went churning at one end of the table.

"Edsel put his meat on my plate when you weren't looking."

"I did not."

"Did too."

"Did not."

Dot sighed. "Ten hours in a hot car with Zoe wasn't as bad as this."

"Trade plates," Dash ordered.

Edsel stared hopelessly at the mess set before him. "I can't eat this."

"Then sit there all night."

"I don't want to."

"Then eat it."

"Why don't you leave him alone," said Dallas. "Who cares what the fuck he eats?"

"I certainly wouldn't expect you to." Dash's voice was quick and harsh, a wire whipping out.

"Good-bye," said Dot. She stood and headed toward the front room. "I'm locking the door," she said. She didn't bother to look back.

"Satisfied?" asked Dash. Father and son faced one another over the dinner remains like strangers in a bar.

Beale and Gwen pretended not to listen. Gwen watched each one leave the table like sentinels falling off a wall. All this space made her nervous.

[65]

"Your lip curls any further," said Dash, "it may have to be pressed."

"I'm real scared." And as Dallas rubbed the gun metal he felt the genie awaken and she was deep inside him where the changes start from and a quickening moved over his body like a beam of cool light and flesh stiffened, cells locking into alien combinations, and his skin took on a strength and an iridescence even as gravity shifted beneath his feet and he was a solid piece, he could walk through the atomic fire.

"What's happening with you? My own son talking to me like this."

The beating under the floor grew louder.

"You're insane," Dallas said, and got up and came around the table, hand fumbling under his shirt, and passed his father and started up the spiral stairs, the beginnings of a smile working the corners of his lips at the thought of what he could have done and yet did not.

"Well," said Dash, looking about the table, "I guess it's just the four of us for dessert"—then noting the other son sullen over a congealing plate—"or three, anyway. I don't know what we've got out there in the kitchen, but I'm sure it's good."

"Could I have another beer?" asked Beale.

"The UFO made him do it," said Edsel.

There were voices now under the floor and the muffled sounds of struggle.

Dash stared at his son for a moment. "I think it's time to get out the old Jap lenses," he said brightly. "Show these folks the real night sky."

Edsel did not respond.

Trinity's voice came up through the floorboards penetrating and clear: "Don't you bite me, you little bitch, I'll knock your damn teeth out!"

"Amazing how well you can see with these binoculars," said Dash. "Took 'em off the bridge of a Japanese destroyer at Leyte Gulf."

"I didn't know you were in Vietnam," said Beale. He had

[66]

reached that point of intoxication where a sense of true clarity prevails, each object emitting an aura of grand discovery, each word a fascinating piece of flotsam to be inspected with sober concern.

Dash looked at him. "Navy," he said finally. "Off the coast."

Beale nodded solemnly.

There was a sharp scream, and someone seemed to be kicking the bottom of the floor.

"Excuse me," said Gwen, hurrying off to the cramped sanctuary of the bathroom.

"She seems to like it in there," commented Dash.

"Reminds her of home," said Beale.

"Yes," Dash went on, "you'd be positively astonished at the sights we've seen, the wonders of the universe." He pointed up at the clumsily painted constellations arching in flaking splendor over their heads. "Chariots of the Gods, Bug-Eyed Monsters, the starship Enterprise." Dry laughter rattled out of him in a long chain. Beale looked around, realizing only now he was alone at this table with a surly kid and a strange, vaguely threatening man he didn't really know and not even sure he could successfully navigate the few yards between his chair and his backpack.

From under the house came the cry of a child, a note of pain so pure it seemed a living thing itself, risen up out of the dark foundation, the fright of stone and wood, the loneliness of matter.

The phone began to chatter again, like a gourd savagely shaken in your face. Its demanding sound went on and on. No one moved. This was a noise that would have no end.

THEY STOOD OUT BACK IN THE middle of the yard in the middle of a darkness that seemed to reduce to tabletop scale the stretch of lawn, the steepled house, the long ripening fields, the whole platter of earth upon which the people themselves were clustered like tiny hand-painted figures set gazing in awkward silence off the edge of a miniature world. The air was still and clear, and the stars burned with a numerical precision, dimming momentarily to dirty gray at the passage of high thin clouds swift as smoke. The binoculars, each lens the size of a mortar tube, were mounted on a tall metal tripod, a prehistoric insect with dark shiny eyes. Dash crouched, cursing, one knee already damp, under the long spindly legs. Poly, the untethered goat, having discovered the open car window, was gnawing enthusiastically on a fibrous seat cover. Zoe went rolling over and over across the uncut grass.

"There's so much of it," Gwen exclaimed. She was wearing an oversized sweatshirt that advertised Gilley's Pasadena Texas across the chest. Her hands were stuffed in her pockets. "It makes me dizzy." But she was unable to turn away from the chance that one of those specks of glitter up there just might become unglued at any moment.

"You don't get skies like this in the city," said Trinity. "You

[68]

come out here and think, this is what an ant feels like crawling across the floor of St. Peter's."

"Right before it gets stepped on," said Dallas. He kept nervously circling the group, dropping sarcasms on each rotation.

"Yes," said Maryse. "We all know you've been to Europe. You don't have to keep throwing that in our faces." She held the baby in her arms as if it were a magnum of wine wrapped in a cold towel. "Why don't we all just shut up and listen for a moment." She looked out dramatically into the fields, out above the flowering heads of the cornstalks, that shadowy mass of closely ranked spectators pressing quietly forward.

"Jesus Christ," said Dallas.

"What?" asked Gwen, turning. "What are we supposed to hear?"

"More of her shit," said Dallas. "That's all."

"Each ear hears what it was designed for." She held her magic doll upright so as to deflect the evil of others.

"I don't hear nothing," said Beale, sitting atop the white Styrofoam cooler, a can of beer clutched in his warm fist.

"There's never nothing," Maryse insisted.

"Get off of that," said Dallas. "You're gonna break it."

"I don't think anybody's in the mood for amber waves tonight," Trinity declared.

Maryse looked steadfastly away. "It's coming in on you whether you listen or not, getting into all of us, but you need ears we don't have anymore, frontier ears to catch the sound behind other sounds, the ones you know. Back then Mother Ivey heard it plain, wrote it in her journal: the whisper of the sod."

"Yeah, right," said Dallas.

Gwen thought she might be able to detect a dull shell-to-your-ear-type roar, something vastly mechanical laboring along under the far ground. "Like a ship?" she suggested tentatively.

"Yes," Maryse responded in a suspiciously quick hiss. *Was that what she had meant?*

[69]

A flat piece of wood went sailing like a wing over the lawn. "Goddamn!" cried Dash. "Could I trouble one of you people for a little assistance WITH THIS GODDAMN THING?" He had a firm grip on one leg of the teetering tripod. "You see," he declared, holding up another rectangle of plywood, "these are the materials we're forced to work with."

Gwen assumed, perhaps wrongly, that he was speaking to her and nodded her head in sympathy. She wondered how he could possibly see anything with those sunglasses on.

Dallas handed his father his board. "Not that one, idiot, does that look like it could fit in here?"

Zoe, running out of open lawn, smashed into the fence, ringing the wire all around the yard.

"It's like a Christmas tree," Beale proclaimed, toasting the universe with upraised beer can, "minilights, a million strings of 'em," and then seemed to surprise himself by abruptly sitting down backward on the uncushioned ground.

The only light this summer night was what fell naturally out of the sky, hard bitter starflakes, the soft laving of the moon. No cheery hearthlike glow on these bare horizons, no comforting sense that somewhere nearby competent people were up and about, taming space with motion, making a human noise, keeping a vigilant eye on things. Instead there was distance and wind and the ever-troubling notion of a total world totally asleep, plunged in unconsciousness, night inside, night outside, a volatile equilibrium of critical elements. Because out here it was actually possible to experience a darkness that was more than an absence, a temporary quality, but a living fluid as vivid as daylight, masked only momentarily by the magnitude of the sun and moving as freely among the sleek shiny spaces between the stars as within the dank textured depths of the mushroom shadow of the big cemetery tree that went thump, bark to flesh, beneath the inevitable collision with Zoe's body, a battery-powered toy that immediately reversed itself and went rolling away, apparently undamaged, in the opposite direction.

"If my child grows into something like that . . ." Maryse

shifted the infant in question from one arm to another, careful to keep the plastic nipple plugged in place.

Gwen's head went up and down in agreement, almost an automatic reflex by now. Were these people really speaking to her? Beale sat huddled Indian-style on the ground, privately worshiping at the pale altar of the beer cooler. "This is great," he was mumbling to himself. "This is fucking great." Here was Maryse's kid, Gwen thought, plus a couple decades. He had the oddest-shaped head. She could pick him instantly out of any-sized crowd. That is, if she wanted to. She wandered out into the yard.

The moon, slightly flattened on one side like a big snowy paperweight, was almost as round and bright as a moon could ever be. It reminded Gwen of a harsh tower light overlooking a grim prison yard.

"Do you know any constellations?" Trinity asked, edging up behind her.

Gwen shrugged. "The Big Dipper?"

Trinity laughed. "Yes, that's one."

"My father once tried to show me when I was about Edsel's age. I told him there weren't any pictures up there, and he told me to make up my own. I still couldn't see any."

"Have you noticed my father's?"

"The painted ones?"

"Yeah, up on the ceiling."

"Sorry, no pictures there, either. I don't know, maybe it's something only fathers can do."

"Good. I like that. Tell it to Dash, see what he says."

"What are you two whispering about?" asked Maryse, lurking near.

"You," Trinity responded at once.

"Oh." She shifted Mignon to the other arm. "They're ready. Dash wants to show Gwen the moon."

"Fine. Do you want to see the moon, Gwen?"

"Sure. I guess."

"Okay, then we will."

Dash was in a portrait photographer's crouch behind the

binoculars, fiddling with the focusing rings. "A little this way . . . a little that way . . . a little more lubrication, please." He stepped back with a flourish. "Here she is, the big-bottomed goddess herself."

Hesitantly Gwen leaned in to the glasses, the black eye-pieces, cold and hard, seeming to leap forward to seize the bone of her face, and the lifeless, boring old moon burst into shocking clarity inside her head, a ball of burning tissue illuminated from within by the eerie gelid light of a consuming disease, the pearly-blue lesions, the thin black spider fractures, the deeply shadowed pox. "God," she gasped, "it's beautiful."

"One of the pair of cosmic eyes watching us day and night," Dash explained. "The sun, bright and quick, the moon slow and milky. That's why night is a good time to hide." She felt his large hand settle gently onto her shoulder.

"Grandpa Warden always used to say the moon was a golf ball," said Trinity, "so whenever I went outside after dark I'd have to put a pot on my head just in case it fell down."

"Yeah, and look what happened to Grandpa Warden," said Dallas.

Beale sat plucking idly at the grass between his legs, rubbing the short fragrant stems into broken pieces he sprinkled on his lap. His attention, shifting in and out of the moment since dinnertime at the apparent whim of playful thumbs twiddling his own knobs, suddenly locked back on, and he looked up at Gwen's head attached to the huge lenses and demanded loudly, "Do you see The Man?" his consonants beginning to slur. "I want to see The Man in the Moon." He got unsteadily to his feet, a longer climb than he would have supposed, the yard swaying perilously for an uncomfortable second or two.

Gwen moved away from the tripod. She could still feel the touch of Dash's hand, a glowing moonprint on her shoulder.

"Lemme in here," ordered Beale, and attempting to assume a properly dignified and well-balanced viewing stance, knocked his head against the binoculars, throwing the barrels out of alignment, the giggles he was certain he had been hearing off and on all evening now returning thick as crickets. He swiveled the lenses wildly about in a grim show of expertise as he tried to focus by twisting a locked nut on one of the tripod legs. "What is this?" he bellowed. "I can't see a fucking thing." Dash stepped in and readjusted the lenses. "Oh," he said, gazing starward, "oh that. Big deal."

"Go get Zoe," said Dash.

Trinity refused.

"Zoe," Dash shouted. "C'mere, Zoe; c'mere, Zoe honey, come to Daddy." He might have been calling a dog. "Where is she?"

"I don't know," said Trinity.

"I think I hear something under the car," said Maryse.

"Come here, Zoe, come and see Daddy." He walked toward the VW, voice large with false excitement. "Come on out, honey, see what Daddy's got."

There was the sound of furtive night creatures from under the car.

"C'mon, sweetie, come give Daddy a hug."

She wriggled out like a soldier under fire, elbows digging into the ground, her body dragging behind, and as soon as she was free began rolling away from him toward the road. Dash was on her in a few quick steps, he lifted her up by the waist and carried her, thrashing and screaming, across the lawn, all the while stroking her hair, murmuring in her ear until she stopped struggling and allowed herself to go limp in his arms, her round-toed Keds dangling loosely against his knees. He nuzzled the back of her neck, inhaling her characteristic aroma: a kennellike mingling of sweat, mud, crushed grass, and animal manure, none of it quite strong enough to overwhelm completely the fresh essential vanilla scent of young child. "Look in here, darling, see the moon." As Dash hoisted her toward the binoculars she stared up at this strange apparatus rearing before her and tried to grab the lenses so he had to hold her to his chest with her arms pinned and, clasping the back of her skull with his other hand, force her head into the waiting eyepieces. "C'mon, honey, you have to look in here." She immediately began to resist the way a dog or cat resists being shoved toward an unpleasant dish. "Look, looky here." She was squirming now, but Dash was able to get her eyes lined up under the lenses long enough for the steady succession of grunts "unh, uhn, uhn" to go glissando-ing away into registers usually inhabited by wounded hogs. When she tried to bite, Dash dropped her thrashing body and she got to her feet and ran off to the house, her cries louder and even more disturbing in the dark, breaking out over the land like something greater than sound, sound crystallized and sprayed into the fields as insecticide. A screen door slammed, the cries went on muffled by the walls of the house.

"Moon really spooks her," said Maryse, rocking little Mignon, who had started to cry himself but lacked the wind or strength to produce anything more than a squeak a toy doll might make.

"I wish you wouldn't do that," said Trinity.

"But what does she see?" asked Dash. "That's the damn mystery. We throw her into moonlight often enough, maybe she'll learn how to swim and teach the rest of us."

"It's stupid and cruel."

"So is life."

Dash repositioned the binoculars, and they each had a turn gazing at the planet Mars: a twinkling dot of unvarying insignificance and luster both with and without magnification. "It's a long ways away," said Trinity.

"Depends on who's taking the measurement," replied Dash.

Then a peek at Venus: it looked exactly like Mars.

"Now," Dash announced with a certain amount of paternal drama, "the jewel in the crown."

Gwen stared into a field of glittering stars no larger than pinheads. "Which one?"

"The big one. Right in the middle."

"Jupiter?"

Dash moved in for another look. "M31," he said as though

pronouncing the classified name of the ultimate weapon. "Home."

"That minuscule point," Trinity explained, "is an entire spiral galaxy in the constellation Andromeda."

"Where we all came from," said Dash.

"And where we're all going back to," added Maryse. "As soon as they bring us the thermium for The Object."

"Want to come?" asked Dallas.

Gwen contemplated the sky. So stars could be galaxies and all look the same. "When would you return?"

"I said it was home," Dash declared.

A light came on behind them, and the dark looming geometry of the house was broken by the yellow rectangle of the kitchen window in which appeared the fuzzy outline of Dot's head calling, "Dash!" pause "Dash!" pause "Dash!" pause, the cries coming even, inflectionless, like planks being clapped together. Finally he turned with reluctant irritation and in a deliberate voice, low and flat, answered, "What?"

"Don't give me that shit. Get up here and help me deal with this. She's banging her head against the refrigerator." Behind her, objects clanged and crashed. Dash stared at the beer cooler for a long while. "Show them Pegasus," he ordered, and stalked toward the house.

Dallas grabbed the binoculars, swinging them to the west parallel with the horizon. "Fuck the constellations. Let's check out the neighboring planets." He peered through the lenses, carefully refocusing, intent as a U-boat commander scanning shipping lanes for unescorted oil tankers. Gwen wondered what marvel of astronomy could be so engaging. Samantha Hostetler's bedroom, explained Trinity. Oh. She hadn't noticed the scattered houses sitting lonely as sheds out along the low distant rim of the country.

There was a pink bathrobe hanging on an open closet door. A pile of clothes on an unmade bed. A wall of pop stars' posters. Last week he and Donnie had caught a flash of freshly showered tit, profile and full frontal, tasty mug shots just for them.

Maryse began prodding him on the shoulder. "Stand aside, Einstein, give somebody else a turn."

"One minute."

"C'mon, we want to see a tube."

"Yeah," added Trinity, "and we don't care whose it is."

"Point that thing at the MacGuffins'. Let's see if Donnie's up." They hunched together like witches, their wild cackles ringing out over the desolate moor, startling Beale at his peasant labors, stooped over the icy cooler, arm submerged to the elbow in black water, numb fingers bumping in vain against the heavy beer cans, elusive as fish. "Fuck you," he muttered, addressing any who would hear.

"Go ahead and laugh," warned Dallas, finally surrendering the scopes, "I told Donnie what you do out here."

"Flattered, wasn't he?"

"He wants to show you the moon."

"I can hardly wait." She studied the house through the binoculars. "Uh-oh, all dark, must be an eclipse tonight."

"Try the Overmeyers," Maryse urged. "They're always good for a grin."

Dallas spoke to Gwen. "Once, this is great, once last summer we saw the mister and missus buck naked in their living room, not doing anything, him in one chair, her in another, just sitting there quietly without a stitch on, watching television."

" 'Course it was a hot night," added Maryse.

"You know," said Trinity, "I've been to that house many times, but going through the front door isn't half as fun as coming in through the window."

Beale, having successfully snared a dripping can from the arctic waters, turned his back on the others, their self-importance, their mockeries, wait until he got Gwen alone later tonight, he'd show her, and without a word made his way cautiously as a demo man across the mined yard, trying not to lose a drop of beer, over to the secluded cemetery, its dull stones lying like oversized children's blocks spilled in the shelter of the tall bushy tree. He was mumbling almost

constantly to himself now, nothing truly audible or even coherent, merely the sound track to the film fermented barley
was running through his empty head. In the buzzing dark the
level of the lawn kept shifting and progress was like ascend-
ing the tricky steps of a feebly lit funhouse, so it was without
much surprise that he discovered himself tripping over an
exposed root, a possible concussion miraculously averted by
one hand (the canless one, thank God) flying out and grabbing at the rough edge of one of the monuments. "Whoa!" he
cried, and eased himself down onto a conveniently located
stool-sized stone, minus only a couple splashes of brew and
the dregs of a dignity he no longer cared about. No one appeared to have noticed his clumsiness anyway; they clustered
still about the tripod, seemingly far away and terribly vulnerable out there in the open. He was cozy inside a leafy tent,
where instead of indulging in childish Peeping Tomism he
would meditate for a while on the Grand Ideas, but even as
he tried to grasp them his thoughts went slipping away one
by one in a disconnected stream on out of sight, leaving behind a blank screen and a body as still and as conscious as
one of the stone angels surrounding it in the dark until after a
time impossible to clock the thoughts returned again as if
bound on wide celestial orbits but so altered he no longer
recognized them. He smiled stupidly, pleased with his own
giddy sense of disorientation. He glanced down at his hand,
noted that it held a forgotten beer which he immediately
emptied down his upturned head, little stars winking know-
ingly back at him from the jagged spaces between the leaves.
He let the can fall from his fingers into the grass where its
curved aluminum edge caught the moon in a cool arch of
comfortless light. Broken mutterings faint as the rustle of the
encompassing tree life stammered from his barely parted lips:
"Bastards . . . kicking me out . . . screw him . . . never ran
away . . . screw all of 'em . . . wasn't my fault . . . dog knew,
always did know . . . Mom . . ." His story, the one you tell
deep in the ladderless hole of tapped-out nights on secondary
roads when there'd be enough money for a couple six-packs

[77]

and your faith in a country as big as dreams had dwindled to the hope the raw sun wouldn't find you in a ditch, hot wind from highballing semis blowing cinder dust and ragged litter over your oddly humped back or the moon catch you in a graveyard telling tales to ghosts and even through impossibly thick boughs its soft penetrating beams pick out the thin streak arching over your own cheek and paint it silver.

Back at the glasses they were finally offering Gwen a turn. She wanted to look but couldn't help thinking of how she would feel about prying telescopes pointed at her windows. "Isn't this illegal?" she asked.

"It's just neighbors," answered Dallas. "Out here this is all we have to look at."

"And we look at it real hard," added Trinity.

"In between long tense periods awaiting the arrival of The Occupants, of course."

"Of course."

Gwen pressed her face against the eyepieces. There was a barn with a hooded light above the open door and inside the twitching hindquarters of some cows in their stalls. A truck sat in the yard, tail reflectors glowing crimson like the un-blinking eyes of a night beast. The big two-storied house was a riot of electrical display, high wattage pouring from every room, a pervert's choice of windows to explore. The kitchen was decorated a grotto green, and the excess color seemed to be bleeding off the walls, submerging the room in aqueous air.

"Well?" asked Dallas impatiently.

She could see plants in the window, a faucet lifting into view like the slender neck of a chrome snake, the upper-right corner of a sickly yellow refrigerator, closed cabinets, hanging potholders, and a red wall clock in the shape of a smiling tomato. She stared at this domestic scene for several minutes. Nothing moved into or out of it.

"Try another window," suggested Dallas. "This is like looking for life on Pluto."

Gwen slid over to the living room. The furniture was all of

[78]

the big brown baggy sort imprinted with vague outlines of the human form. There was one brass floor lamp and a dangling overhead and a bookcase half-full of records and on top of the television a gleaming collection of framed photographs. The television was on. There was no one in the room.

"What do you see now?" asked Dallas.

"This is boring," said Maryse.

Gwen discovered she was enjoying her maiden adventure in voyeurism even without the undressed walk-ons. The objects themselves were fascinating enough, these props for other lives handled daily by mysterious strangers and now touched by her probing eyes acquired at this distance and in this manner a forbidden aura that transformed the most mundane article—a bag of golf clubs, a shovel leaning near the door, a container of Diamond salt, a heart-shaped trivet—into an intriguing thing of charged complexity. She felt like a detective pondering clues. "Who are these people?"

"Farmer Bill and sweet wife Irene," said Trinity. "Only she never comes outside anymore, and he goes around in a filthy jumpsuit with a big cowboy six-gun strapped to his waist and a big silver skull for a belt buckle."

"Everyone around here," said Maryse, "is either in debt or half-crazy or both."

Gwen drifted slowly upstairs. The shades were pulled in the bedrooms, but she found the bathroom window open far enough for a glimpse. White walls, white tile, white towels, then something moved. "Uh-oh," she said, "I think somebody's taking a bath."

"All right!" cried Dallas, nudging her aside. "Here we go! Yeah, seems to be some definite skin here."

"Probably Irene," said Maryse, "soaking her twat."

"Or her bruises," said Trinity.

"Shit," complained Dallas, "you can't make out anything, the damn crack's too small."

"I guess," said Trinity, "there's no points for anyone tonight."

"Hey," called Maryse, "catch this act."

Behind them a dark shape draped itself over a tombstone to the sound of vomit splattering on dry grass.

"Jesus," muttered Dallas, "ain't he got no respect for the dead?"

Gwen went over and helped him up to the house (all quiet now, parents and daughter apparently resting peacefully, Edsel asleep at the dinner table, head cradled in his arms beside the still untouched plate of food) and got Beale out of his clothes and washed him off and tucked him into his sleeping bag, and by the time she finished the others had come in from outside and dispersed to their various corners. She went into the kitchen for a glass of water, and when she turned around Dash was standing in the darkened doorway staring at her.

"Oh, you scared me."

He smiled with half his mouth. Even with the sunglasses gone the eyeballs themselves seemed to be hiding behind tinted contacts. "Enjoy the stars?"

"Very much. It wasn't what I expected."

"It never is." He came toward her like a part of the shadow in the next room detaching itself and moving into the light. The kitchen seemed painfully bright, the sputtering fluorescence overhead glazing surfaces with a hard inhospitable look. She stepped out of his way and stood leaning against the sticky counter, sipping nervously at her water.

"I've been pointing my finger at the sky for decades now, but I might as well be squatting out on the interstate with it up my ass. Most people are either stupid or cruel, don't you think? On second thought, I'm not sure there's a significant difference." He filled a battered copper pot and set it on the stove to boil. "How about some coffee?"

"Thanks, but I'm afraid it would keep me up all night."

"Tea, then." Up close she saw that she had been mistaken, the eyes were gray and soft, like bits of eraser.

"I guess one cup wouldn't hurt." She sat down at an enamel table cluttered with piles of dirty dishes and smudged, half-empty glasses.

[80]

He rinsed out two cups in the sink and placed them on the counter. "When I was young I used to drink whole pots of it at a time—coffee, that is. 'Course in those days I only slept three hours a night. Guess I was afraid I would miss something."

Suddenly this wild orange mass came leaping out of the silence onto the table and Gwen cringed.

"That's Minerva," said Dash. "I think she looks like an owl, don't you? I think most cats do, look like owls with fur."

"She's gorgeous."

The animal looked at her for a disapproving moment through big amber marbles, then began to pick her way among the stale dinner remains, pausing to sniff daintily at the dried clots and crusts. She crossed the table and seated herself directly in front of Gwen, puffy tail curling neatly in about the white paws, the oversized elliptical pupils expanding and contracting as if taking breaths, the glimmer of intelligence inside low as a pilot light.

Dash was pulling tea bags out of a jar. "Seems I need something warm in my belly these days before retiring." He set a steaming cup before her, nudging the cat aside, and took a chair across from her. "Sleep little enough as it is."

Gwen watched the tea vapors go writhing away into nothing. "My father was like that. Warm milk every night. Because of his stomach. Finally it got so bad all he could eat was stuff without any color to it—milk, bread, cottage cheese, like that." She sipped at her tea and paused, the most curious taste.

"Was he ever able to work his way back into the spectrum?"

"Huh?"

"Colors."

"Oh. I don't know. I haven't seen him in four years." She looked into her cup at the floating leaf debris. "They're divorced."

"So he doesn't know what's been happening with you?"

"No."

[81]

"And your mother thinks you're crazy."

She smiled. The words sounded funny in his mouth. "Yes." She put down her cup. "Look, I'm sorry about what happened at dinner, I'm not usually like that."

"So what happened?"

"All that emotional stuff. It kinda caught me by surprise, too."

"Surprise is our business. You knew that. That's why you came."

"I don't know. I'm not sure anymore what I'm doing."

"You're a pioneer, you've witnessed the crack in the egg, and that's enough to twist anyone's head. So don't apologize, you knew enough to come to us and get your story on record, the official history, not the one the mole people keep. Most everybody these days seems to have settled, settled for good credit, settled for processed cheese, settled for too damn little, if you ask me. As if we've already finished with this world, cleared out all the woods. But a big surprise is coming, and they're not going to be able to handle it, they're not in the business."

"Will I have to witness that, too?"

Dash smiled, professor to favorite pupil. "You already have." He leaned toward her. "Watchers like us, you know, are the last true Americans."

"I've never felt that important."

"You're a heroine, and it's an honor to have you as a guest in my home."

She bent over her cup. Was that her future swirling about in dark bits and pieces on the bottom? "I've always wanted to meet you," she confessed without raising her head.

"Disappointed?"

She looked up at him. "Are you kidding? You're like a movie star."

"Really?" He seemed to be enjoying himself immensely. "Which one?"

"I can't remember the name. He killed a lot of people and he never smiled."

His laughter erupted like something released from long confinement.

"He usually died at the end," she added.

"Yes, don't we all."

The cat lifted a paw and dipped her head, licking repeatedly along one rippling flank, scaly pinkish tongue drawing out the long hair into pointed orange tufts. Gwen placed her cup on the table, and the cat ceased its grooming and stuck its nose beneath the rim. Then it settled back and looked at her again, cold, unblinking.

"You know, I thought when you came back that you'd kick us out. I mean, probably you've got people showing up at your door all the time and it must get tiresome."

"Not so many." His own cup was cradled between hands almost as pale as the porcelain. "Interest waxes and wanes. Like the stock market. And why should we mind? Fresh faces are always welcome around here, particularly ones as pretty as yours."

She looked away. "Thank you."

"Your mother must be quite beautiful."

"I guess."

"Skin like that runs in families." Beneath the merciless kitchen glare the surface of his own face appeared bloodless, rough and pebbled, the skin of someone who was, well, older.

"Another cup?" he asked.

"Oh no, no thank you. I think I'm about to fall out of this chair."

"Well, listen, Dot and I are scheduled for a segment on *Night Chat* next Friday. How'd you like to come sit in on the gig?"

"I don't know. I didn't think we were planning on staying that long."

"I was serious, what I said earlier."

"What about Dot, the rest of the family?"

"They love company, couldn't you tell?"

"Let me talk this over with Beale."

"I think Beale wouldn't mind moving in."

[83]

"I think you're right." She pushed back her chair and stood up. She was more tired than she had thought, the kitchen wobbled briefly, then clicked back into place. She put her empty cup in the stained sink and paused in the doorway. "Well, good night."

"Good night," he said. The smile on his face seemed to be aimed in other directions than solely at her. "Don't forget to wish upon a star."

She locked herself in the bathroom and brushed her teeth and washed her face, trying to ignore that other Gwen moving around inside the mirror. In the morning she would tell Beale they had to leave immediately. When she came out the kitchen light was off, the entire house lost in darkness, and she had to feel her way across the room with her feet like a blind person. Beale was snoring incredibly loudly, as if the plastic mouthpiece of a party horn were stuck in his throat, but when Gwen crawled into the sleeping bag beside him as quietly as she could, he came awake, arm clutching wildly for her in the dark.

"Zatchoo?" he croaked in an exaggerated whisper. She was instantly enveloped in a rainbow-colored cloud of toxic fumes.

"Yes," she gagged.

"Maya." Now which old girlfriend was she supposed to be tonight? "Mica," he repeated.

"It's all right." She patted his clammy hand.

"Mygah, I can't find mygah."

"It's all right now. Go to sleep."

These were magic words, for even as she spoke them he mumbled something unintelligible and dropped off again, mucus-rattling snores trailing after like noise from a bad muffler. It didn't seem possible he could be taking in enough air through that obstruction, but she supposed she should only really start to worry when the sound stopped. It wasn't so bad, anyway, she'd certainly rather share her consciousness with something recognizably human than one of Maryse's spooky nonsounds: like the faraway urgent crackling of cellophane that can grow out of a dark room up into black flame eating at the walls. Oh God. She couldn't bear another night in this horrible place. She closed her eyes, opened them, closed them, opened them, the quality of darkness remaining precisely the same, a huge roofed presence arching high overhead, already the second time flat on this floor and still not used to lying down for sleep in the middle of a church. Her mother was religious, never missing a service except for illness, but she had stopped going with her when she was fourteen, the year the pastor, Smiling Jack, touched her once after choir practice in a distinctly unspiritual way. Probably she would have quit going anyway, churches were places of perfumed boredom, places where dead bodies lay rotting in polished boxes, places where people got married. And if God was taking down her thoughts this very minute (to be branded in fire upon her flesh in the hereafter), that was fine; she had already taken down enough stuff on Him.

After a while her body started to sway in a pleasant floating manner that she rather enjoyed. Perhaps finally she was beginning to relax. She imagined herself adrift on a blue air mattress on some warm tropical swell, trying to feel, not to think, all the inner knots going limp, coming loose, sinking slowly into the ease, breath drawing deeper, thought losing outline, when suddenly awareness sat bolt upright out of the void like a prematurely buried body crying, What? Who? Where? Up above, the high dark ceiling seemed even higher, the floor now plummeting quickly downward. Sweat broke out across her palms, her heart throbbed in her teeth. If she got up and turned on the light, it would awaken the others and reveal her secret: here she was going freaking schizo in a strange house of strange people at a dead hour in the absolute dead center of nowhere, U.S.A. But she could not move. She lay there, helpless, face up into the ominous peak, the fall of the blade. She watched, fascinated, as her panic, raving on undiminished, detached itself from her, stretching, thinning, snapping off like a length of elastic, all the little nerve creatures scampering away into the gray indistinct. She must have

[85]

slept then, a light fitful doze, dreams tumbling around her too rapid to sort from the hints of another world only Fever could have ruled and maintained: sudden light spilling across her eyes to the crash of a refrigerator door, rattling trays, shattering glass, the thunder of feet brushing past her paralyzed head, Dot screaming, Zoe crying and crying and crying down a tunnel and out while above in the loft the measured creak of pacing steps, the ghost of a mad organist hunting for the stops, and occasionally she would become aware again of Beale's snoring, the simple sound of phlegm seeking an exit become a lullaby sweet as the mechanical beat of a clock, something to cling to on the long rollicking ride to dawn, but then the feet would rush by, Zoe's rapid feet, the refrigerator door bang, the fragile things go crash over the screaming and the crying, but was this now or before? Which was the dream? And how to comprehend the frozen image of Dallas posed before an open window, his nakedness as bright and close as the pale light of heaven trapped inside monstrous lenses and within The Object the sibilant murmur of voices rising together like engines warming for lift-off and behind the altar wall the weaving of domestic argument in shrill call and response: sensations arriving and departing in busy rush-hour numbers at the saucer terminal in her head where she was an Occupant and all the members of this frantic family aliens. Later, she awoke in calm darkness with a dry throat, a full bladder, but without will or power, the ensuing moment of fear subsiding like a bubble back into tenuous sleep and a sense of her body changing out from under her, growing, swelling, limbs bloated, muscles slack and useless and unable to resist when at last the thing emerged out of the night and lowered itself clumsily onto her chest, a penetrating fullness sweeping over her as the shadows bloomed crimson and she strained against the weight but her arms wouldn't work and the weight began to move, rocking back and forth, drawing her in and out, and she saw Zoe in a yellowy patch of sun, hugging her knees and rocking on the scarred hardwood floor among echoes of stale hymns and Bible must and a thick voice, male and loudspeaker harsh, announced directly into her ear, to her alone, tick tock tick tock this is the way the universe fucks, and the moon swung grandly into view like a big silver ornament turning on a string and the Man in the Moon had the features of Dash himself and there were craters for his eyes.

IT WAS RED AND POPPING WITH pain bubbles, so this must be it: the hollow interior of your very own head. There was pink quartz here sharp as razors and veins of black tar and knobs of forgotten muscle sticky as warm window putty. There was movement, a quick recoiling, also your own, and you opened her eyes and, groaning, flung a ponderous arm over her clammy face. The shades were up like raised theater curtains all around the room, and the sun was standing right outside, just beyond the glass, monstrous, naked, shockingly near. Her head seemed to be some sort of useless organic object peeled, discarded, and left out to dry. Her throat was stuffed with stiff blotting paper. Woozy puddles of vile fluid sloshed about in her stomach. She couldn't handle alcohol, everyone knew that, why did she persist, and what poison was it exactly she had—the night was on her like a collapsing wall. Oh god oh god oh god oh god. She reached a frantic hand down between her cold thighs.

"Oh, hi," called Maryse, breezing through the room with pale Mignon connected to an even paler bottle, "you're up. Look outside, what a gorgeous day."

From the kitchen came the horrifying smells and sounds of a family breakfast: spitting bacon and burned toast and the first tentative fender benders of a long summer day's quota of emotional collisions, the pit stop for dreams and refueling having been indecently short.

Gwen squirmed into her clothes inside the sleeping bag and rushed to the john before anyone could invite her over for a plate of runny eggs. The bathroom door was locked.

"Who is it?" asked Beale.

She shook the handle. "Let me in."

"All right, all right."

She pushed her way in and quickly rebolted the door.

"My God," he was exclaiming to his face in the mirror, "I feel like I've been plowed under one of those fields out there." Then he saw how she was looking at him. "Okay, what the hell's wrong with you?"

"We've . . ." she began, and stopped, already out of breath.

"Let me go get a paper bag, you're about to hyperventilate."

She grabbed his arm and held on. "Listen, we've got to get out of here. Now." Her eyes were moving around in her head like trapped birds.

Beale sighed. Slowly he squeezed a large white pimple bursting above one eyebrow. "Haven't we had this discussion once, more than once?" She said nothing. He pressed a wad of toilet paper onto the oozing hole in his head, then examined the tissue with interest. "You know, I think if we offer to help out with the paperwork, their correspondence and manuscripts and stuff like that, we just might be able to hang around as long as we like."

She waited for the silence to accumulate properly. "Dash raped me last night," she announced simply, reciting an equation.

"What?" They looked at one another. The mirror between them was flecked with dried toothpaste. She could see herself still clutching her sweatshirt as if it were some small animal she had just strangled.

"Dash came into the room in the middle of the night and crawled into my sleeping bag and raped me." This is how you explain things to a child.

[89]

"Are you kidding?" He saw how she looked at him. "But I was lying there right next to you."

She explained again, she had patience. "He got you drunk and he put something in my tea and he raped me. Obviously his plan all along. He could have fired a bullet into my head and you wouldn't have heard."

Beale considered her words. None of them made any sense. His eyes blinked in the mirror. "Have you seen my gun? I can't find it anywhere."

She stepped up to him then, the top of her head just level with his shoulders, and began to beat on his skinny corrugated chest, the pleasure was immediate, the blunt meaty sound, how the skin came up red under her fists, she was inside her body in a new way, the very force of it an enclosing spinning out of which she communicated by beating jungle messages on a gooseflesh drum, three months on the road, three days in this house, prune for a heart. She had never been so serious about hitting, despite the loose arms of the sweatshirt she couldn't let go of flapping about in comical confusion, she wanted to make marks visible and sore enough to remember for a time and when she finished she whipped the shirt across his face in a last gesture of contempt and charged out of the bathroom, out of the church, out of his life. Zoe bounded up from nowhere, eager as a puppy, a fresh bruise the color of spoiled eggplant decorating one cheek, her dress (the same one as yesterday and the day before that) filthy and dragging kite tails of raggedy material. "No, no," said Gwen. "You can't come with me." The girl stood just out of reach, head tilted at what appeared to be an especially uncomfortable angle, eyes averted. "Do you understand? You have to stay here with your mommy and daddy." She stood like a robin listening to worms underground. Gwen started across the yard, the girl running about her in wild circles. "No," she said. "Go. Go home." As she mounted the bank the girl at last broke away, veering off toward the back of the house, a renegade missile, screeching like a monkey, a sound Gwen was only too glad to leave behind forever. It didn't matter which direction she chose, road ran two ways, both of them leading straight out. Howl, you rotten kid, maybe someone'll come out and knock your ratty teeth in.

She walked rapidly, almost at a run, watching the gravel skip on ahead of her, scattering like thought, then suddenly to look up and around, the eyes into a dizzy roll, nothing to hold them out here in all this terrible flatness and space, like a palsied hand reaching out for support and sliding wheeee! across a sheet of oiled glass. She had to stop for a moment, bent over by the side of the road, arms braced against her knees, waiting for the buzzing to stop. When she turned for a curious last glimpse back, the house had become unexpectedly diminished in size, little more than a dunce-cap triangle of black roof and pointy steeple topped by that ridiculous dish revolving still, searching her out, the whole awful place already too distant to return to, and find the gun and shoot the maniac—she could see herself acting this out in fleshy clarity, how she would look marching back into the church, boots thumping loudly across the floor, right up to his startled pasty face, and raise her arm, carefully memorizing his expression for the rocking chair years, pull the thingamajig, watch his forehead go smash. But there wasn't a gun because the idiot in the john had lost it on the road somewhere, lost the gun, lost the way, lost the keys, lost her.

She wiped her eyes on her shirt and went on. The sun burned white and ruthless over silent fields of green haze. Stare too long into this light and you risk corn blindness. But there wasn't much to look at along the road, either: the flaking orange shell of a battered muffler, the scaly S of a flattened snake, a shredded tire or two. No sign of a vehicle or any hope of one.

She must have gone miles before happening on her first farmhouse, a strangely stunted two-story affair constructed of randomly alternating bare and painted boards that seemed to tilt slightly forward as if searching anxiously for overdue visitors. Rising out of a knee-high yard on uneven pedestals of gray cinderblock was a bleached-blue Datsun truck, sway-backed and wheelless. Mechanical chickens strutted aimlessly along the driveway, pecking at pebbles with amazing persistence. Out back a crumbling barn sagged against the big bullet of a brightly domed silo. In the hot wind the black rooster of a weather vane pointed a black unwavering arrow straight westward, the blades of a windmill were motionless as the hands of a broken clock. In the daylight Gwen recognized nothing, the house hid its identity behind the reflections in its windows. She supposed this was the place where the woman had been in the bath. Where was she now? Where was her husband? Who fed the chickens? Who tended the crops? The country was a mystery she would never penetrate.

She walked on. What would happen was this: the road would run on into another road and that one or the one after would run out to the ramp of an interstate where she would climb into the first car that stopped and ride until she was told to get out. She had a wad of bills stuffed in her pocket and when that was gone she would improvise.

Heat hung on her like an ill-fitting suit. Dust clung to the moist skin of her face. Her scissoring legs made a steady rhythm over the ground. Beale and Dash, Dash and Beale, Beale and Dash. She looked up and a point of light clear as one of last night's stars fallen accidentally out of the darkness streaked at impossible speed across the empty sky exactly parallel to the trembling line of bare horizon. Her mouth began to work as all sorts of possibilities opened up in her head, not least the realization cold and precise: this is not a hallucination. Without the slightest reduction in speed the light executed a crisp ninety-degree turn and headed directly at her. She dropped to her knees, flooded by revelation. The experiment was over, the maze run, here came the extraction. She prayed there would be no pain. Then, almost on her, the light pivoted again and, gracefully banking away, extended a pair of sleek flashing wings on which she read without comprehension the word USA and actually wondered to herself, USA, pronouncing it Oosa, what planet was that? She got up slowly out of the dirt, angry, foolish, relieved. So. The experiment was not over. She wished they'd toss her a few crumbs of cheese now and then, these shocks were getting harder and harder to take.

She went on. Beale and Dash, Dash and Beale, Deale and Bash.

She heard a car approaching from behind and turned, already offering a hopeful thumb. It was the blue Bug. She bolted off the shoulder, skidded down a steep grassy bank, hopped a stagnant ditch, and threw herself into a six-foot-high wall of solid corn. She came out on the other side in a tropical nightmare of green humidity, thrashing her way down a dense endless aisle of sharp leaves that slapped and cut her hands and face, stumbling on hard dry clods of dirt until the momentum that had carried her deep into the stifling heart of the land burned to vapor and she lost her balance and went sprawling down into the baked earth, one raw ear pressed up against a crack in the sod. She listened. It whispered, just as Maryse had promised. It whispered. "Gweeeeeen," it called in an old raspy woman's voice, "Gweeeeeen." She lay still, face flushed and wet, panting like a dog, and transfixed by her first close-up view of the bizarre stiltlike structure of a corn root, it looked like it could break loose and walk away. "Gweeeeeen." There was only one voice, and it kept moving around. A drop of sweat slid off the tip of her nose and disappeared into the dry ground. The voice called and called, quite serious apparently about receiving an answer. Under her for the first time she *felt* the earth, a solid thing, a big thing, a thing of being. This was you dead. "Gweeeeeen, Gweeeeeen." Her name squeaked through her like the sound of a mausoleum door. But as she listened she became gradually aware that this voice that would not stop was a voice she knew. She struggled to her feet. "What?" she cried. "Where are you?" answered the voice. "I'm coming," shouted Gwen, pushing her body between the flapping stalks. When she emerged at last into open sunlight she saw Trinity far away down the road, peering off into the dense field. There was a moment of hesitation when she could have taken one short

[93]

step backward and disappeared into the landscape, but there was something in Trinity's attitude and look that held her until it was too late.

"Oh, there you are," she cried, smiling easily at her mistake. "God, I was sure you were down here somewhere." She approached Gwen, the soles of her boots crunching along the gravel shoulder. "Are you all right?"

"Yes." A wary smile flitted across Gwen's features. "I think so."

Trinity laughed. "You don't look all right."

Gwen turned her head aside. "Don't look at me like that."

"Why don't we get into the car?"

"I'm not going back, so don't think you can get me back because I'm not going."

"Okay with me, I'm no cop. Why don't we just get in the car, cruise around, and we'll go wherever you want to go, all right?"

"Take me to the interstate."

"Fine."

The inside of the car was as hot as an attic. Gwen angled the window vent toward her, aiming the wind right into her face. It felt so cleansing, as if dirty pieces of her were being blasted off.

"I'm supposed to tell you how concerned everyone is, especially Beale."

"Then why didn't he come with you?"

"He wanted to, of course, but Dash has got him involved in some sort of intense discussion. You know how Dash is."

Yes. Gwen stared out on the passing scene. For her it was always passing, no matter what it might be. Suddenly the night in the parking lot opened up before her, unfolding out of the blazing center of the day, and for one long nearly unendurable instant the asphalt was cold and hard against her frantic shrinking from the light, a huge bright shower of light and she gripped the handle on the dashboard so she would not fall. She looked at Trinity and the door of the glove compartment popped magically open, spilling pretty maps of the states across her lap.

"Are you all right?"

The story came out in a rush, the confusions of the night, awareness rising up and sinking down, dream pictures of actual events outside her head, the loss of motor function, the weight on her chest, the flight of the moon.

Trinity kept her eyes on the road, saying nothing.

This time Gwen heard herself telling the story, and sometimes what she heard sounded odd. She doesn't believe me, either, she thought, and began to cry.

Trinity looked over at her. "We've got to get you two out of here," she said, She sounded worried.

Up ahead black shapes started lifting up out of the fields, familiar angles and planes. Gwen's head began to shake back and forth. "No," she said firmly. "No."

"I think there's some Kleenex in the glove compartment," said Trinity. "Listen, it's all right, no one's going to touch you, okay? Trust me."

"You've already lied once," said Gwen, sniffling into a ball of wet tissue.

"Yes." She smiled. "But I didn't know it at the time."

They came bumping into the backyard and stopped, the bug-splattered windshield filled with the sight of a grimacing Dallas down on one knee, arm locked around Beale's struggling neck, seeming to squeeze the blood out of his mangled mouth. Dash stood to one side, observing, the indulgent parent, faintly amused.

Gwen leaped from the car, screaming, "What's this?!" her face a violent red, veins swelling into plastic tubes, buzzsaw voice louder even than Zoe's. "What's this, huh? What's this?!"

She ran up, arms flailing as if herding pigs out of the pen. Everyone, including Beale, looked over in surprise. When no one moved or spoke she spun around and bolted for the house.

"What's the matter with her?" asked Dash.

Trinity followed without replying. Gwen was already in the john behind the locked door. Maryse's head poked from the top of The Object. "What's wrong with her?"

There were loud shouts from outside. "She thinks Dash raped her last night."

"Oh God."

Wreathed in a tangle of uncombed curls, Dot's sleep-pressed face thrust itself around the doorjamb. "This slamming?" she barked gruffly.

"Gwen," replied Trinity. "She went to the john. She's upset."

"Might have known. Girl lives in the toilet." Dot disappeared. Then her door slammed, too.

Trinity and Maryse looked at one another in resigned silence. Trinity spoke. "What's with the wrestling?"

"Oh, that." The lines of Maryse's mouth lengthened and thinned. "Some kind of loud and ridiculous boy scene. One said one thing, another said another, then they yelled and ran outside. I think it was something about the beer."

For a moment Trinity felt herself drastically reduced in size, an injection molded figurine in a cardboard house whose giant owner might be glimpsed at one of the paneless windows, straw hair tied in stiff paintbrush braids, eyes enormous, round, noon blue, and glassy as ice. She looked at Maryse. "I think it's time to go on a trip."

"Oh goody, I'm going, too."

Inside the bathroom Gwen stood, too cranked up to sit, holding on to a towel rack, forehead against the wall, trying to recall something useful she had read in a book once, a couple lines of Zen nonsense resting at the bottom of a page under a bowl of inky plums, you are not you, you have no face, bad thoughts come and go like clouds across the mirror, keep the mirror polished bright, or something like that. Yes. Better than a towel rack. Certainly she could imagine a mirror, she could imagine clouds, drifting thick and deeply shadowed, blue and gray and black, billowing, bunching, speaking to one another across strokes of fire. It began to rain. The night, the light, the moon, the dish ran away with the spoon.

She jumped at the furious rattle of the doorknob.

"Who's in there?" Beale demanded angrily.

She pulled back the bolt.

"So," he said, forcing himself in past her, "you came back."

"Yeah, I did. What happened to you?"

"What does it look like?" He leaned his bloody face in toward the mirror, inspecting the damage. "I got cut."

"Let me see." She turned his sweaty head into the light. He yelped and pulled away. She wet a stiff musty-smelling cloth and dabbed it gently under his nose. "What were you two fighting about?"

"I don't know." He pushed her hand away and touched the lip himself. He winced. "I think he's crazy."

"They're all crazy." She caught an unexpected glimpse of herself in the dark glass. She looked like someone she wouldn't want to know.

"He's been after me since we got here. Jesus, look at this, do you think I need stitches?"

When she didn't answer he turned around. She was watching the water drip into the rusty sink, one, two, three. She looked up. "What?"

He went back to studying himself. "This is great. You've been raped and I've been beat up. What a pair." He laughed at their reflected images. "And Etherians were supposed to be such gentle peace-loving folk."

Water gathered in the ring of the faucet tip, a clear trembling bubble that bulged and broke, releasing the drops in measured succession pop, pop, pop, into the stained enamel sink, logical, inevitable, musical. Her voice was soft and even. "Why don't you kill them?"

"Hah, hah, yeah, well, the gun, there's a problem with the gun, problem being there seems not to be one anymore, like it's plumb disappeared or sprouted legs and walked off or maybe someone found it accidentally and accidentally put it in his pocket. You know he jumped me from behind when I went outside looking for you. Think I got him a good one in the eye, though. Hope I did, anyway."

"Why?" she asked in a near whisper. Down the dark drain dropped the lonely drips.

"Why? 'Cause he was choking the hell out of my throat, that's why."

There was a long silence. Then she said, "No. Why'd he jump you?"

"He's nuts. Look at the sister. Who can figure any of these people? He and Dash are in the kitchen eating waffles and I go in to find out if anybody knows where you went and we talk, everyone real friendly, and I go out and suddenly he's on top of me, biting my ear. So then Dash comes out and just stands there gaping like a fool. Christ, look at my face."

His upper lip had swollen into an ugly pink larval thing, beard hairs bristling in every direction like poisoned barbs.

"Listen, here's what we'll do. You stay right here, don't go out, don't let anyone in. I'm gonna go talk to the little fucker and then we'll leave, okay? Once we get out we'll stop in town and send the cops back. But first I gotta find out what happened to my gun. Don't let anyone in, okay?"

She nodded her head. Whatever. Securing the door behind him, she perched on the edge of the toilet seat and thought again about being a mirror. The best she could manage was a ghostly replica of an aluminum plate. Suddenly she leaned forward, staring at the wall. There was a small hole she had never noticed before bored through the side of the house. When she looked into it, she could see part of the yard, the road, the bracketing corn. She imagined Dash standing out there, hands in his pockets, eyeball twisting around in the wall like a separate creature. A bile-colored cloud settled heavily onto her aluminum plate. The night, the light, the

[98]

moon, memory shuffling, reshuffling the same old greasy deck in which all the suits had been replaced by murky rectangles depicting not just the previous night but all her famous nights, the one in the parking lot, the one on the beach, the one in Mechanicsville, the one in etcetera, etcetera, and all the face cards reduced to two: grinning Men in the Moon and glossy left-profile mug shots of her.

A quick tap on the door. "It's me." She got up and let Beale in. "They're gone," he announced excitedly. "Dash took off in the car somewhere, Dallas just left to go visit some stupid friend of his down the road, one of those houses you looked at last night. So here's the plan. You stay here, get all our gear ready to go, and I'm gonna try to catch up with him." He moved in close to the mirror. "God, I look like hell." He pressed his fingers gingerly to his lip. "Ow. I'm not even gonna be able to chew for a couple of days. Shit, I can't believe he did this to me."

Gwen was looking at herself in the glass and didn't realize he was finished. "Oh," she said, glancing up at him. "Yes, I'll do that."

He frowned and winced and was gone. She stepped out blinking into the big sunny room, bright dust falling like snow through great diagonal planes of lemon light. The sun broke across the curving metallic surface of The Object into a hundred twinkling stars that whispered urgently to one another in human voices. There were people inside. She picked up Beale's dirty clothes off the floor, stuffed them in his pack, and got down on her knees and began rolling up his large unwieldy sleeping bag. The cat, licking whiskers tough as fishing line, ambled out of the kitchen to rub its soft hairy flanks against her leg. The telephone rang with a shattering abruptness. Trinity climbed out of The Object. "Oh hi, you feeling any better?" She picked up the phone, listened for a moment, then carefully placed the receiver down on the splintered windowsill. She smiled pleasantly at Gwen and climbed back inside The Object. The cat purred. The black receiver lay on its side as if stricken in a pool of liquid sun, emitting the muffled squawks of a parrot in a curtained cage.

From between the peeling bars of the loft railing Edsel watched the funny lady. She acted like a clown. First she rolled the sleeping bag up, then she let it get away. She rolled it up, it stuck out its tongue. It was difficult not to laugh. When she bent over to tie up the strings her breasts swung about inside her shirt. His sister's were bigger. She turned the bag on end and sat down facing the TV. The set was off. She didn't move. This was boring. After a while he snuck back to his stool. Under the smudged glass the green hand went round and round. He watched. They're here! he saw himself shouting from the rail, family faces beaming up with pride. He watched, but the screen was always empty. Then he crouched on his bed, knees digging into the lumpy mattress, head hanging out the open window. The sun was everywhere, and he could see forever, all the way to Timmy's house, a bike ride away if Mom would only get up and let him go. They played terrorists in the spooky barn. He could see the funny man with b.o. walking far away down the road. Grown-ups could come and go without permission, but all they ever did was fight and shout and make ugly faces at each other. He already knew what he wanted to be when he grew up—happy. He leaned out, chest flat against the sill, until his head was directly above the steps. He brought up some spit from the back of his throat, puckered his lips, and let drop a nice juicy hawker. It made a dark star on the dry cement. He puckered his lips again, and suddenly something made him look up. The funny man was gone. The sun was everywhere, and he could see forever. It had been a sound, a new one, like one of Arnie MacGuffin's M-80s. He waited, watching. It did not happen again. He let the gob fly from his mouth. Boom! A direct hit. Boom, boom, boom. Saturation bombing. He went back to check the screen. If people had radar eyes, instead of black dots in the middle, there'd be fuzzy little

[100]

green windshield wipers clicking around in circles and everyone would be able to see vast distances and know in advance about storms and missiles and aliens. It could be fun. He slipped over to the railing. The lady was still there, digging at the back of her head with her fingernails. This was the most boring house in the world. When would Dad get back? When would Mom ever wake up?

■■■■■■■ "GOOD EVENING, YOU'RE ON
the air, what is your question, please?"

"Huh? Hello? Am I on?"

"Yes, sir, you're on the air, go ahead, please."

"Uh, what? Hello?"

"Turn down your radio, sir."

"Oh, oh yeah, uh wait a . . . okay?"

"Yes, sir, go ahead, please."

"Yes. I was wondering, uh, about this electricity business?
There was a fellow on the tube the other night said no one
really knows how the stuff works or even what it is. Now
I was thinking, seems these UFO things spend a lot of time
out in the country buzzing around those big utility poles,
and I was wondering like maybe they feed off them or something, like electricity is maybe sacred to them like water
maybe."

"What about that, Dot, Dash?"

"It's interesting the caller should mention this, it's one of
the reasons we live out where we do, although we believe
they're not feeding so much as just listening."

"Our daughter, you know, spends hours sitting quietly beside the wall sockets."

"Really? The wall sockets?"

"Yes, and it's highly likely that people who die by electrocution are actually killed by an inability to process such a concentrated dose of pure information."

"The Occupants tell us that electrocution is a most spectacularly pleasant form of death. You go over in possession of everything you need."

"So wait a minute now, what are you saying here? Electrocution involves some sort of divine ecstasy and maybe what—since it's such a rush, we should perhaps consider executing capital offenders by some other, more punishing method?"

"I suppose that's for the state to decide."

"Fatal injection?"

"Well, that's a whole other issue, what the chemicals would do to your pilot."

"Your pilot?"

"What is it that differentiates us from this table, for example?"

"The table has four legs."

"Electricity. Look at the Frankenstein myth. That's what life is, amps, juice, a steady current. And human thought? Sparks leaping a gap."

"I am shocked."

"Excuse me, excuse me, please."

"Yes, sir, go ahead, get in on this, it's your question."

"Well, I just had a thought, what about that pointy thing on top of the Capitol dome, what is that, anyway? Looks like some kind of lightning rod to me, pulling all that electric down out of the sky. Messages, maybe. Probably they know all about 'em in Washington, always have. Maybe the next step is plugging into each of our heads, suck out the juice in there."

"All right, sir, thank you for your call, I guess we might all consider wearing metal hats."

"Whole dome looks like one big skull to me, anyway."

"Thank you, sir, we have to be moving on now. All right,

then, let me see, before we suffer a grid failure here. These so-called Occupants which you both, which your entire family has apparently seen, communicated with on numerous occasions, yet you refuse to describe—"

"There's nothing to describe. Human words are a by-product of a specific human environment, arising like our plants and animals out of exceedingly local conditions in a universe of a billion billion environments. The Occupants are a product of an entirely different set of options. As such, they exist beyond our language."

"Beyond language?"

"Certainly."

"One is struck dumb. As in our own family."

"All right, but whatever they are, they visit our planet in spaceships that might be said to resemble giant amoeba. True?"

"Blue."

"Giant blue amoeba."

"That's why you rarely see them during the day without special equipment. They blend right in, hovering over us almost constantly."

"You know, another reason so many sightings occur at night on lonely country roads is because they're out there waiting for accidents to happen. An accident is a rather special event. Who has ever come up with a theory that adequately explained the meaning of accidents?"

"When worlds collide."

"So what are you saying, if you want to get to Mars quick, drive your car into a telephone pole? Or maybe stick your finger in a light socket?"

"Who said anything about Mars?"

"Who indeed? Well, we'll try to get our planets straightened out during this commercial break. You're listening to the Night Owl on WHO-AM/FM, all-day, all-night radio."

. . . .

"Yes," said Dot, "I thought that went rather well, didn't you?" Her braceleted arm reached out briskly to close yet again the gaping mouth of the glove compartment.

"I didn't like his attitude."

"You don't like anybody's attitude."

"Rub my shoulders."

She shifted around uncomfortably in her seat and began kneading the cords of his neck. "God, you're tight, it's all knotted up in there."

"Any time, darling, just say the word, and we can stop and trade seats."

Dash hated driving, especially at night when the effort of holding four bald tires to a shifting road surface he could barely see in the vague wobbling beam of their one unaligned headlight keyed him into such a state he'd spend a good part of the rest of the night tossing in bed reliving the whole trip in grim hallucinatory detail from ignition to final brake unless the dream was happening now, in which case those fast approaching high beams might be real enough to require evasive action. He swerved. The car shook in the roar and blast of a cannonballing gas truck passing inches off their left side.

"Look out!" Dot yelled.

Dash eased his foot some off the accelerator. "Driving this thing is like a blind man trying to tap his way home with a rubber cane."

"Well, watch where you're going, for God's sakes."

"I'm in here, too."

There was a moment of silence.

"You know I don't like to criticize."

"Sixty-two miles," said Dash.

They sat facing ahead through a windshield speckled with tar and exploded insects. Soft darkness rushed at them, screaming.

"Now where were we?" asked Dot. "You always change the subject whenever I ask a question. You'd think you were running for office or having an affair."

"I said he thought we were fools."

"So when has that ever mattered before?"

Home was on her mind tonight and homeyness and the decided lack of, and as usual she was irritable. It seemed now as if she were tired all the time, fatigue radiating out of her bones in long nagging waves. She needed rest, rest and silence and solitude, and where was she going to get that? And when?

"You know what I mean," said Dash.

"It doesn't matter. They can laugh or cry or curse or smash their radios, but the one thing they don't do is move the dial and that's why we're invited back despite what he may think of us. What are you complaining about, anyway? The electric stuff was wonderful."

"I did that last time."

"A golden oldie, they loved it."

"And why start in on Zoe and the Institute? They'll try to get her back, you know that." She subtracted: one from four equals three, not counting the two she had no responsibility for who could be kicked out at will. If Trinity ran off again, that would leave the other two. Two. It had been years since the numbers were that small. Her equations tended lately toward the rounded harbor of placid zero.

"It was good for her," she said.

"The box was good for her?"

"It was good for us."

"She didn't sleep for a week when she got back. You know who funds that place. They want her, they want all the kids like her. I'm not discussing this again. We're not discussing this again. End of discussion."

There was an image Dot had of herself when young, standing alone out in the open, in a flowing field of golden waist-high wheat, sculpted face turned into the clean wind, hair streaming back, sharp eyes fixed on the blue distance, an assertive image out of an old painting or bronze engraving or head of a coin, never quite clear enough to determine whether the look was one of expectation or dread.

And what did this mean, and why was she thinking of it just now?

Daughters are a disappointment, she remembered her mother remarking casually over afternoon coffee with friends.

Strange the things that came and went through the mind.

Damp wind howled across the open windows unable to muffle the steady tick tick tick somewhere behind that had puzzled mechanics in several states. We'll drive it 'til it dies, Dash had said. The car, the saucers, the family.

Clouds of bugs swarmed up continually over the hood, thick and brilliant, as if they rode upon a vast bed of embers.

"Must you drive so fast?" she asked.

"Yes."

The car hit a bump, and the glove compartment popped open.

"I'd like to get there in one piece," she said, gathering up the spilled maps.

His mumblings were drowned in car noise.

She stared unseeing for a moment at the white blips of the center line flashing urgently at them, then turned to him and said, "I don't like being cut off, either, if you don't mind."

There was a long pause.

"I give up. Cut off from what?"

"The show. Several times tonight right in the middle of some important explanation of mine you deliberately—"

"What do you mean? It was all I could do to keep you from stepping all over me."

She turned abruptly to the window and was momentarily startled by the pale reflection of her own face speeding along beside her out there in the dark. The tires thumped, the glove compartment fell open. "You're a real shit," she said to the night. "Do you know that?"

"Why not, you remind me often enough."

The brakes squealed for an instant as a sharp curve leaped suddenly into the light.

"We didn't need Hitler and the hollow earth hypothesis, either. Talk about playing the fool."

"What do you mean? Nazis and UFOs, what America's all about."

"Oh please. Mister Night Owl almost swallowed his microphone."

"But you were the one who said it went so well."

"Well, what do I know?" She turned her head. "Gwen, dear, what did you think of tonight's show?"

A figure stirred from the shadows of the backseat where her greasy head leaned against the vibrating window glass, gazing out at the darkness that moved, the darkness that did not. She sat up and shrugged her shoulders. "I don't know," she said. "I never saw one before."

"Well, regardless, you can surely render an opinion."

She sat up straighter. Lights had already appeared on this empty road, had revealed themselves personally to her, had danced, had winked. She had kept quiet. She wasn't feeling well. "Okay," she said, "I guess it was okay."

"There," Dot grunted. "The considered opinion of an unbiased observer."

Dash's glance came up immediately into the rearview mirror, bone features dim green in the grainy dashboard light, her eyes touching his for only an instant before darting away like shocked fish. Eyes that knew something she did not. Such eyes surrounded her now without cease. In them was the record of events begun in cold distant places and the suggestion that the implausibility of the truth was disguise enough. Her eyes knew nothing. Since coming among these people she had left one life behind and been born again into ignorance and incomprehension. Mysteries thrived about her like weeds, and clear views were difficult to obtain. What had happened that night long ago? What happened any night? The past was a jigsaw readily assembled into any shape. What was happening now? She kept watch, muttering to herself. For conclusions, such as they were, now had to be pieced together in solitary.

So he ran out on you, Maryse said. So what. I didn't like him anyway.

[108]

It's all for the best, said Trinity.

He was a creep, said Dallas.

He might come back, said Edsel.

Not with what's baking in that oven, laughed Dot.

His tan and bundled pack stood stiffly upright in a corner beside the door, unclaimed still, a curious object beached there from an awful catastrophe far away.

"Stop!" Gwen cried. "Stop the car!"

"Huh?" Dash tried to watch her and the road, too.

"You heard the girl," said Dot. "Pull over."

The brakes squeaked, the wheels wobbled to a halt, the glove compartment popped open. "Now just what's the—"

"Let me out!" She pushed impatiently at the back of Dot's seat.

"All right, honey, hold on here 'til I get out."

She squirmed from the car, hand cupped to her mouth, and rushed away from the headlight to stand hunched in the brush, vomiting into the dry grass until empty and exhausted she turned away on unsteady legs, loops of saliva dangling off her lips. Dot walked her back to the car, patting her gently, "Now now, now now." Dash had remained inside behind the wheel, radio turned up to the news out of Chicago. Another abortion clinic bombing. The U.S. rejected the latest Soviet arms proposal. Dot found her an oily rag under the seat she could wipe herself with.

"I'm sorry," she said. "I don't usually get carsick."

"No, I'm sure you don't." Dot glanced meaningfully at her husband.

Gwen curled up on the backseat under a scratchy wool blanket smelling vaguely of cat piss. She tried hard to concentrate on ideas of firmness, stability, lead weights, ships' anchors, slabs of granite that never budged. Under her the car sped on through darkness so complete it was easy to lie there looking up backwards out the window and imagine you were traversing the great vacuum at the edge of the universe where the stars stopped and the real nothing began.

Then all at once they were back at the place even she now

thought of as home and she was safe inside the zippered cocoon that smelled of her, hard against a floor she had vowed to quit how many days ago? looking up at church roof and church beams and the familiar darkness trapped within, waiting patiently for the rock of night to soften and dissolve and bathe her sore eyes in a few hours of lidded peace before the light and morning clamor roused her again into yet another loud long fretful day, anxious and confused.

Later (whatever that meant, time grown tricky and headstrong between these old walls, a magical juncture eerie as the site of an accident) she heard or thought she heard a noise yanking her from sleep or whatever related mental state she happened to be occupying at the moment, creak-creak-creak down the tall spiral staircase. No, she thought at once, and it was more than a word. Her body hardened, inside and out. They'd have to break the shell to pry it open this time, and by then she'd be dead. Huddled there in the bag, she tried to see what was coming with her ears, but it was impossible to penetrate beyond the frantic bounding of her heart. Blind and frightened, so intent on anticipating the cold touch and the moment of sharp pieces, she became aware, only after they had passed, of the steps' quiet progression across the complaining floor, the soft slap of the screen door. Cautiously she turned and peeked out into the room. There was nothing to see. Had there ever been? Light sizzled blue white above the door as a large beetle hit the current in the Bug Buster. She settled back down and after a while her antenna slowly retracted and blood rapids subsided into the wide lulling swell of a dazed calm she had learned to accept as actual sleep.

The moon, minus a nice bite-sized piece, shed a weak fluorescent glow across the land. A quick black shadow slid over the silver grass, stretched itself out, monstrous, spindle-limbed, along the bright surface of the road. This was Dallas, strolling down the center line with all the confidence of a property owner who knows the country at night is his alone. As he passed he counted off the telephone poles to a certain number and then his steps and when he stopped he executed a smart right-face his father would have been proud of and plunged through the crackling brush into the high corn where it was very dark. There was nothing there. He looked all around, then squatted to peer in among the stalks. Yes, the thing, a heap of crumpled black, lay on the dirt two rows away. He pushed through the leaf walls and stopped. A dark odor settled over him like a hood. From his pocket he slipped the penlight his parents used to inspect crumbling teeth and inflamed throats and squatted down again on strong webbed claws, the smell a clotted ball of twisting forms in his mind. He clicked on the light, its thin beam filling with the sudden image of (here was a good shivery thrill) a human eye that neither glared nor gaped, squinted nor blinked. Its function had changed, its color had faded, it resembled a spoiled egg. The face itself had gone to blue, a new blue absent at least from the media palette that furnished color to Dallas's world. The rest of it, the attached body, was a broken lump that seemed to have been dropped from a great height, a space-man perhaps, tossed out a hatch by laughing barbarians in iridescent suits. The thing had lain here for three nights now and each night Dallas had made his pilgrimage, a scientific excursion, really, out to this spot to record privately the organic changes. He was an obsessive student of process. The slow shift of color across a spectrum of nameless energies. The dark bubbles blooming on the peeling cheeks, the ballooning body, shirt stretched taut across the rigid shoulders, pants inflating around the thighs. And the rich and infinitely varied aroma of nature's gourmet kitchen. Dallas crouched there in the bottom of the tasseling cornfield and looked on in wonder, the yellowy circle of light playing up and down, experiencing the flushed sensations of an anthropologist stumbling unexpectedly upon a wholly new form of life. He tore a strip of cloth from the thing's fraying shirt and tied it around his ankle. He sat on his haunches like a native and contemplated his find. Left here this specimen could age naturally into whatever shapes and hues awaited at the end of the process, but time was also pushing its hours up the stalks

[111]

and soon Old Man MacGuffin would be out for the harvest and what a scene that would be—discovering the surprise vegetable in the patch clogging the blades of the combine. Dallas switched off the light and put it in his pocket. Working as carefully as he could, he managed to heave the thing up onto one shoulder and trudge out of the field onto the road. Muscles developed at work made the job easier than expected. Wouldn't all be amazed at the bacon he was bringing home now? Halfway there a cold liquid began seeping through the back of his shirt. He smiled. Better and better. The hard shiny road was a length of chrome. There was a handful of neon moons burning behind a grill of tightly strung wire in the open sky. In the cities there's ash on the roof and a fine sprinkling of metal from clouds black as chimney soot. His eyes are yellow with vertical pupils of red. The hollow ground trembles through padded feet. The impatient concert crowd at the sold-out Polydome is chanting his name. They are waiting for him, tonight's superstar.

He approached the house from the shadowed side and slunk up along the wall, a sweating Santa with a big bag of goodies, stooping beneath the windowsills, ever alert to the dangerous curiosity of naughty little boys and girls. He rounded a corner and stopped, listening hard for a moment, before easing his load to the ground. He stopped again and looked behind. The cemetery tree looked back, displayed its incurably arthritic arms. He got down and crawled in under the church on his belly, dragging the thing behind him. There was a wall in here where steps from a trap in his parents' room led down into a dank closet-sized space just right for a wine or tornado cellar or handy "counseling" room for "disturbed" female parishioners. It was hard work pulling that weight along the ground, shoving it tight against the bricks, covering it with sticky clods of dirt, piles of damp leaves. He sweated like a miner and when he was done he went out and sat on top of good ol' ALPHEUS PAGE and chugged the two beers he had hidden there after dinner. He lobbed the empty cans twinkling in the moonlight out into the shadowy corn and wiped his lips on the back of a hand and tasted dirt—what night is made of, he thought. Back inside he paused, pondering the dark enigmatic shape on the floor that was Gwen. Then he climbed the stairs on soft catlike pads, stripped, and eased into bed beneath the perpetual astonishment of Larry, Moe, and Curly. Headphones clamped to his ears, he withdrew down stone tunnels of sleep to the amplified clang of metal on metal and the screams electricity makes forced through a wire.

SHE CAME TO IN DARK WATER, clawing for air and a strange silver surface rippling far, too far, away. The weight of an ocean pressed down across her, cold salt tide tugging at her belly. She couldn't see, she couldn't breathe. Blackness gurgled through an open pipe. Dash unzipped her bag and spit inside. This was every night now. Real as death. But by dawn he was a ghost and at breakfast merely a dream. What was true? She didn't know.

When she left the bathroom the others were already in place, more or less, around the long table, chewing, sipping, smoking, fluid stems of blue and gray twisting into quick complicated spirals too giddying to consider at this unassembled hour. It was a gray morning, and the early light lay like powder on sleep-wrinkled faces. No one spoke, entertained as they were by the audio portion of The A.M. Show already well in progress behind the closed wall of the mysterious room at the altar end of the house:

"Pick what up?"

"Try using your eyes for a change."

"That? I didn't put it there."

"Oh no, of course not, you never leave anything out for me to trip and break my neck."

"I see the bullshit's flying with the crows today."

"See what you want to see."

The pale tepid orange juice tasted as if a nail had been dissolved in it. The toast was cold and slightly damp. She went to the kitchen for an apple and discovered the cat on top of the stove, lapping out the bottom of the frying pan. She wasn't really hungry, her stomach hurt.

From behind the wall:

"Selfish? Selfish?! I've devoted my life to that child."

"Oh, just forget it. I don't know why I bother. You haven't heard me for twenty years."

Zoe reached out, overturned her cup, and began banging her head on the edge of the table, strands of lank hair whipping through the puddles of spilled milk. Dallas tapped a spoon against his plate in time with an irritating rhythm inside Gwen's head.

"Do something, for Christ's sake!" shouted Trinity. "It's your goddamn turn."

"Shit!" He leaped from the chair, seized his baby sister by the wrists, and dragged her off into The Object, where, using frayed rope the goat had chewed on, he tied her securely to the pilot's seat, command central to the stars.

When he returned, the voices had stopped. "They're screwing now," he said, licking butter off the blade of a knife and looking right at Gwen, and it was scary because there wasn't any way she could stop his eyes from going in as deeply as they wished.

"Just the image I want to have between me and my corn-flakes," said Trinity.

He shrugged. "It's what they do."

"Isn't it time for you to go to work?" asked Maryse. She poked at the swaddled mess lying motionless in her lap. Only the head was visible, a lumpy, somewhat round object sprouting transparent wisps of crinkly fiber. Eyes and mouth firmly shut, Mignon resembled a soap carving of a baby. Maryse pinched the colorless cheeks with intensifying force until the lips jerked open, emitting a brief rodentlike squeak. Satisfied,

[115]

she plugged the hole with the stubby nipple of a plastic bottle and settled back, glaring around the table, daring anybody to utter one word.

Dallas pointed the wet knife in Gwen's direction. "So, what now?"

Carefully, she focused her gaze on a spot at the center of his forehead. "I don't know."

"Have trouble without dickhead around to decide for you?"

Behind her, like some monstrous motorized sculpture, The Object came eerily to life, began to wobble slowly back and forth, its cheap metal skin buckling and popping on the hard-wood floor. "Not at all," she replied, trying, as usual, to ne-gotiate the least hazardous path through the familial wood. "It's just I can't think too clearly here."

"Yeah? Tell me about it." He dumped an incredible amount of sugar right out of the bowl and into his coffee cup, stirring it in with the knife.

"What'd you dream about last night?" asked Maryse inno-cently.

Gwen hesitated. Was it actually possible this weird woman with the bad complexion and dirty fingernails could help un-ravel the disturbing mystery of her nights, sort event from illusion, cast the cataracts from her inner eye? "I can't re-member," she said. "I think I dreamt I was awake."

"Oh, really? But that can be quite revealing."

"Help!" came a small voice from the closed room. "Help! Help!" growing in volume, the muffled cries of Dot behind the wall. "Someone help me!"

The Object continued to rock, a big ball bobbing on a big ocean.

The phone rang. On the tenth ring Dallas lunged at the noise. "Fuck you!" he screamed into the mouthpiece. "No one's home!" He opened his fist, let the receiver go crashing to the floor.

Tall white clouds long as ships passed in magisterial re-view across the row of open windows.

"Let's go to the mountains," suggested Maryse brightly.

[116]

Trinity stared at her in bleak silence.

"Hitchhike," Maryse added. "Who needs money?"

"The mountains suck," said Dallas.

The screen door flew open bang! and in rushed Edsel shouting, "Look what I got!" waving a length of old rubber tubing in Gwen's face. The tube moved, stuck out its tongue, and Gwen flinched.

"Only a garter," laughed Dallas.

Trinity remained at a respectful distance. "They still bite."

"Yeah," agreed Edsel, proudly exhibiting the fresh pair of blood freckles decorating the web of skin between thumb and forefinger.

Maryse peered at the wounds. "Now you'll need a tetanus shot," she said. "And they really hurt."

"Look, he shit on me, too." A twisting trail of whitish slime ran along the underside of his arm.

"That's come," said Dallas.

Maryse pointed sternly. "Don't let that stuff get in the bite or you might get pregnant with a big bunch of snake babies."

"That's not how you get pregnant," protested Edsel. "And besides, I'm a boy."

"But you forget," Maryse reminded him. "You're not from Earth."

Edsel paused. "Yes, I am, too. You're the one with the alien baby. You're the one the monster fucked."

"Shut your mouth, you little shit."

"Get it out of the house," ordered Trinity. "Now. Let it go."

"I hate you," he shouted, heading for the door. "I wish this snake would bite you in the foot and it'd turn black and fall off."

"So." Dallas looked over at Gwen. "You wanna ride in to work with me?"

She could imagine his work, a chaotic meeting ground of steel and flesh. "And what would I do—mop up?"

"Naw, they wouldn't even let you in the building. You could wander around town, meet us at the truck after."

"That'd take a good five minutes," said Maryse. Mignon

had finished sucking and been deposited like a bulky hand-
bag at the foot of her chair.

"She's already been through town," said Trinity.

"It's quiet. She wants to think."

Something warm touched Gwen suddenly under the table
and again she flinched.

"Jesus, are you jumpy," Maryse declared.

"You wanna go or what?"

"Help!" called Dot inside the wall. "Help me!" Since no
one had ever given the slightest indication they had heard
these cries, Gwen wondered if maybe she hadn't begun hal-
lucinating aurally, too, and when a horn sounded outside,
stopped, sounded again, she waited for a sign from the others,
but they were all looking at her.

"So?"

She noticed now how the light concentrated in Dallas's
eyes like night stars or the little bright X's on a cartoon character who is drunk or knocked out.

"Help . . . help . . ." Dot's voice grew steadily quieter, fading with repetition in a pleasing echolike effect. But the truck
was here and Beale was not and she was struck by the realization that his presence simply did not matter, had never
mattered. In this situation every person was on her own. So
when Dallas's chair went scraping across the bare floor, and
there he was, looming over her with that maddening bland
expression she had given up trying to decode, she got up too
and followed him without a word out back where an aging
pickup truck she recognized instantly waited, idling noisily,
its engine trying and trying to clear its throat.

"This is Gwen," Dallas announced, opening the cab door.
She slid in quickly across the cracked leatherette seat. "That's
Donnie."

She thought she recognized him, too, the one in the window at the 7-Eleven, only now his hair was shorter and a
haystack brown and his thick converging eyebrows were
dead white and fuzzy as caterpillars. He nodded, "How's it
going?" and jerked the stick into gear, heading out for a

smeared blotch of green perched on the horizon like something left unrefrigerated too long.

She bounced along between them, gripping the seat edge, six warm denimed thighs jostling together there side by side as a peace medallion dangling on a chain from the rearview mirror swayed in benedictory arcs over them. Donnie punched a cassette into the tape deck, and familiar music assaulted their faces, Vic and the Vectors, "Who Put The Baby In The Microwave?" When Donnie inquired, shouting, what she did, she screamed back, "I'm on hiatus." The ride ended in a mammoth asphalt parking lot flanked by identical rectangular warehouses of industrial red brick. On one side the chain links of a tall concertina-topped fence were clotted with knee-high drifts of snowy white feathers.

"Chickens over there," Dallas explained. "In here we do the hogs."

The air had a sharp taint to it, the taste of ozone and hot iron filings. A procession of sallow-faced men and women in T-shirts and jeans passed one at a time through a narrow monitored gate.

"There's a guard?" Gwen asked.

Dallas smirked. "Don't want you civilians to get too good a look at our secrets."

Donnie laughed through his nose. He didn't seem too bright.

"Albert's that way. When you run out of town, come back and play in the truck. When you get sick of the truck, go ahead and walk home."

"But watch out," Donnie warned. "There's guys like to run strangers off the road for a couple of kicks." He looked at Dallas.

"If you're not here when we get out," said Dallas, "we're gone."

"Sure." She was watching the women filing in, searching for a face like her own.

"Okay," said Dallas.

"Fine."

"Yeah," said Donnie.

They lifted their rubber boots out of the truck bed and walked off in a rolling sailor-on-leave swagger meant to impress her. She started to picture them inside at their jobs and abruptly stopped. Maybe if she could walk like that . . . A whistle shrieked and a cloud of sparrows burst from a neighboring tree, wheeled over the painted meadow of glaring auto tops, and disappeared back into the dark fluttering leaves. Such freedom, she thought. Because they were too small to eat.

Downtown Albert was three stunted blocks of abraded brick and commercial disappointment, persisting with seedy stubbornness between the boarded facades and gutted interiors. There was one bar, one restaurant, one pharmacy, one beauty shop, willing to "tease" all heads. In the window of D&C Hardware a string of Christmas minilights framed a dusty display of red-beribboned claw hammers and among drifts of Styrofoam snow a tiny Santa was about to be seized in the nasty teeth of a giant monkey wrench. It had been years obviously since the one theater had glowed with the spiritual light of manufactured miracles, the marquee was bulbless, the ticket booth a smashed cylinder of damp plaster and charred wood. Who had occupied the stool that last night? Did she look like me? What was the movie? Unfed parking meters cast a grim row of sad lollipop shadows down the potholed street. A big bright car cruised slowly by, every nice white face inside turning to absorb in an instant all they needed to know about her. She felt an unexpected pang of homesickness (or was it some physical complaint?) and suddenly remembered that it was her mother's birthday today or tomorrow or sometime last week.

She slipped into Ace Drugs where a flimsy wire rack of lame greeting cards revolved with protesting noises in the cool artificial air. The place, all shiny and fluorescent, smelled of bleak hospital corridors and dry medicine in capsules and tablets. The door opened and an elderly hunchbacked woman with tight flesh-colored bandages encasing each leg from ankle to knee shuffled in and down the clean, well-lit center aisle, the rubber cap on her aluminum crutch making a violent sucking sound on the gray linoleum floor. Gwen thought of lungs and phlegm and black drains under autopsy tables; she saw Dallas, stripped to the waist, in a close, windowless room under a naked bulb, slippery blade in hand, scraps of tissue clinging to his boots, he looked straight at her, a pig upside down on a steel hook came in between them and when it cried the sound was exactly the same as that of a human baby. "The discharge should clear up in a couple days," said the bald pharmacist, who had been eyeing Gwen carefully since she walked in. "What?" squawked the woman, crinkling her well-floured face. Gwen looked at the card in her hand. The pond was wax, the ducks stuffed. With Love For You On This Your Day went hastily back on to the rack and she out the door, the single word "prognosis" making a quick escape with her.

Social life in Albert was represented by a cluster of un-washed pickup trucks tethered before The Bent Fork Cafe, the last outpost marking an abrupt end to the "commercial district." Inside this murky cave were tables of large bib-jeaned men in grain caps, sipping from chipped coffee mugs, rattling newspapers, and debating in unemotional tones the immediate advisability of carpet bombing some irritating palm-treed obstinacy where neither the weather nor the government changed often enough. A young woman with a sleepy face and a cigarette in her mouth sat at the counter, spooning lumps of cottage cheese into the infant on her lap. An older woman in a charred apron stood with her back to the room, scrambling eggs on the grill.

"Excuse me," whispered Gwen, her small voice assuming intrusive proportions in this strange, suddenly silent space. The pie under glass was filled with a pale gooey substance impossible to name.

The woman turned and spoke, but unfortunately only half her face was in full working order, the other side seemed to be sliding slowly off her head, the lid on one eye drooping so badly she couldn't possibly see out of it. The good eye studied Gwen with a cat's indifference.

Gwen smiled.

The hand holding the metal spatula twitched once, twice. So the problem was confined to the facial area only.

"I wonder," Gwen began, and felt something cold and wet on her arm—the pink hand of this remarkable child gazing up at her with full baby strength in two clear baby eyes that passed her in that moment an important message she would have to think about later when she was alone and less confused. "I wonder," she began again, "if you've seen a guy about my age, a little taller, come in here any time in the last week. He has curly black hair and—"

The twitching ceased. She spoke out of the corner of her mouth, and it was both hard to look and hard not to. "I've been standing behind this counter seventeen years for someone like you to wander in and ask me a question like that."

"Tell her, Iris," shouted one of the rural lookalikes.

"Is he lost?" Iris asked her.

"I don't know."

"Are you lost?"

"We were traveling together and got separated."

"I know you," the woman said suddenly.

Gwen smiled without much conviction.

"I knew you the minute you walked in. You're one of those space people."

"Sheeeeeit," called an anonymous voice from the floor.

"Oh, let them laugh," said Iris, leaning over the counter. "Who cares? I've seen two myself, just before my operation, right out in the middle of Yellowstone National Park. The bears howled all night. My mother says it's the Russians, but I for one don't believe so, I think they're buzzing them, too."

"Could you tell me, is there a bus terminal around here?"

"Friendley's," said Iris. "The gas station. Two blocks that way. You buy your ticket from the driver."

"The driver?"

"Ask Sam about them. He saw a pair of them last summer on a fishing trip to Arkansas. Then he started showing up at church. Maybe he'd tell you what really happened."

"Thank you. I will." She could feel the eyes, unblinking dozens, on her unprotected back, gross as hard-shelled, quick-legged bugs. When she turned to go, many of them looked her straight in the face, rapists all.

The gas station attendant was an old man with sun-coarsened skin and oily rags dangling from his pockets like a magician on the skids. He held in his hands an auto part of some kind, a big metal ring his scarred filthy fingers kept nervously working themselves in and out of. She stood in front of him, patient as a private eye, quizzing him about the bearded boy, recent arrivals, departures. When she finished talking he reached into his right pocket, all the while steadily returning her curious gaze, and removed a blunt black object the shape of an electric razor that he pressed up against his neck in the crevice beneath his chin. He pressed a button and replied. His voice, vibrating through this plastic box, was the largely indecipherable cackle a toy chicken might make when you pulled the string on its back. He seemed to suffer from the same condition as the grill cook, but in a more advanced state. He pointed up the road. He looked at her. She thanked the Friendley man. She hadn't understood a word.

For variety she decided to walk back through the town on the sunny side of the street. She passed a feed store reeking of fertilizer. The door was wide open. No one inside. It was so quiet she could hear the clicking of bicycle chain as a group of tanned boys in mismatched baseball costume pedaled solemnly along, repeating the deliberate stares of their elders. And of course, now she knew what this was. She'd heard of towns like this before. There was a whole seminar on them at the last Ft. Smith Convocation—Ditto-lands, an Etherian idea of small town America mass-produced on huge space platforms and transported to Earth for jiffy erection in remote locales, on abandoned land. There were supposed to be hundreds of them all over the country inhabited by a skillfully integrated population of human collaborators and Etherian copies of real Earthlings. In Dittoland out for a jog you just might run into yourself.

She hurried back to the truck and locked herself in the cab, where, after several suspenseful minutes, she succeeded in convincing herself that Albert was Albert; Dittolands, if they existed at all, waited in lonely distant regions for strangers far unluckier than herself. Eventually she fell asleep to wake much later with an aching head and the afternoon sun broiling the exposed side of her sweaty face. She groaned, sat up, popped open the door. Before her stretched the long, neat, innumerable rows of employee cars, bright tortoiseshells of steaming enamel and chrome, then the dark brick wall of the Green Farms Packing Company, behind which she could see herself in greasy hair net and stained apron at a sleek polished table, stuffing mashed pig into intestine casing day after day after day; at night she manned the backyard telescope. Railroad tracks curved gleaming through a high-wire gate to vacant loading docks in the shadows of the building. End of the line. Conveyor belts. Hooks. Vats. Did the chickens know? A new clean refrigerated world. No pain, no fear. Drumsticks.

A siren shrieked. She cringed, missiles always in her future. Banks of double doors crashed open, releasing an impatient mob to the freedom of their cars.

"I told you she'd be here," shouted Donnie, tossing his soiled boots into the back.

"How'd you like Albert?" Dallas asked. She'd never really seen him smile but knew that smirk quite well by now.

"It's nice."

The engine and the music started simultaneously. The sinister throb of heavy machinery. A pile driver's percussive clang. The thunder of collapsing walls. A high-speed dental drill. The lead singer sounded exactly like the man at the gas station. On bad shocks they bounced down a bad road, Dallas's shoulder rubbing, rubbing, rubbing against her own.

"So what was your favorite part?"

"The water tower with the skull and crossbones painted on it."

His eyes, those quick dark weapons, were only inches from hers, and she had to look away. "I did that," he said.

"God!" Donnie exclaimed, spewing cigarette smoke. "You're as big a liar as your old man."

Dallas's arm snaked around behind her back, punched Donnie on the shoulder. "Hey!" he yelled, holding the wheel with one big-knuckled hand, slapping back at Dallas with the other. Gwen crouched forward on the edge of the seat as they grappled behind her and the truck veered to and fro across the road.

"Hey, hey, hey," Dallas shouted, connecting on each word. Then the arm withdrew, Gwen settled back into the space between. "He likes to fuck around," said Donnie.

"Step on it," Dallas urged. "Follow that tractor."

They sped across the landscape, animating emptiness with mindless speed.

Outside the 7-Eleven Gwen had a vision. She was alone in the cab, watching the boys horse around in front of the cooler inside, when there was Beale as vivid and goofy and lonesome as he always appeared in real life, trapped in the interval between the filmy windshield and the tinted store window. The muscles of her throat contracted on a cry that would never come. He was standing at the edge of a baking highway in the middle of a great barren desert, looking uncertainly up the road behind him. He extended a wistful thumb. A gray car stopped, he got in, the gray car disappeared. In the vision he was wearing his old backpack. How could that be?

They roared away from the store like stick-up artists, their feet propped on cold six-packs. Pop, pop, pop went the first cans, rapid as gunfire.

"Where we going?" asked Gwen. After two chugs the beer went down like spring water. This was fun. One of the guys.

Dallas raised his can in a mock toast. "To the moon." He drank.

Gwen looked out the window.

"You've already been there, right?" Donnie asked.

She didn't understand.

"Outer space, man. Whoosh, bang!"

"Something like that."

"So what were they like?"

"Who?"

"Those Occupant things."

"I don't know, they weren't *like* anything. It's hard to explain, I guess you just have to experience them."

Donnie nodded, looking serious. "Sexy," he said. He hit the brakes with both feet, and, skidding sideways, the truck lurched off the highway into the deep ruts of a hidden dirt lane that wound through a narrow aisle of plump bushes and monstrous trees whose branches clawed at the truck, scraping paint, tapping at the windows. In the dappled shade of an unexpected clearing stood a small wooden shack with a sway-back roof and broken windows and one crumbling corner where a giant had paused to nibble on the gingerbread. There was a thriving garden of assorted weeds and a couple emaciated cars sunk to the axles in black mud, and the postage stamp yard was strewn with tooled chunks of rusty metal from a machine that must have blown up here at least a century ago.

"Anyone home?" called Donnie, and laughed his funny laugh until beer foam dribbled out his pointy nose.

"What's this?" asked Gwen, nudging a soft orange mushroom with her toe.

"Our summer place," said Dallas.

"I meant this plant."

"That's a basketball," he said with a naturalist's seriousness.

Counting in unison, they pushed together on the heavy warped door. "Eeek!" screamed the frightened wood. "Eeek!" They slipped in sideways one at a time through an opening a foot wide. There were two rooms: the remains of a kitchen containing a fixtureless sink, bare cupboards hanging off the walls by their nails, and an overturned refrigerator packed with dirt that now served as a jumbo planter for a dozen or so tender shoots of marijuana; and the front "parlor," a drifter's lounge, a delinquent's party den. Where the walls weren't dense with spray-painted slogans and band names (Oi!, Megabone, Vectors Rule), the plaster was broken into fist-sized holes. Soft gray webs thick as cotton candy hung from the corners of a ceiling cracked and buckled and discolored by what appeared to be tremendous urine stains. Covering the floor, as if carefully sifted there in a deep even layer, was a carpet of dust, dirt, ash, butts, scraps, grounds, rodent turds, condoms, rags, papers, six-holed sets of plastic rings, cups, cans crushed and whole, and beneath the milky panes of a window where a couple of fat flies buzzed in futile commotion a mattress black with grime that Dallas kicked, prompting a mad stampede of many-legged bugs.

"Oh my!" Gwen exclaimed, though she had slept on worse, had huddled one frosty night on a piece of damp cardboard below an interstate bridge outside Indianapolis, spinning wheels in her dreams, singing songs she almost knew, just like the voices she could sometimes pick out of the noise of an air conditioner, voices she almost recognized.

They sat together on the foul mattress, cans of cold Bud between their thighs, and compared families. Donnie's mom was pretty much okay except sometimes when she was on the rag and half-crazy and they all had to go to church on Sunday or she shouted and broke plates. Daddy was in the fields all day and out to political meetings most every night and cried sometimes alone in the combine, but no one was supposed to know about that. Sure, they believed in the saucers, each had seen one on several different occasions and was quite convinced of their other-worldly origin. The pastor said angels were at the controls, said it was sorta like a convoy, semis to the stars, hauling souls back and forth, pickup and delivery. Donnie wanted a ride in one, just like Gwen and Dallas had done. Donnie's sister wanted them all to come at once, world being what it was these days. What we needed, a glimpse of the fleet. Because afterwards, she said, it would be like a tiny nightlight had been turned on inside everybody, and the earth couldn't help but be a friendlier place. Yeah, interrupted Dallas, 'cause we could all find our way to the john in the dark. Donnie hated school, but he liked his job, Green Farms treated you square. But why work at all, claimed Gwen, when you could float through the days? Disappear away like her father had done, but she didn't say that part. She talked about her mother, her crazy mother who talked out loud to the goldfish Stan and Ollie; actually stooped in public to pick up pennies off the street; had been threatening for the last decade to get her real estate license; and her boyfriends, the amazing dozens, walking cologne wicks with luxuriant nose hair, any one of which she would gladly marry if one only asked. She wanted Gwen to marry, too, joked about a double ring ceremony. Too bad she never met Beale, said Gwen, he would have been the perfect date for her. Dallas said he'd marry her, she sounded like Doris Day compared with his family. No drinking, said Gwen, she doesn't believe in it. I hate atheists, said Dallas, and demonstrated how to swallow all twelve ounces in less than a minute from a hole poked in the bottom of the can. That's nothing, said Donnie, once at the mall he finished off a fifth of Seagram's, jumped out of the car crawling around on all fours barking like a dog, and bit a lady on the leg who kept whacking him with her purse 'til he rolled over and threw up. They couldn't stop laughing. Dallas could chug a six-pack quicker than anyone in the whole school, then take a leak Tommy John the coach's son once timed at four minutes twenty-two seconds swear to God. Out at the quarry one weekend he drained the kegs and ten minutes later started pissing off the ledge and everyone fell asleep and when they woke up he was still standing there whizzing away and R. J. said if we hadn't run out of brew he could of filled it to the top.

[128]

Stop, Gwen moaned, don't make me laugh, struggling to her feet, I gotta go, the wall she leaned a hand against until the seesawing floor quit playing with her having momentarily lost the sturdiness of wood, and the dull dented doorknob, the axle of the room, grinning maniacally as if about to slowly turn. She found herself searching the corners, counting them off so as not to miss a single one, but since she could never remember where she started she had to keep beginning over and the count kept coming out differently. Beale, Beale, Beale, a name repeated like the strokes of a clock in her brain or in her mouth but he wasn't it, what she wanted right now. What did she want? Oh, a pee, yeah, that was it, she needed to take a pee, she needed a john, where was john, john, John, Johnny. He didn't appear to be around either. Isn't one, giggled the awful boys, rollicking together on the ratty mattress like a couple of deformed twins, do what we do, outside in the grass. Beyond the door the light was dazzling, a christening of the day, and she could feel air on her eyeballs that knew better than to attempt anchorage on any one object. Keep moving and things remained in place, stop and the world would rear up on powerful legs, gallop out so far ahead you'd never find your way home.

This patch of moss under a friendly sycamore tree looked inviting and somehow she got her jeans down far enough to squat there in the cool shade, water running out of her, lemon seltzer bubbling on the grass, two stupid doughy faces leering at her from an empty window frame, but she didn't care, either about them or the fact her pants now seemed to be hopelessly wet. By the time she found her way back inside they were both on the mattress again, ignoring her, arguing over the plot of a splatter movie no one that summer could quite figure out. She looked down at them from towering alcoholic heights, pressed a fist to her stomach, and belched loudly. "Beer," she said.

Later she noticed her feet were bare and bleeding from numerous cuts she didn't know she had. Maybe she'd been outside again, in the cluttered yard, wandering through the open-air museum of exotic space junk lying exactly where it had fallen out of decaying orbits and damaged ships. Oh my God they were out of beer. She tiptoed to the window, tripping twice on the chaotic cemetery of aluminum empties, bloodprints dark on the sordid floor. The guys were out by the truck, talking, reenacting for her color cameras a scene from *The Grapes of Wrath*. Wherever there's a cop busting a guy's head, I'll be there. Dallas's own head, a spiky globe of light, was the texture of spun sugar. Then their mouths turned ugly and Donnie climbed into the cab, slammed the door, and the truck ground furiously away, weaving backward through the shaking bushes. Dallas came around the door, six-packs dangling from his fingers.

"What's wrong?"

"He's an asshole. Don't worry about it. Look at all the brew for us."

When Dallas drank, she drank. It was easy.

Sunlight skipped across the shiny rims of discarded cans, their dark puckered mouths going "ooooh, ooooh."

The mattress was a raft.

Her legs were attached to Dallas's feet.

The sky in the window was pale, an unchanging cream, deep with enigmatic burdens, irrecoverable longings.

A broken chair stared insistently at her between splintered slats.

"Dumb," Dallas muttered.

Inside this room, nestled at the center, was a large black dot, hard and round and compact as a seed. To keep it from growing you watered it with Bud.

I don't care, I don't care, I don't care.

Suddenly all the trees lost their leaves and didn't know where to find them.

"Stupid," Dallas mumbled.

The air was alive, swarming with bright wormy shapes, larvae of the gods.

On the shingled roof of a doghouse abandoned for so long there wasn't even a trace of doggie scent stood an old Heineken bottle they took turns throwing rocks at. It was a smart bottle, sidestepping each time just enough to avoid getting hit. Gwen wiped her sweaty face on the sleeve of her T-shirt. Dallas opened his fly and, bending backward, one upraised fist pumping madly above his head, the other gripping his cock like the saddle pommel on a rodeo bull, shot a streaming arc of warm piss flashing toward the target. Inspired, Gwen undid her buttons, hopping precariously from one bloodied foot to the other, freeing herself with difficulty from the harsh fabric of her jeans. Together they'd extinguish that damn green flame. She spread her legs and let go in fair imitation of Dallas who whooped and applauded. Then all the clothes were gone and they were romping through a sunny field of flowering goldenrod, feathery yellow clusters tickling her breasts. She could see the sky, a high dusty blue, sliding around behind the seething plants, and realized she was on the ground, a hard shape defining itself through the pain in her back. It was a beer can, of course, empty and lost, trying to find its way back to the party. Dallas sprawled across her, his exploring mouth nibbling at the tight edges of what no one had ever been permitted to know. Then his eyes found her and she let herself tumble all the way in, it was a pressurized cabin actually with protective padding and conveniently located handholds and weightlessness not at all as frightening as she might have supposed, exhilarating free fall through neuronic fire, the vapor of dreams. "Tie me up," she ordered in a raspy, unfamiliar voice. He drew back, suspicious, scrutinizing her flushed face. "It's what Beale used to do." She pointed to the neglected clothesline drooping from one corner of the shack to a withered limb of the sycamore tree. "Yeah, sure," he agreed, astounded by his luck. She followed him into the yard.

Worried by the seasons, the rope kept breaking, the knots coming apart, which Gwen found hilarious, and him and his ridiculously throbbing tube scrambling around her in typical male haste, pinching and tugging at her until somehow her outflung arms were strung to the trunk of the tree, legs spread in wishbone fashion between a pair of railless fence posts, a human star with points of flesh. She was hypnotized by the perfect black fly clinging in immutable equanimity to the slope of his shoulder, and when he settled down against her she recognized that the odor on his skin and hair—she sucked in deeply—was of the plant, eau de Green Farms.

"Ow!" she cried.

He pulled away, lubricated himself with a handful of spit, and tried again.

"It hurts."

"I'll be right back." He dashed inside, emerging seconds later clutching a glass jar with a corroded lid.

"Peanut butter?"

"It was all I could find."

She stared at the jaunty emerald elfin figure on the label and thought of reindeer, thought of snow, thought of flying off you go. But what was going on down there? It felt so gritty. Chunky style? He wouldn't dare. As bad as Beale, all this huffing and puffing, poking and grunting—whoops! he was in. She closed her eyes. The darkness behind them was incredibly soft, tactile, the down on the skin of a peach. Her body felt pleasantly elongated, like warm taffy. Now let the world go shuddering as it would, she was fastened down, she couldn't be thrown. Arousal was building, block by block, a luminous pyramid of electrified stone. Out of the budding darkness cords of light drew near, curving inward, embraced by her magnetized body. Wind strong and sure shook at the struts of her heart. Dallas was gone, a figure forgotten at the terminal, stale newspapers and yellow candy wrappers blowing away down wooden rows of varnished benches barren as pews. Something was coming and she struggled in her bonds to receive it, hardly aware of the sudden accompaniment of distracting pops and bursts as if a hidden camera quite near were stealing snapshots of her back rooms, across the white flaring a distorted glimpse of the black-nostriled mask of Dash's face, an immense parking lot ominously vacant of all cars but one, a deserted beach at low tide, fat gulls riding the gray swells, important scenes perhaps, but it was too late to linger because right now she was undergoing illumination, right now she was fully Occupied.

"ARE THESE CANDIED YAMS OR what?"

"Doesn't the aroma of fresh bread remind you of a nursery?"

"It's Romaine, dear, not Roman."

"If there aren't any lumps, they're not authentic."

"That's my spoon she has in her mouth."

"It is so what Popeye eats, look it up."

"Corn on the cob hurts my teeth."

"Stop throwing grapes at your sister."

"But the pork is pink in the middle."

"No one leaves the table until all this . . . whatever it is, is gone."

"Pass the ketchup."

Dinner: the day's centerpiece, The Unit in full cry about the groaning board.

"Mashed turnips, again?"

"Get her grubby fingers out of the Jell-O, for Christ's sake."

"Is Thousand Island supposed to be orange?"

"Let it ring, let it ring, we do not accept telephonic communications during mealtime."

"No, radishes won't keep away vampires."

"I am, of course, referring to Major Mantell, the first casualty of The War of the Worlds."

"The check is in the mail."

"Look at her makeup, it's like eating with a dead person."

"Not another tornado watch."

"I've been to forty-six states, twelve countries, and four planets."

"I just love this . . . this creamed stuff."

"More salt, please."

She saw him at breakfast, of course, often in the same bloodied clothes he had worn the day before and sometimes the day before that, nudging bits of congealed egg onto his fork with an auto mechanic's perpetually grimy finger and smiling secretly to himself but not at her. Beale had rarely smiled; he was serious; the world was serious—we are here to be eaten, he said, dreaming of living on air beyond air among creatures you could trust. She had thought of Caspar and Cheshire cats, but now, during the long, lonely hours when Dallas was at work, the tang of his scent, a sheltering sac, fluttered invisibly about her as she moved in aimless unrest through these last hot days, fag ends of an unusually warm summer, waiting for him (the physical touch of him) to return.

She sat in the humid dark of the locked bathroom amid the drip of thick clear fluid off the bowing tips of imagined leaves, broad elephant's ears, symmetrically latticed, greenly green, his lean body flashing across the spaces between obscure trunks of ? and Doric columns, her concentration breaking up into a mental static so prevailing here it seemed to emanate from the charged foundation of the house itself.

The hole at eye level in the wall before her was the exact size a bullet might make. Each time she leaned into it she somehow expected this tiny circular field to explode with event and surprise and was always disappointed by the same boring view of the same insignificant grass and the corn and the more corn. Around the corner in the shade on the side of the house she couldn't see was the cemetery she was learning to know through her skin, spine all shivery, buttocks flattening against the cool plane of solid stone, their bodies shaped by the moon, fluorescent limbs brushing against the night's velvet, discovering she liked to fuck on mortuary marble before a hushed audience of the attentive dead. Once he strung her with rope between the stones, and when he moved into her, his large dark head, momentarily eclipsing the moon, bristled with the rays and spikes of an angel's aureole. She thought that probably she was in love.

"Butter beans, anyone?"

"The rice is all sticky."

"Zoe, honey, let Mommy smell your hair."

"That was a *hospital*, not an asylum, Grandpa Warden was sent to."

"Oh, I get it, your dream quotient's like your batting average."

"Tofu, stupid, not toe food."

"So what is your point?"

"If I ever find cigarette butts in my frying pan again . . ."

"Toss me one of them hush puppies."

"Stuffed what?"

Once a week The Unit squeezed into the battered VW for its regular run to the mall, a magical kingdom of mirrors, chrome, escalators, and the phantasmagoria of mass production cunningly housed inside a low windowless I-shaped structure embodying the contemporary architectural ideals of corporate chicanery and state detention. Each family member was permitted two hours and one purchase. Outside, the parking lots were vast solitary tracts of black asphalt. Gwen declined the trip. They understood.

One day Edsel demanded to stay home, too. Why? his mother asked. I hate you, he replied. My head hurts, he confided to Gwen after the others had left, there's too much talking here. So they sat quietly together on the warm steps, sharing an apple, watching the corn thrash in the dry wind, the high uncluttered sky playing variations in blue, blackbirds on the telephone wire shifting nervously about like beads on a busy abacus string. A nice meditative day of surges and flux, openings too vague and elusive to be named with any accuracy—soft, summery sensations out in the country, a pleasant straw-headed boy at your side, and for a moment the thought: this is what it's like to be a mother, bound forever to a body that had come out of your body, life preserver, maker of worlds. And what of him? Was the feeling reciprocal, or did he always assume the attitude of a son in the presence of any reasonable adult?

"What's that?" she asked, catching a glimpse of silver between his restless bitten fingers.

He opened his hand. It was a flat, star-shaped disk of metal with sharp, ugly-looking points. "Here's what ninja do," he said, standing quickly and hurling the thing across the lawn right at the orange cat daintily high-stepping her way through the uncut grass. The disk whistled. Gwen screamed. The cat bolted over the road into the field. Edsel laughed. "I was just kidding."

"That was awfully close."

"Not even." He retrieved the weapon and motioned her away from the steps. "Watch this." He leaned back and pitched the star like a fastball. It made a terrible whirring sound and slammed against the side of the house, burying itself halfway into the peeling wood. Gwen watched him. "Do your parents know you have one of these?"

"Shuriken," he said. "All the kids have 'em." He wiped the star carefully on his pants. "They're not my parents."

She didn't know what to say.

[137]

"I'm an orphan." He slipped the weapon back into his pocket. "Want to see where the monster lives?"

"Wait a minute," she said, following the whorl of fine hair on the back of his head into the house. "Dash and Dot are not your mom and dad?"

"I live with them now," he explained, leading her past the table piled with dirty breakfast dishes, the dusty gray eye of the television set, the slowly oxidizing surface of The Object, right up to the green door, mysterious threshold to the "parents' " room. "My real mother and father are going to send for me as soon as they get jobs." The door was locked, but he produced a key and escorted her in. Red tubing on the ceiling bathed the interior in the plush warm light of the nocturnal mammal house at the zoo. Twin sets of simple furniture had been arranged identically on either side of the room in a failed attempt at symmetry, one half clean, trim, precisely ordered; the other a funhouse mirror image, the bed unmade, the table a mess of books, magazines, paper, amber vials of prescription medicine, and an assortment of variously sized half-filled drinking glasses. On the floor between the beds was a white circular rug decorated with strange geometric designs. Against the wall rested a giant glass thermometer that glowed with a soft, snowy radiance when Edsel turned it on and emitted a low electronic hum that changed tone periodically. Up on the wall in an enclosed frame of thorns was a stylized portrait of a Caucasian Jesus displaying the holes in his palms, the sad face askance yet oddly distanced as if the bloody hands were not his own. He was also wearing a clear round space helmet.

"So where's this monster?"

Edsel yanked the rug away, revealing a trapdoor set into the floor. "Down there."

Gwen stared at the brass ring embedded in the wood. "What is that—a fruit cellar of some kind?"

"We don't eat fruit."

"What do your parents—I mean, Dot and Dash—what do they keep down there?"

"A monster," Edsel repeated with emphatic impatience. "I already told you that." He stood well back from the trap. "You can hear it sometimes at night. It cries a lot. It wants to get out."

"Have you ever seen this monster?"

He turned away toward the dark closet, its door ajar and hung with wrinkled pants and shirts. "I only saw it once."

"Well, what did it look like?"

"Something you weren't supposed to see," he said. "A monster."

"I guess I should watch out, then," said Gwen. "I think I've seen it, too."

He looked at her for a moment, then quickly nodded his head. She was a funny lady.

"That's not hair, that's sprouts."

"I don't like food from France."

"What difference does it make whether his teeth have come in or not, you never feed him anything he needs to chew."

"Who broke my curtain rod?"

"Then pick out the raisins, for Christ's sakes, you'd think they were goddamn rabbit turds or something."

"Money only comes to those who act like they don't really need it."

"Quiet everybody, Edsel's about to do his Elvis impression."

"Too bad your friend Beetle isn't here to defend himself."

"Does the tablecloth stink or is it me?"

"It's the glop inside the shell you're supposed to eat."

"I think it needs more thyme."

Alone in the house she stretched out on the hard naked wood of the long room, bare legs warming in a trapezoid of sun, attentive eyes fastened on the astonishing array of silver stars above. Must have needed a big ladder to ornament that plaster heaven. A lot of patience. Much devotion. She had dreamed of Dash again. He had come to her abruptly, materializing out of the dark, a figure in black the night had stitched together and sent on to her bed. He had lain down beside her, gently, as if he belonged there, and once more she had been unable to move or to speak, her body rigid and detached with no more will or sense than the hollow limbs of a child's doll, enduring his bloodless touch, cold as the spaces between the real stars, while beneath her embalmed skin the shrinking heart of her, no larger than a tissue specimen in a test tube, writhed helplessly as if prodded with a needle. When she woke, drenched in the lather and scent of fear, the house was as dark as a mine and as empty. What commentary this dream might provoke at the breakfast table: that Dash was an obvious double of her father, haunting her sleep in a guise that rendered horror to permissible levels; or that he must be an earthly stand-in for one of The Occupants, a masked clue to what really happened that long ago evening in the California parking lot. But what if Dash were simply Dash? The unblinking stars stared down upon her, mute as stone. Scalded by light, drowned in darkness, the twin halves of a single experience. Nausea she thought she had successfully suppressed hours earlier billowed through her like a damp green cloud. Flu? Food poisoning? Bad thoughts? She couldn't remember the date of her last period, life on the road too frantic and improvisational to keep track. Last month? The month before? She tried to imagine growing a baby, Mother Nature working a basketball pump on her thin body. No, it wasn't a game she wanted to play. Her arms were extended wide as wings in a block of light the color of unvarnished pine. The house was a different place emptied of its inhabitants, a theater after hours, hushed, expectant, the props ready to assist in new roles. In this space larger than the claustrophobic confines of the gurgling bathroom her mind expanded, moods flowing easily one into the other, thought a gas filling up a vacuum. She pictured the congregations of the past, that succession of believers who had once occupied this very room, bewhiskered and bonneted faces lifted up from their hymnals, alert as flowers, drinking in the light of the Word. All plowed under now. What would they think of their church (raised with their own callused hands out of wood carted miles from places where there were trees) today? Now she too was a part of the history of this place. She glanced away for a moment at the chalky blue coating the flawed glaze of the window, and when she turned her head back again the curious puzzle of the constellations was abruptly solved. The stars on the ceiling were a connect-the-dots version of the family itself. She could see the father, the mother, towering above a galaxy of silhouetted children, at their feet a modest gathering of suns representing a little dog, a cocker spaniel, she imagined. What had happened to that animal? And in back, where the flecks of paint were fading into vapor, the hint of a shape, something taking form and approaching the others. She knew at once that that must be her.

"Beets?!"

"But all the vitamins are in the skin."

"The roast is burnt."

"No, I won't speak any louder, I refuse to compete with the goddamn television set."

"Quit doing that, that's disgusting."

"The rest of us have opinions, too, you know."

"This broccoli smells like old tennis shoes."

"Can I have twenty dollars?"

"No, I can't say that olives ever reminded me of eyeballs."

"Pass the ketchup."

His body. Even alone at night in her musty sleeping bag in the lee of The Object, she dreamed of it lying warm beside her. "I wanna jump your bones," he hissed into her ear one starshot night out in the cemetery, jolting her own body into the ascents of an orgasm so intense she thought she might briefly have lost consciousness. Later she could usually hear him snoring away in the loft above her and once she crept up the creaking spiral stairs to his narrow bed under the robed trio in stained glass and they made love there without uttering a sound, the emerald glow from the radar Edsel used as a nightlight washing endlessly over their tangled bodies, the dish on the steeple scanning the skies with the incurious tenacity of the purely mechanical. But many a night he never returned at all from work and the only place she could touch him was in her dreams. . . .

"Shut the fuck up. How many times I got to tell you? They're sleeping there right above your head."

"But what is it, man, what you got in there?"

The sheer blackness of the house loomed up beside them like the stone face of an unscalable cliff. Before the darkness floated a shifting curtain of white dots pale as dandelion fuzz. Donnie lost his balance on the wet leaves, skull thumping hard against the brick foundation. "Shit!" All the dots flared together like hundreds of synchronized flashbulbs. He sat back on the ground, shaking droplets of beer from his hand.

"Hey!" Dallas cuffed him on the back of his head. "Quiet!"

Donnie grabbed for the hand he couldn't see, missed, and spilled more beer on himself. "God, have you got bad breath."

"Shut up and get in there."

"Sure. I'm gonna crawl under that."

"Scared?"

"Fuck."

"I'll be right behind you."

They worked their way in under the house like plumbers on their hands and knees, grunting through their noses, the dank earth sticky between their fingers.

"Jesus, you people ever clean this crap outta here? Feels like fresh shit. Smells like shit, too. And I left my fucking beer outside."

Dallas flicked on the penlight.

"Holy—!"

"Sssssh."

The face was mostly gone by now, bright ridges of bone cresting through unrecognizable layers of peeling gray; sockets sunken to dry cocoons whitish and webbed, lipless teeth locked in perpetual grin. The clothes were rag bindings almost indistinguishable from the body itself, woven by time and weather into one soft, uniform shape. Hordes of sleekly carapaced bugs fled the thin beam of light into the tunneled interior.

"Who is it?"

"Guy that came with her. A jerk."

"You do him?"

"He kinda did himself."

"Kenny has got to see this. He'll freak."

"I decide who sees. It's mine, I own it now."

"He's leaking oil real bad. Lemme that stick."

"It changes. I've been making Polaroids with my father's saucer camera. You can watch it disappear. Pretty soon there'll be nothing left."

Donnie poked tentatively at it as though testing for doneness until suddenly the stick plunged with alarming ease deep into the squishy mystery of the thing itself. His hand jerked back as if from an open flame. There was a short bubbling sound, and dark liquid ran out of the hole and was sucked away instantly into the porous ground. Donnie's eyes were big. "Ooooo," he whispered in simple wonderment. "Biology."

Later, squatting solitary atop ALPHEUS PAGE, bare skin flowing lean and luminous under the absolute cool of the moon, toes curled birdlike over the edge of ancient pitted stone, Dallas raised the dripping stick, a wand of celestial magic, over the unknowing land. In this sign you will be as gods. In the darkness of juice, in the smoke of goo. The sky was bisected into perfect halves, one green, one red. The lobes of the Master. Pulse. Deaf. Spasm.

"Hot muffins, oh boy!"

"This turkey has three drumsticks."

"We had money before, we'll have money again."

"You can't make a meal on animal crackers."

"Rejoice, kiddies, it's the Age of Arnold."

"There's French fries in her nose, for Christ's sakes."

"They won't let us on television anymore because of calls from Washington."

"You dip the leaf into this brown sauce and pull off the pulp with your teeth."

"It's not the blast, it's the shock wave."

"Don't you dare speak to me like that again in front of the children."

"It must be the cheese."

"Who broke the goddamn pepper mill?"

She stood transfixed before the open refrigerator door, paralyzed in the generous spill of frosted light and cold celery air between the last of the Granny Smiths and a runny wedge of yesterday's coconut cream pie. He was behind her before she could even register the presence of another body anywhere in the house.

"Oh," she blurted, rather too quickly, turning and stumbling against the door, killing the light, her suddenly frail hands seeking at her back contact with the power humming from the walls of this big white enameled appliance. "Hi," she said in a lower tone.

Dash was wearing soft round-toed shoes with high rippled soles, and there were silver bands circling each thick, hairy wrist. "Relax. I'm not the bogey man." He looked like someone attempting to smile through a botched face lift.

"I didn't know there was anyone here." She curled her fingers around the edges of the door, digging her nails into the insulation so he would have to pry her off this machine.

"Why are you so afraid of me?" He remained just inside the doorway, poised against the weakening light of late afternoon, the crumbling gray erasers of night already beginning to smudge the planes and edges of the room. Someone should turn on the overhead.

"I'm not."

He hadn't moved, he stood across from her as if waiting for her to make the first move so he could act. "Don't be. I hate that."

"I'm sorry."

"I hate that, too."

She had begun recently to think of the topography of his face, so big, so bloodless, so blank, as a species of foreign sky rarely troubled by the drift of a mood, the ragged wisp of an emotion. It was a surface knowable only with the aid of instruments. In the silver pools of his sunglasses she was split in two, distinct and identical images of herself peered back out of convexities of opaque aggression.

"You make me nervous," she admitted finally. "I don't always know what to say."

He stepped closer. "That's obvious." The table, cleared of dishes and wiped clean, was still between them. She gauged the distance to the knife rack. "And quite silly." He turned his back to her and rummaged through a counter drawer. When he turned around again he was holding a Phillips screwdriver, twisting the blade between his fingers.

She shrugged helplessly. "Just a jumpy girl, I guess."

"Yeah. It's that kind of world."

The silent cat appeared in the doorway, regarded each separately with an Oriental gaze, and decided in favor of retreat, slipping quickly away behind the throbbing refrigerator.

"I . . ." she began, and stopped. He was as still as a mantis on a stick. "I wondered if there was any salad from last night."

His silver mirrors looked at her looking at him. "My wife has a talking vagina," he said. But he didn't say that. He said, "Sit down."

He eased cowboy style into the chair opposite her. She

watched his face. Was this what a daughter felt like, waiting for Dad to administer the dreaded punishment?

"The situation here," he said, "in all probability, is approaching critical proportions. The time frame will be relatively brief. I thought you should know."

"Yes?" She continued to look at him, this strange man in quasi-military costume; the dark doorway, the gray stove, the fading butcher's chart on the wall, all streaming in taffylike attenuations across those insect eyes; his strung presence, insistent as a magnet, drawing her out in deformed shapes she could neither easily recognize nor quickly control. She never understood, she never knew how to respond.

He contemplated the starred tip of the screwdriver. At the window behind his burr head the sky was darkening but still blue, dark blue, a simple undisturbed blue. Summer was shrinking but not yet done. The corn still had its ears.

He looked at her. "My son fucks my daughters," he said. But he didn't say that. "For instance, Zoe," he said. "Been checking her out lately?"

"Yes. Someone should stop her from scratching and banging so much. Her face doesn't look so good. She could get a bad infection."

"Thank you, we are touched by your concern. I was referring, of course, to her transmissions. Have you noticed?"

She pretended to shuffle through recollections. "She's at a different window every time?"

"No, no, the gestures have changed configuration entirely. All new signs, new messages. I've only been able to catch about half of it, her hands are moving with such urgency these days."

"What does it mean?"

"You know what it means, you toothsome cunt." But he didn't say that. He said, "The Intervention."

The Intervention: a Dot-Dash title she had read by the orange flicker of crackling pine one mosquito-plagued night in the chilly Appalachians, wide awake in the damp sleeping bag, feet numb, joints stiff, orderly formations of brittle light

[146]

crossing the black pane of space, mating fireflies winking back at her in prearranged signals, and next morning for breakfast a pallid Beale bringing her dirt-encrusted mushrooms he swore were edible and which tasted like an unwashed crotch and must have been hallucinogenic because every other person she saw for the rest of the day was a scary government dero like in the book, intent on silencing her and the extraordinary truth of the amazing Occupants.

She considered the hands fiddling with the screwdriver as if trying to find some novel use for it, wondered again if eyes could remember what flesh had known, the revelation of a touch bursting through dreams into certainty.

There were zones, he was saying, one should flee to in the Zero Time, his voice penetrating memory, sound and cadence evoking a time before her own father departed into a private zone of his own. She looked up at the impervious masquerade of his face, strange lips forming strange words in familiar ways. She produced a vague smile of interest when he looked at her, nodded intelligently when he paused. She knew nothing about this man.

The good news, he was saying, is that WE ARE ALL GOING HOME, the Ark hidden in readiness high in the Catoctin Mountains, wherever that was, final boarding instructions via the channel Zoe, who must be guarded with special zeal from those who would interfere with her circuitry in this period of rupture and ruin. The threat could develop even within The Unit itself, a brain undergoing cosmic bombardment being capable of the most unexpected and vile activity.

Let me tell you a story, he said as she sat there immobile on a red plastic seat under a cracked ceiling, the frosted ring of fly-specked fluorescence, the room undergoing that long slow steep into summer night. It was so cold the day she was born that the little frozen car, a scrim of ice dangling from the running boards, lurched and creaked like a wooden ship down the slick white streets. When he turned on the heat the interior filled with snow, condensed crystals blowing up in their faces out of the vents so that it was like sitting inside

[147]

one of those glass balls you shake with a winter scene in miniature inside. They had to lean forward, breathe on the windshield, to see out. It was beautiful. Blocks from the hospital the car hit a sheet of ice, the brakes locked, and they skidded sideways across a double intersection, clipping a cab, bumping the front grille of a Buick, and shuddering backward into a bank of snow as tall as the roof. Dazed, they crawled out, stumbled the rest of the way through drifts and gusts, blood from where he struck his mouth on the steering column freezing like cherry ice on his chin. The abandoned car, barely visible in the mound of white beneath the saffron swirl of the street lamp, protruded at an angle halfway out into the road, emergency blinkers crying out to the passing world in staccato pulses of regulated color dash-dash-dot-dot, dash-dash-dot-dot.

The birth was quick and efficient, without complaint from mother or child, a wet blue baby arriving in eerie silence on the planet. Her adjustment to this alien environment was difficult and prolonged, days of decompression in a closed chamber, tiny electrodes cemented to the soft bulging head, and spindly chest now a sort of bruised yellow panting with avian rapidity. Two weeks she shuddered there in a nest of tubes and wire, shit the color of pureed pumpkin squeezing out of her in neat toothpaste coils, no matter what happened the last of a line, the mother had spoken, no more. This was in Circleville in a pit of spiritual malaise and financial depression. He played the organ Sundays in the Methodist church, the rest of the week pop piano in the Rose Room of the Round Table Motor Lodge. She was a disillusioned RN who scorned MDs and disliked the company of the sick. She was tired of nursing, both strangers and her own. So it was the father who learned to hold her, to rock the frail, distressed infant in his arms, to slip the rubber nipple skillfully into the toothless mouth, to soothe her with homemade lullabies, so that science was rebuked and surprised when she lived. And he performed these devotions cheerfully, without resentment,

[148]

because the child wasn't even his. Fatherhood was earned, a conscious act of appropriation. And that was why her name was different from the others, the naming of the tribe a crucial task of religious care. He knew he had been properly guided when, in the second month of her second year, the first brief hesitant communication manifested itself, disguised cleverly, of course, as a constellation of medical symptoms. He understood at once in a way no doctor ever could the true meaning of her anomalous behavior. Her first word, do you know what it was? "That!" with one saliva-coated finger directed calmly upward at the tensed blue membrane of perfect sky. "That, that, that," repeated with echoic persistence until the morning the mother heard an answer and went to respond, her small daughter clutching unsteadily at the sill, the slippery finger pointing out, "dat, dat, dat," the notes of a clock jammed on the hour, even as the mother crossed the room in a rush of air, seized the thin diapered body in both hands, and without pause or exclamation hurled the child out the open window and not even bothering to witness the impact lay down on the unmade bed, one pillow under her head, one pillow over her head, and still the clock would not stop. The child landed in a hedge of sufficient density to break her fall and a couple of her bones. Of course she attempted no further experiments with tellurian language following that episode, but her destiny could not be denied. Her arms came up and began to move like a robot struggling to dance.

The inscrutable sunglasses regarded her like miniature television monitors that had been turned off. "I'm the only one who can interpret her signs." His mouth, when it moved, reminded Gwen that she too was an unwilling prisoner in a skin suit.

"Daddy's girl," she said.

He was staring toward the doorway as if listening to movement in the other room. The monitors flashed silver as his head came quickly around. "And what the hell's that supposed to mean?"

She glanced at the knife rack. "I'm sorry. It doesn't mean anything. Just that she likes you and you like her. That's all. What did you think it meant?"

"I bugger my son in the ass," he said. But he didn't say that. He said, "I've got a radar device to adjust." He stood up, towering over her, tapping the shaft of the screwdriver against an open palm. She wondered if he used Trinity's makeup to achieve that glacial mask effect, there was a grainy quality to the underside of his jaw as of excess powder beaching there. "Oh," he added, pausing theatrically in the doorway. "It might be wise to keep your kit packed. We may have to evacuate this station on a moment's notice."

He was there, then he was gone, leaving behind a black rectangle of shimmering space. The sun had set. A thin gray moss of last light clung stubbornly to the surfaces of things. Across the window the sky had gone out. The cat meowed. She jumped from her chair, lunging for the wall switch. The kitchen snapped back into place, rescued just in time from the terrible tow of the night. She leaned against the smudged yellowy wall, a damp hand gripping the cold greasy edge of the stove, watching faucet water falling monotonously into the empty sink, the hollow metallic ring of each separate drop like the ghostly tapping of a fingernail deep down the line and the dead tone of its song accompanying in impeccable sync the crazed beating of her heart.

"This melon's all slimy and gross."

"Au gratin, that's French for eat it if you know what's good for you."

"No, I don't want the shrimp or fake food of any kind."

"Rat casserole, my favorite."

"Of course the world, such as it is, exists solely at the whim of The Occupants."

"How much noise can you make eating a goddamn carrot stick?"

"Asparagus causes warts."

"I'm old enough to do what I want when I want."

"There's enough animals at this table without feeding the goat through the window."

"The water tastes like farts."

"No peanut butter for me, thanks."

"My chicken is red raw."

"So smother it in cholesterol, see if I care."

"This is cozy," she exclaimed, settling comfortably into the down of a pillow as big as a suitcase.

"Our blue heaven," said Maryse.

Gwen was inside The Object with Trinity, Maryse, and Mignon, her first "official" visit, no need to explain those furtive explorations during The Unit's shopping absences. Today's invitation to the girls' clubhouse had come only after all three had shared a grueling morning trying to attend to Zoe while Dot and Dash drove hundreds of miles, the backseat of the car loaded with overflowing boxes of their books and pamphlets, to address the Fourth Annual Abductee Assembly and Galactic Picnic held this year at a rented racetrack just over the state line. Zoe was asleep for the moment, sprawled across her moldering piece of foam rubber in the corner of the room she had territorially marked with teeth and claws and stained permanently with body fluids resistant to even the latest supermarket cleansers. Her snores reverberated through the house like the banging of tenement plumbing, a comforting sound to those gathered inside The Object. After she had overturned the refrigerator and tried to throw Mignon out the window, Trinity and Maryse had quickly agreed to overrule Dash's explicit instructions and dose her good with the medicine Dot kept hidden in the kitchen cabinet behind the spice bottles. "Speed?" Gwen had asked, incredulous. "Yeah," replied Trinity, "it has an opposite effect on kids like her. Nobody really knows how it works." So now the old homestead was quiet for at least an hour or two. There were angry bruises and stinging scratches on all of Gwen's arms and legs. Her body ached, she felt like a tackle after the big game.

The floor inside here was heavily padded with countless layers of rug: wool, acrylic, phony Persian piled one on top of the other in lumpy strata of color and texture. Walls and ceiling were hung with rippling sheets of satiny blue material. Not a glint of metal anywhere. She might have been trapped inside a giant balloon or reclining within a royal tent pitched at the distant edge of some important desert struggle. Mignon lay almost invisible in a heap of gray swaddling that nearly matched his skin tone, a sick inverted turtle without the energy or desire to right himself, his scent an inescapable perfume, persistent, cloying, hard to place.

The surrounding shine and flutter of deep, decidedly unskylike blue was both claustrophobic and oddly pleasant. Gwen liked The Object, this domestication of high tech. Is this what a sister felt like? "But where are the controls?" she asked.

Trinity pulled back a curtain, revealing an empty computer console, an unreliable-looking arrangement of tarnished panels, uneven rows of mismatched switches and dials, some of them remarkably similar to oven knobs; clumps of red and yellow and green insulated wire dangled out below like spilled spaghetti left to dry and harden. Between the panels was bolted a small metal wheel of a type ordinarily found steering a child's toy car. The entire assembly offered up the spectacle of a trendy artistic construction abandoned in midflourish by both inspiration and will. Behold! the gateway to the stars.

"Don't make a face," said Trinity. "Just window dressing. For those who need that sort of aid. We are the power, Maryse and I. When it's time, we lie on our backs, lift up our legs, and press the soles of our feet together. It's bumpy at first, but yes, it flies."

"We have to be naked," Maryse added, smiling down at the baby who never smiled back.

"Yes," Trinity agreed. "Starkers."

"No one wears clothes in outer space."

"She knows that, she was there."

"I? Well, yes . . . but I didn't see—" She felt herself begin to blush and was embarrassed further by the emblems of embarrassment. Trinity, who was now engaged in the absorbing task of painting her fingernails, paused, applicator poised quizzically, and looked at her.

"Any people," Gwen concluded.

"You must have been on a special flight." As she finished a nail, she leaned over, blowing on the polish as if cooling a spoonful of soup. The paint was drying to a dull even black.

"Off peak," Maryse suggested.

"There was a whole lot of light. I couldn't see very well."

"When we went, there was just this nice white glow. Sort of creamy. And it was everywhere. They don't believe in shadows. They say shadows are defects in our primitive perception."

"Their organs are astonishing," Maryse declared.

"Yes, and ever since I first laid eyes on those Etherians I've wanted a tail."

"And what would you do with a tail?"

"I don't know. Hang from rafters. Brush away flies."

"The whole idea's disgusting. Why don't you just get a pet monkey instead?"

"What—like yours?"

Maryse reached over to stroke Mignon's head. His prematurely wrinkled brow was bathed in a queer perspiration slick and heavy as glycerin. When his mother touched him he let out a squeak of ill-fitting parts rubbing briefly together.

"You shouldn't make fun," said Gwen. "He's a beautiful baby." From that old Zen book she couldn't remember the title to or the author of: the adept who would something something practices sincerity and something something at every opportunity.

Maryse picked up the child and settled it in its rags on her

[153]

lap, gazing down tenderly, wondering if the others noticed any resemblance to the Madonna.

"The grandparents must be proud," said Gwen.

Maryse looked at her blankly. "What grandparents?"

Gwen could feel the rush of blood into her cheeks, the heat spreading. "But aren't Dot and Dash—?"

Trinity laughed. "Oh, yeah," she said, "the grandparents are quite proud, especially the *grand* father."

"We're not sisters," offered Maryse in explanation.

"I'm sorry, but I just thought . . ."

"We're blood sisters," said Trinity firmly. "To the death."

"But he looks so much like the rest of you."

"He is one of us."

"I don't think I understand."

"Dash is the father," said Trinity.

"He is?"

"Yeah," said Maryse. "We think it happened one night when he mistook me for Trinity in the dark. I don't really remember too well. That whole day's kind of blurry."

"But—" And then she couldn't seem to find the proper levers for verbal generation. Lights were dimming in important centers everywhere.

"We didn't want to tell you before."

"We thought you'd probably freak."

For an instant she saw them both, bared on their backs, feet elevated and connecting, sole to sole, twenty toes spitting blue current, the cushioned floor in a tremble, about to tilt, and crouching there in a shower of hot sparks beneath a triangle of bone and illumined flesh was a young woman with yellow eyes who looked like her, stroking the erect fur of the cat, voided expression opening around the kind of mirthless grin that just might contain real fangs.

"The soup is real soupy, Mom."

"He threw noodles at me first."

"You've never liked any of my friends."

"Jelly doughnuts for dinner?"

"This surprise loaf looks surprisingly like cat food."

"I'm old enough to do what I want."

"My, what a big sausage."

"Boring, boring, boring, boring, boring."

"Don't threaten me, young lady."

"If we're so poor, why do we keep on having these ridiculously gross meals?"

"Can I have ten bucks?"

"Apple pan brown dowdy cobbler, a traditional recipe."

"Sauerkraut's like eating skin."

"And don't ever come drunk to this table again."

"What *is* that smell?"

"Out of ketchup? We're OUT OF KETCHUP!"

Gwen scrubbed her face over and over with a dwindling bar of lavender soap—the cleanest face in the family, Dot said—she used the word "family." She looked at herself in the mirror. That is me, she said. She watched her hands dry themselves on a musty towel. Dash had been right, the Zero Time was drawing near. She flushed the toilet and composed her shining features. Her kit was packed.

Zoe was already in her chair, sticky fist brandishing a spoon bright as a crucifix against the last blinding rays of the lowering sun, knots of light twisting in dizzy spectacle around the walls.

"Hi, Zoe, whatcha doing?"

The spoon flew glittering across the room and out an open window. Gwen laughed. "Good shot."

Dash shuffled in from the kitchen. Sometimes he walked like an old man, age draped suddenly over his body heavy as a winter coat. "What's so funny?"

Her pleasure dissolved. "Zoe," she said. "She just tossed her spoon out the window."

[155]

He stood there, looking evenly at her, hands stuffed in his back pockets. "I'm sure she had a good reason."

Gwen shrugged.

The Object shuddered, creaked, shuddered again, and Maryse appeared, clutching a brown bottle of vitamin B complex. "Great news," she announced. "Mignon crawled today."

Dash stared at her, expressionless. "Well, call the neighbors." He glanced impatiently around the room. "Where the hell is everybody? I'm ready to eat." He shuffled back into the kitchen.

"One of these days," whispered Maryse, "we're going to poison his food. Don't be surprised."

"We eat at six," they heard Dash shout to his wife, "no exceptions."

Gwen looked at the television. The set was on, so Edsel couldn't be far. She realized that not only did she recognize all the characters on this dumb show, she could accurately identify them by name.

The screen door opened and Trinity and Dallas rushed in breathless from one of their frequent tussles on the back lawn. Trinity's latest ambition: to be a TV wrestling star.

"He showed me a British commando hold," she declared. "I can put any one of you out in three seconds or less."

"Do it on Gwen," urged Dallas.

Dot, pausing to scowl deliberately at each in turn, carried in a platter of meatballs, followed by Dash, rattling the ice cubes in his vodka glass.

"Where's Edsel?" he asked.

"He was here a minute ago," said Trinity.

"Fine. He gets no dinner."

Dash stepped to the head of the table, and everyone hastily assumed their places. He intoned the blessing: O merciful Occupants, Horn of Plenty, aluminum 19, Cygnus X-1. Gwen no longer paid much attention to these recitals, he sounded like he was barking out optionals in a celestial football game. Her eye wandered over the yard litter adorning the center of the table—the usual miscellaneous pile of brittle leaves, pocked stones, stems of grass, wilted weeds, a dried thistle pod, the cartridge from a ballpoint pen, shards of blue glass, a corroded D battery, one half-inch screw, a light bulb filament, a glazed strip of perforated metal, some rusty Nehi caps, the rubber seal off a Mason jar, four cents' worth of tarnished pennies, a piece of a robin's egg, and poking out from under a torn sheet of waterstained notebook paper on which Edsel had drawn in purple and green crayon the descent of the mother ship, an odd cluster of stubby little sticks all gnarled and gray and around one peeling worm-riddled twig a thick ring crusted in black where linear forms seemed to be struggling into letters and, fascinated, she edged forward, Dash droning on about thermium and cosmic string, and thought she could decipher a V or a Y and a G and an H, curious consonants scratched in the dirt, what could they possibly—and oh no, VALLEY, and oh no, HIGH, and oh no, it wasn't a twig, and her head jerked back, and she was on her feet, frenzied eyes seeing nothing, mouth in silent stutter, the others staring politely, waiting for her to speak, but what she wanted to say was outside and she was through the door and down the road before she even heard the sound that had been lurking here all along, braided among the laughing corn, woven into the smiling sky, the sound she fled toward with fluttering arms as if what lay before her were only a facsimile, temporary, paper thin, she could bust through into respite from the voice of the landscape itself, the total sound of a permanent shriek.

EEEEEEEEEEEEE

Zoe was screaming and no one could stop her. Wedged in back between Trinity and Maryse, she tossed her head, the greasy ropes of her dark mane, snapping with crooked teeth at all the arms that wouldn't let go. "Watch the nails!" warned Trinity. "They're sharp as claws!" Short scrawny legs bruise-ripened yellow and brown shot savagely upward and a pair of Mickey Mouse Keds slammed flat into the back of the front seat. The VW swerved wide, lurching out of control into the oncoming lane, horn blaring, brakes in pain.

"Jesus God!" Dash yanked on the wheel, a quick glance up into the rearview mirror. "I'm trying to drive the goddamn car here."

Trinity stuck out her tongue at the back of his head. "We've only got two hands each, Daaaaad"—her voice braying in mockery—"case you haven't noticed."

"Why don't you just get off their backs?" Dot shouted. "We're all doing the best we possibly can." With the ball of her thumb she pressed a soft pink plug deep into the canal of one ear.

Dash turned to study for a moment the puzzling shape of his wife's profile. "You wanna drive?"

She ignored him. Hair tied up in a gaudy paisley scarf that coincidentally duplicated in its pattern the very form of those mysterious amoeba patrolling in invisible splendor the oceans of Earth's sky, Dot stared through her own matching Ray-Bans at the county road sliding on beneath them, a black arrow aimed at the low clouds squatting like dusty chickens in the far haze. Through the muffled booming of her blood she was dimly aware of the noise her daughter made.

EEEEEEEEEEEEE

"Use the knuckle grip," suggested Trinity. "She hates that."

"Shit!" Maryse shouted. "Look what she did to my cheek."

Dash leaned forward as if to urge the wheezing vehicle on, though the accelerator pedal was already hard upon the floor, his mutterings lost in the general confusion and complaint of The Unit. "Why a carful of grown people cannot manage one little girl . . ."

"Quit yelling!" yelled Edsel, hands clamped in desperation to his head. "Everyone just quit yelling!" He was on his knees in a corner of the backseat, blinking through tears no one should see at the creepy demon face of his brother leering down at him from the elevated wheel of Donnie's pickup truck and off in the clear country distance beyond, curds of black smoke roiling high against the flat September sky, talons of fire even now reaching up for the glittering prize atop the steeple, the silver dish revolving on as it fell, scanning still for signs of intelligence all the way down into the roaring ruins.

"Ow!" Maryse screamed. "Let go my ear!"

Trinity expertly seized a pinch of Zoe's exposed thigh and squeezed and did not stop until long after Zoe had let go. Her shrieks were horrible, but Trinity smiled.

Dash raised his voice. "You know what will happen if I have to stop this car."

Dot fished around in her purse for the brown bottle. "Here," she said, "give her two of these."

"No dope!" Angrily Dash batted the vial away. "What the hell do you think you're doing? You know that's just exactly what they want."

[159]

"Who?" Dot's expressionless face set severely forward to withstand the scourings of the meanest wind. "Who's this they?"

Dash gaped at his wife in rare astonishment.

"Is there blood?" asked Maryse. "I feel something wet."

Edsel turned around for a moment, wiping furtively at the corners of his eyes. "Are The Occupants after us?" he questioned his mother, shouting.

"No, dear, no one's after us."

"What was Dallas putting in the ground?"

"A UFO pilot," answered Trinity, the bones of Zoe's arm thin and brittle as dry sticks under her aching grip. "So the Air Force won't find it."

Baby Mignon, all but forgotten on a pallet of rags stuffed into the luggage well behind the backseat, bleated on unheard in futile protest at the harsh pillow of sun smothering his face.

"My leg's going to sleep," Maryse complained.

"Like how long are we expected to hold her like this?" asked Trinity.

Dot looked at her husband. "Moon-stoned," she said. "Utterly."

EEEEEEEEEEEEE

"Let's throw her out," Maryse suggested.

Dash's hand kept checking the position of the gearshift. "Hell will be a resort after this," he observed.

No one disagreed.

From his balcony seat in the cab of the truck Dallas watched the dumb masquerade unfolding up ahead with a connoisseur's delight, a comedy of flailing limbs and distorted mouths performed to the headphone-delivered accompaniment of electronic surf, garbage-can-lid cymbals, synthesized thunder, cranial drills, sonic booms, steam compressors, and a grim doomsday voice chanting in Teutonic accents, "The rusted arm, the page of night, the Palace Guard spills into the street, burn it up, go too fast, what you know is in your eye," Vic and the Vectors: the sound, the truth, the life.

Suddenly Zoe got loose and wrapped an arm around her father's neck. "Fucking Christ!" The car seemed to leap out from under them, fishtailing all over the road, a moment of pure panic, skidding off onto the shoulder in a ricochet of pebbles and exploding dust, Dash's sunglasses humorously askew, salt of blood flavoring his mouth, Trinity cuffing Zoe's head, Edsel crying, Maryse cuddling dazed Mignon, Dot rubbing her nose, everyone shouting too loudly to notice the flash and whine of the cruiser coasting to a stop behind them, the tap on the glass—"Oh no, no problem, Officer, just the girl here, minor temper tantrum"—the cop bending down, examining license and registration, their startled faces, the sanctioned gaze of official eyes, Dot leaning over: "We're on vacation, sir."

From behind Dallas watched, slipping the revolver from glove compartment to at the ready between his thighs, the one who would do what had to be done. The roar of a cement mixer rattled his head, chunks of lyric tumbling around inside.

"Where the hell did he come from?" asked Dash of no one in particular after the cop had left them with a hard stare and a warning.

They fed Zoe the medicine, twice the usual dose.

"Are we going to jail?" inquired Edsel.

"Only you," Trinity answered. "For bed wetting without a permit."

"The numbers on his badge added up to 11," noted Maryse. "Ditto sign."

"No one's going to jail," said Dot.

Checking the mirror, Dash edged the car cautiously up over the speed limit. "We'd better change the plates. That extra set still on the floor back there?"

Trinity felt around with the bottom of her foot. "I think I saw Zoe playing with them in the yard the other day," she said. "Out near the fence."

"Of course. Why did I even bother to ask? You can't keep anything in this fucking family."

[161]

"Whose fault is that?" said Dot.

"Maybe I just should have told him to follow the smoke, check out the fresh hole in the cemetery."

"Why not? They're going to think we did it anyway."

"Oh, we know who did it all right."

"That boy was disturbed. It was obvious from the beginning."

"I'll tell you who's disturbed."

"Meaning what?"

"You've got a brain, you figure it out."

Maryse made a funny face at a black-hatted bearded man on a tractor they passed. "This is like Bonnie and Clyde."

"What about Poly?" asked Edsel.

"Poly can take splendid care of himself, don't you worry about that."

"But what about Minerva?"

"Minerva never cared about us anyway. And she's too stupid to even realize we've left. By tomorrow night she'll have already found another family of saps to fill her bowl and she'll think it's still us."

Edsel listened carefully, but he didn't believe his father. He knew the goat and the cat would both die long, solitary deaths and their bones would rot unremarked and all that held his tears in check was the image of the monster in the cellar, preceding his pets into pain and darkness, burnt up good and dead.

They came through Albert at dusk, rounding the town square, the gutted and defaced jet welded to iron struts in memory of the county war dead, scattering shy dogs and surprised pedestrians and nearly colliding with a horse and buggy that appeared out of nowhere, a wild commotion of hooves and spokes, to frighten them all before vanishing again into the mirage of the rearview mirror.

"You want to meet more cops," snapped Dot, "keep on like that."

"Well, hell, did you catch the kid driving that thing? And the idiot sitting next to him?"

"I think you want to have an accident."

"Of course I do and go to Rio and live off the insurance money."

"Makes as much sense as most of your grand plans." She stared out the window at the color draining from the world. "We shouldn't have left the girl behind. She couldn't have gotten far. We should have found her and taken her with us."

"She could be anywhere by now. Besides, who's going to take the word of a deranged fool, anyway?"

"Maybe she'll get lost in the corn," offered Maryse. "Plenty like that died of exposure back in the Ivey days."

"Never should have let either one of them into the house in the first place," said Dash. "This is what comes of assuming your grown children are mature enough to make responsible decisions."

Trinity jammed her knee into the bulging driver's seat. "Fuck you, too, Dad."

At the approach to the interstate Dash brought the car to a full stop in the middle of the road.

"West," said Dot.

"The west is crazy with lunatics and desperadoes." He turned onto the graded ramp beneath the big white arrow pointing dramatically to CHICAGO.

All their money, $3,059.21 in cash, was locked in a steel box on the floor between Dot's feet.

"I've got cramps," Maryse announced.

"Are we there yet?" asked Trinity.

A procession of beaded light howling eastward over warm concrete. The backwash from passing semis rocked the little car, and the wind through the cracked windows buffeted their faces with fumes and grit. Words had to be screamed to be heard, so they sat mute and still like wired mannequins awaiting a collision test. The flat fields on either side fled away into the night. Nothing out there to distract you from the mad round of thought.

Edsel propped himself up between his parents, arms dangling over the seat backs. "Where are we going?"

[163]

"Ask your father," said Dot.

"This is an adventure," Dash explained. "And like all pioneers, we'll know when we get there."

"Shit," grumbled Maryse.

"I think I'm getting carsick," said Trinity.

Dot handed her daughter a paper bag.

Dash drove on, ear keyed to the nervous chatter of the engine, anticipating the eccentric notes, the arrhythmic prelude to inevitable breakdown. The plan he refused to divulge was simple and manifest: speed, distance. The lights of America after dark merely a constellation to sail through on a journey destined to end elsewhere. But he hated driving for all the miles he had logged. His back ached, his palms itched, the muscles across his shoulders felt like a harness.

Edsel reappeared with another question. "Dad?"

"Yes, Edsel."

"Why didn't we fly to where we're going? In The Object?"

"Yeah," said Trinity. "Where are The Occupants when you really need 'em?"

"It's a big universe," said Dot.

"But we're supposedly these personal friends of theirs, they use our sister for a goddamn telephone, for Christ's sakes. We're talking some kind of priorities here."

"It's not time," said Dash.

"By whose clock?"

"We're not their only concern," said Dot. "Perhaps at the moment there are more important affairs to tend to."

"Like what?"

"Shit," said Maryse.

A hundred miles and one state line later, after everyone in the car except sleeping Mignon and drugged Zoe had complained at least twice, Dash pulled off into the light-hollowed, bug-choked space of an all-night Exxon station. As he managed the pump, Trinity and Maryse squeezed out of the car and raced laughing toward the restroom.

"Thank God!" Trinity exclaimed, slamming and bolting the heavy metal door behind them. She opened her mouth and

pretended to scream once, twice, shaking her head vigorously, trying to temporarily free herself of the family loa.
Scratched into the walls were primitive depictions of the
male tube in assorted dimensions and clever attitudes along
with names and initials and jagged hearts and misspelled
jokes. The air reeked of disinfectant and stale urine. A full
roll of sodden toilet paper lay capsized in an iridescent puddle of suspicious content beside the lidless stool. "I've passed
out in worse," said Trinity. She examined her makeup in the
tarnished mirror. "Mother is going orbital. It's in her voice."
She could see Maryse in reflection over her shoulder, watching the brush scattering powder across her cheek. Then Maryse's thin beige lips began to move: "Well, I don't know
myself how much longer I can go on impersonating a sack of
laundry in that impossible car."

"We should have left last week when we were talking
about it." The lipstick appeared to be drawing blood.

"We should have left last year." Maryse spread paper towels over the grimy floor, settled Mignon on his back, and
began changing his diaper. "Do you think he did it?"

"No, not really, but that doesn't mean he didn't."

"I know, it's hard to be sure about anything that goes on in
this funny family."

"They're all insane." With her tube of Magnetic Red, Trinity printed in neat letters across the glass: HELP! WE'VE
BEEN ABDUCTED BY ALIENS FROM OUTER SPACE!

Outside in the flickering glare of the harsh gas station light,
skin tone reduced to a cadaverous hue, Dallas leaned arro-
gantly against the front fender of the truck, a sweaty beer can
hanging casually from one hand. He took a swallow and
smirked at them. "You two look like a couple of goddamn
tourists."

Maryse gave him the finger.

Trinity opened the car door and before she could close it
again Zoe was out quick as a cat, scampering without a backward glance over the oil stains and on toward the darkness of
the road. Dot shouted her daughter's name. Dash dropped

the gas nozzle and sprinted out after her. She was fast and surprisingly difficult to catch, zigzagging with athletic dexterity across the concrete apron into the first lane of traffic where a matched set of round lights burning white and pupilless came bobbing down the hill at terrific speed, air brakes begun too late their pneumatic hiss, when Trinity seized an arm and yanked as tons of shrieking metal roared by, horn blasting, unintelligible cries flung from the cab window, scraps of aural litter. Dot bore down in fury upon her daughter struggling still to escape Trinity's grasp. "She's impossible," Trinity remarked, sadly aware of the bleak insignificance of those stale words. For answer Dot pulled down Zoe's ragged panties and, in full view of the elderly occupants of a Dodge Dart with Georgia plates looking on in affected middle-class horror, spanked those raw bony cheeks until Dash stepped forward, restrained her arm. The attendant stood in the office door, slapping the wooden dowel with attached restroom key softly against his palm like a billy club.

From the dark interior of the VW erupted a threatening series of gagging noises.

"Let's go," Trinity urged. "The fumes are making Edsel sick."

Dash got in and gunned the engine, curved screeching out into the night. "Well," he shouted, "we'll certainly be remembered here. Nothing like a nice quiet getaway to cover your tracks." In seconds he had rejoined the flow on the interstate and even at double digits over the speed limit a steady show of impatient vehicles passed contemptuously on the left.

"If you have a plan," Dot declared, attempting to contain on her lap the squirming body of her youngest, who was punching at the radio buttons, chopping the mellow strains of "Heartland After Dark" into disconnected bits remarkably similar to the famous sound of Vic and the Vectors, "I think that this would be an appropriate time to share it with the rest of us mortals."

"Oh, Mother," groaned Trinity from in back.

"The plan," Dash repeated as if speaking to a small child, "is to place as many jurisdictions between us and a pile of suspiciously inert remains as quickly as possible."

"Is that it?"

"What did I say? It's an adventure."

"Drop me off at the next rest area."

"Afraid not. No one gets out until the end."

"Look at Dallas!" shouted Edsel, pointing behind at the flat grille of the truck charging down upon them to within inches of the Bug's gasping tail pipes, high beams in the mirror blinding Dash's eyes, the interior gone suddenly all black and white, art deco cutouts twisting across the illuminated leatherette, the rear bumper tapped gently three times before the truck paused, the space between the vehicles holding steady for one long moment, then Dallas and his machine seemed to slide rapidly backward like something seen in a reverse zoom lens.

Dash glared into the mirror, nostrils twitching. He spat out curses and extravagant threats everyone had heard before.

"He drives just like you taught him," Dot commented.

"There's a baby in this car," Maryse reminded her fellow travelers.

"Oh, shut up," pleaded Dot.

"Hey," said Dash, "he's already done it once, the ice is broken and chopped into cubes, so maybe he figures he may as well go on ahead and do the rest of us, too. Penalty can't be any worse, and who knows—he might just plain *like* it."

"Yes, that's what you would think."

"Like what?" asked Edsel.

"Tell you this, sports fans, he tries a stunt like that again and we'll see who does who." He slapped Zoe's hands away from the radio knobs and turned up the news: killerkickback-faminescareinflationtornado.

"Must we?" moaned Maryse in her best suffering-child plaint.

"I'm tired," Trinity declared. "I want to lie down."

Edsel leaned eagerly forward. "Can we stay at a motel? Can we? Can we, please?"

"One with a pool," added Trinity.

"Too expensive," said Dash, his eye beginning to blink in time with the canted beam of their one good headlight joggling along in front at an angle too steep to expose much road surface. "Look for a campsite."

"That's a laugh. There aren't even any trees."

"Part of the plan, no doubt," mumbled Dot.

"It's too dark to put up the tent."

"We'll use the flashlights."

"What flashlights?"

"A hot bath would sure help these cramps," whined Maryse.

"We don't even have any food," complained Edsel.

"All right, all right. We'll stay in a room this one night only. A cheap one."

There followed a contentious hour of disappointment and futile appeal, the big friendly beckoning lights of a dozen Holiday Inns and Quality Courts falling away one after the other into distant darkness as Dash drove on, searching for what no one knew. He found it at last beneath a pink-and-green face carved into the night, the pulsing head of a neon Indian presiding over a twitching sign announcing LINCOLN MOTOR LODGE, the promise of low rates in the fact they weren't even in Illinois yet. The rooms were small and dank as monastery cells with a lingering canine aroma, the beds lumpy concavities of little comfort, but lapping at their door was a patio-sized pool of blue water seasoned with enough chlorine to sting the eye and bleach facial hair. Dot stripped Zoe to her gray skin and locked her in the shower stall under a warm needling spray whose tranquilizing effect usually lasted for a merciful hour or two. Dash switched on the antique television set, two channels, two colors (purple and green): tanks in the Mideast, riots in Asia, bombs on Wall Street, Do You Know Where Your Children Are? Dinner was a bag of burgers from the McDonald's across the road. "I hope they have Weightlesse wherever we're going," said Maryse. "I'm down to a dozen cans."

During the night the air conditioning failed, and by morning everyone was spread out on the fusty carpet like victims of a hotel fire seeking the last pockets of available air. Awakened at dawn by a revivified Zoe rattling the doorknob as if sheer noise and fury could free the lock, they staggered about gritty, surly, without any sensation of having actually been asleep. Even Maryse had no dreams to report. In the parking lot, while reloading the car, Dash passed out brochures to departing guests: Facts You Should Know About Etheria.

An hour later, tired and hungry, they crossed the Mississippi in a thin gray mist that speckled the window glass and lay dark and sleek on the paving of the road. "Father of Waters," Dash announced grandly.

"It's dirty and smelly," commented Edsel.

Maryse read to them fantastic tales of horror and inspiration out of her Frontier Log, documenting the great westward trek of the previous century. "Hah," Dash snorted, "what a bunch of fools." Lunch they assembled on unsteady laps from packaged meat, bread, a jar of mustard purchased at a corner grocery store in a small town exactly like the one they had fled through—was it only yesterday? Off to the north the sky was decomposing into an ugly yellow nebula that seemed to be tracking their progress, bitter wastes of stricken cities lying vast and unseen and foully gravid.

By afternoon hardly a word was exchanged. Dash kept the name of their destination, if there was one, to himself. Trinity and Maryse dozed fitfully upright against the backseat, awakening occasionally for brief glimpses of land and horizon so similar in aspect the sense of movement, of distances successfully traversed, seemed merely an illusion. Lulled into limp acquiescence by the rocking of the car, Zoe sprawled across her mother's legs, glazed eyes turned up toward the windshield and the nameless and gentle wonder of the clouds. Edsel deployed armies of little men among the denim folds of his jeans where a momentous battle was being waged. If the grays won, he would go; if the blues, he would stay. It shouldn't be that difficult to find his real mother and father, they were down the road somewhere in Ohio, scene of the original mix-up a long time ago.

Back in the truck Dallas was bored. He closed on the family car, ran for more than a mile less than a foot off the rear bumper, daring contact and whatever lurid punishment his dithering father could have had in mind when warning him last night in the motel room of the wages of recklessness both behind the wheel and without. He let his foot ride back on the accelerator pedal, and the VW seemed to soar away until it was little more than a blue smudge on the long white concrete. If he wished, he could turn off onto any one of these exits to nowhere, he could disappear, he could return. The world was a labyrinth of tunnels to worlds beyond numbering. There was a sufficient beer supply stashed under the seat. The headphones held his skull in their tender grip, the cave of his body reverberant with the cries, the thuds, the moans, the bangs of joyful sound. At his back the wounded sun dragged its stain across the whitewashed sky and out of sight beneath the uncertain flooring of this derelict planet.

Signaling, the VW turned away off the interstate, the truck trailing dutifully behind close as a shadow but strange and distorted as if the product of light cast upon some other fugitive object. The signs they followed were cut to resemble log pyramids with painted lettering of a rustic hewn quality. The yellow arrows led miles down a crumbling road to a secluded park of dry grass and clustering trees—The Happy Valley Campgrounds.

Maryse immediately claimed exclusive rights to the backseat. "Mignon and I are not sleeping on this icky ground."

"No?" inquired Dash. "And what would Mother Ivey say?"

"She wouldn't have said anything. She'd have stayed in the car. With the doors locked."

"They got a toilet here?" asked Trinity.

Dallas approached, headphones looped casually about his neck. "This where we draw the wagons in a circle?"

Dash studied his son with the cold eye of a stranger. His voice was quiet and painstakingly slow. "Get the tent out of the truck."

Since all were required to pitch in—"pretend you're at a barn raising," suggested Dash—it took twice as long as it might have to pick the spot, arrange the poles, pound the stakes, set the ropes. The canvas, after years of faithful service up and down the busy Believe It Or Not circuit, was sieved, seamed, torn, and patched, and once erect with the lantern glowing inside, the weathered material took on the mottled transparent look of aged skin. Home. The darkening wilderness around them already beginning to seem familiar. Trinity and Maryse wandered off together down a narrow winding path carpeted with wood chips. Dallas slipped away, unnoticed, not a word to anyone. Zoe was tethered to a sturdy tree. Dash unfolded a lawn chair and reclined, fresh drink in hand, watching the last light pour down the western sky like sand through a funnel. After a while the stars began to peek out shyly, one at a time, like the diminutive buds of a rare and delicate plant, but blossoming then in such numbers as to mock calculation, and soon the body of night was studded with the icy glint of their fabulous light. He watched the ancient patterns emerge into place, the Bear, the Dog, the Ram, the Whale, heaven's menagerie, creatures of fire and void and timeless terror. You could see too the Milky Way, a twisting strand of tissue stuck carelessly to that dark dome. "Hey, come out here a second," called Dash to his wife, who was sitting on the edge of a cot inside the tent, rubbing her temples with short, vicious motions. She continued on without pause.

Edsel appeared from around in back of the tent. "There's no place to plug in the TV," he complained.

For dinner they roasted hot dogs over a fire an hour and a half in the making because of tiresome quarrels about the proper kindling; the type, the size of the twigs; how to stack the wood; how much newspaper to use; repeated laments that no one had remembered to buy charcoal or lighter fluid; and so on, ritual as much a part of their outdoor meals as the actual eating.

"Only nine left," warned Maryse, tossing her drained dinner can of Weightlesse into a handy trash bin.

"Life can be hard out here on the range," commented Dallas.

In the orange firelight their rapt faces were the same color as the wieners. "Isn't this cozy," Dot remarked. It didn't seem to be a question that required a response. She looked at each in turn and, sighing, got to her feet and trudged back into the tent.

"What's eating her?" asked Maryse.

"Menopause," said Trinity.

Edsel pointed a mustard-smeared chin at his father and asked, "Dad?"

Long pause. "Yes?"

"Can we go back?"

Dash pretended to look puzzled. "Go back where?"

"Home."

"You know home is what we're always moving toward."

"I mean where we lived for a while with Poly and Minerva. Can we go back there someday?"

"No, I'm afraid not."

Edsel considered this information and then asked, "Are there dero there now?"

"Yes. Probably more than we can guess."

"With guns?"

Dash looked at his son. "Yes," he said.

Dallas poked irritably at the ash-encrusted embers with a sharp stick. "Too bad we don't have any fucking marshmallows."

The fire crackled and a horde of sparks was sucked helter-skelter up the flue of the night. Trinity was remembering a different campfire in Pennsylvania the summer after Zoe was

[172]

born when she was sent away to learn how to socialize with other girls by making fun of Fatty Franny and singing the same dumb songs every night and weaving strips of smelly leather into bracelets no one would ever wear and shining a strong flashlight into a latrine hole and discovering a big green turd. That was the summer she ran away for the first time and met the boy with the speckled tube.

"Look at that sky," Dash exclaimed, craning backward. "The mobile of time wheeling over our heads."

"God's dandruff," muttered Dallas.

Dash stared back at him. "Go on. That's good. Give me another one."

"Shit."

"Frankly, I don't think you're in any position to be shitting anybody."

Dallas scrambled to his feet. "I don't need this."

"You need whatever I decide to give you."

Dallas turned abruptly and started away, hands balled at his sides. At the edge of the firelight he spun around, glaring at Maryse. "We were out in the country, lost for days and days. We fell asleep under a big tree and sometime in the middle of the night all the branches lit up like they were made of glass with wire inside and an army of chuckling dwarves rushed in and stuck a needle in Dad's eye and carried him off and we never saw him again. They sent a robot to take his place but Mom had already remarried a bail bondsman from Albuquerque. Everyone was very happy. Zoe grew up and went to Harvard." Then he was gone into the dark. They heard an animal cry and a second in response. "Coyotes," offered Maryse, but no one laughed.

Dash tossed a paper plate into the flames. "He's not mine," he said. Trinity watched the thick paper blacken and curl as if there might be signs in the shape of the ash. Maryse fussed with Mignon's blanket. Zoe was now locked in the truck cab and could occasionally be heard beating on the dash with an empty Hires can. The father looked into the fire, then up at the glittering sky. He went into the tent where his wife lay as if dead on her cot on top of the unzipped sleeping bag, arms folded over her stomach. He stood there until her eyes met his and in them were neither questions nor answers but sharp facets of light glimpsed for the first time, the deeps of a stranger. The others, outside in the dark, he knew who they were—poisoned spawn. "Guess I'll check out that road for a ways, see if there's a store open somewhere," he said. She seemed to regard him across a hazy uncertain distance. "You are," she said softly. It seemed to be a statement of some kind. He was going to ask if she wanted anything but instead turned and went out to the car, jangling the keys in his pocket.

Dallas crouched behind a tree, watching the red taillights go bouncing away down the dusty gravel road. He pulled the revolver out of his jeans and slumped against the ribbed trunk, cradling the gun in both hands. He couldn't look at it enough; it gave him the same clear pleasure as peering through a telescope into the Hostetler bedroom. Edsel was beside him in an instant. "Whatcha got?"

"Nothing," said Dallas, twisting his body away, the revolver suddenly too large to get back inside his pants.

"Show me."

"None uh your business. Ouch!" He was tearing hair in his groin.

"I'm gonna tell."

"No, you're not."

"Yes, I am, you've got a gun, and I'm gonna tell."

Dallas shifted about, displayed an upraised pair of empty magician's hands. "See, nothing there."

Edsel lunged forward, grabbing for Dallas's fly. "Whatcha got in there?"

"Oh, all right, you little shit." He produced the revolver with a ceremonial flourish. "Happy?"

"Wow!" Edsel reached out greedily.

"No, no, you have to promise not to tell."

"Okay, I promise."

"No, you have to mean it. This is the biggest secret you've

ever had to keep." He seemed to consider the trickiness of the situation for a moment. "What if I let you shoot it?"

Edsel's eyes widened. "You won't."

"Yes, I will, but we're gonna have to be extra careful, sneak far enough away from here so nobody will hear it. Promise?"

Edsel's head bobbed in solemn agreement.

Out by the fire the girls in lambent silhouette passed a joint back and forth. "This way," Dallas whispered, pushing off into the snarled undergrowth. Edsel kept his head down and stayed close to his brother. These woods were thick and dark and crawling with red marble eyes to spook you and slimy tails to wrap around your ankle and raking claws and dripping teeth. He was sure something was following them, but every time he glanced around it was only a tree offering to shake hands. A chorus of crickets paused in midconcert in eerie salute to their passing. Dallas began making choking noises in his throat like someone either having a heart attack or turning into a monster. He wanted to make Dallas stop but was afraid if he touched him it wouldn't be his brother anymore. When they came out of the trees Edsel kept right on as though he were still dodging branches, slapping away leaves. He didn't stop until he hit asphalt. Then he dared to look back. The eyes had to stay there in the woods, out in the open they'd explode like Occupant eggs in water.

They followed the empty rolling highway uphill and down —a novel experience for longtime flatlanders—until Dallas judged a comfortable distance had been inserted between themselves and the unwanted notice of inquisitive ears. He pointed theatrically to a diamond-shaped Warning S Curve sign. He assumed a shooter's crouch in the middle of the road. The barrel wavered between his hands. Edsel's face crinkled into an anticipatory wince. There was a flash and a crack, the sound of an ax splitting a dry plank. They listened, staring somberly at one another, pondering the mystery of that long, long echo down to the final faint fuzz tone that passes for silence at the human level. Punched into the metal sheet of the sign was a perfect round hole they touched with reverent fingers, a genuine manifestation of the wonder about which the universe itself was constructed.

"Now can I?" pleaded Edsel. "Can I? Let me do it, please."

Dallas positioned him out on the road, demonstrated the grip, the stance, how to squeeze the trigger as if milking a tit. The gun spit and jerked in his arms and the shot went wide, but Edsel was as thrilled as if he'd made the metal ring. He'd entered grown-up land where the power was and you stayed up as late as you liked and smoked cigarettes no matter what doctors said and stuck your dick into girls and there was no school. "Wow!" he exclaimed, giving up the weapon reluctantly. They took turns until all the chambers were empty and a second hole (Dallas's) had appeared in the sign. On the way back Dallas cautioned, "Now remember, this is our secret. Don't tell anyone, not Mom or Dad or the girls, because if you do, something bad will happen."

"What?"

"Try me and see."

Several steps in musing silence. "I want one, too."

"When you're older."

"I am older."

"Tell, and you'll never get one."

Two yoked disks of brilliant light sailed up over the ridge at their backs and down upon them. They bolted for cover, squatting behind a rotten log until the car, sputtering like a sick beast, hurried past.

"I think that was Dad," said Edsel.

Boldly Dallas stepped out onto the pavement, planted his feet, and brought up the revolver in both hands, police academy style, aiming into the dark slot between the fading coals of the taillights. He fired. Click! Click, click, click, click.

Inside the Bug Dash hunched cursing over the rattling wheel. The shimmy in the steering column was getting worse, the muffler noise growing louder, the configuration was breaking down. Even the kid in the paper hat at the checkout had laughed, watching him chug into the lot. If he had had a weapon, he might have drilled him on the spot, rifled the cash drawer for kicks. He bought a sixer of cold Bud, downed two in quick succession as if gulping cans of soda water. It was one of those cotton-candy nights with humid darkness packed in around you deep and dense, emotion leaking in a slow faint hiss. There was a queer tightness arching across the roof of his mouth. As he drove, the only radio station kept cycling in and out, an open forum on modern virginity. He had to shift into first on some of these unexpectedly steep hills, but the downslopes he took at speed, coming up out of his seat on the drop, running his own juices through the internal combustion. He missed his turn and had to double back. "Where the hell's the goddamn sign?" In the dark the camp road looked like the approach to the local dump. Gravel crunched like nuts beneath the tires, popped against the belly of the car. He bounced along down a winding tunnel of pine. Up ahead the tent glowed peacefully, like a paper lantern. The fire was dead, there was no one in sight. He swung the car around, lone high beam raking the hedge, a stand of elegant poplar, a couple of umber picnic tables, and stopped, coming to rest with ordained finality upon the incomprehensible spectacle of some fleshy creature struggling there on the dewy grass, insensate, unholy, many-limbed. The thing rose up, and out of its unfolding reared the startled heads of Trinity and Maryse, deer eyes flashing gold in the bright auto light. For one protracted instant Dash was aware of the serrated outline of each separate black leaf hovering in formal suspension over this scene and the finely particled nature of the cloud of pale dust drifting serenely past the window and the hood of night enclosing all and it was not he who thought, who acted, but a disconnected foot out of mazy dream that hit the accelerator, raced the engine, sent the deadly mass of a car hurtling through space and into a tangled wall of trunks and branches. He awoke against a glass of crushed foliage and the noise of an alarm clock that really someone should heed. When he lifted his head off the wheel, the horn stopped blowing. He touched his face and in the smoking light marked fingers slick with blood. He yanked on the handle beneath his elbow, pushed hard against the door, it wouldn't budge. He pulled himself over into the passenger seat, heaved his shoulder into that door, branches tearing, scraping at the paint. He covered his eyes with his hands and stumbled out through the bushes, shouting, "I'll kill you, so help me God, I'll fucking kill the both of you!"

Dot stood there barefoot in the clearing, trying to fathom the sight of her husband staggering away from their wrecked car like a drunken bully with a torn shirt and bloodied face. "What in hell is going on? I thought we were under attack."

He stalked on past her. "All right, where are they?"

"Where are who? What's happening here?"

"Your daughter. Your daughter and her goddamned . . . her goddamned . . ."

"What's wrong with you?"

"Did you see them? Do you know what the two of them were doing out here in the dirt?"

"Go wash your face. You look like a lunatic."

She never saw his hand, only the stars bursting over her head, the shower of sudden light, breaking, cascading, as she reeled away from this private vision of the Perseids.

Down the road ran Edsel, shouting, breathless.

"Don't you ever hit me again," she hissed at her husband. He moved toward her. "Don't touch me. You don't know what's coming down on you, you pathetic fool."

"Guess what?" Edsel cried.

She swung around on her son. "What the fuck do you want?"

Used to that tone of voice, Edsel looked immediately at his father. "Guess what Dallas has got?"

Dot drew the back of her hand across her mouth, examined what stuck to the skin.

"Dallas has got a gun." And without waiting for a reaction. "Can I get one, too? He said I could. Can I?"

"What?" shouted Dash, incredulous. "What?" He looked back and saw his eldest son sauntering in out of the night as casually as a hayseed reveler just returned from or about to rejoin a noon picnic. "What gun?"

Dallas's eyes blinked once. "So you told, you little fucker."

"Don't hit me." Edsel ducked behind his mother's legs. "Don't let him hit me."

"Where'd you get a gun?"

"I found it."

"Found it where?"

"Out on the road. Before we left home."

"Out on the road, huh. Well, let me see this mysterious gun you just happened to find out on the road."

Dallas stared at the hand extended toward him. "No," he said, and with careful feline movements started to edge away.

Dash took a step, then another, arm outstretched straight as a board. "Let me have it."

Dallas shook his head. "I said no. It's mine. Nobody else gets it."

"Okay, we all know whose it is, give it up now before there's something to regret."

Wary as scorpions, father and son sidled about one another in awkward dance, the gap between as constant as if each were attached to either end of a long pole, the gun barrel steady as a compass needle on the magnetized stone of Dash's chest.

"C'mon, Daddy Dick, Zero Time, mess with this you wanna make it happen so bad." The language already harsh and exotic on Dallas's mutating tongue because something *was* happening, upward sweeping toes to scalp one-instant-you're-you-the-next—backtracking without a glance the ball of the foot (the fin? the paw?) finds the spot that is always correct, slumbering eyes awakened and vigilant now in skin knitting into glassy carapace for the corrosive atmospheres of acid moons where silicon-based sinew tugs against gravity strong enough to warp light. They were on his planet now, there would be no more mistakes. Howling, he raised a claw. Dash leaped. He pulled a trigger. Dot screamed. And surprised at finding himself yet hostage to provincial laws of nature, Dallas was pitched violently onto his back, an ingot of pain hardening in his ribs, paternal fingers grasping at his throat. Fascinated, he observed his own hand, the one clutching the gun, describe a series of furious arcs down into the burred prominences of a head as constant and familiar as the sun in the sky. He wielded the barrel like a brick, the only sound that of the wind in their lungs and the disquieting crack of metal on bone. They clung fast to one another, legs thrashing in the dirt like the tails of archaic monsters. Then Dash's teeth found the flap of an ear and closed. A bolt of red shot across Dallas's temple. The gun tumbled easily from his hand. Still gripping him by the neck, Dash sat up atop his son's heaving body. The fist broke across Dallas's face like a wooden bat. When it came again exactly the same, Dallas got scared because he knew it was never going to stop. The light turned fuzzy and dark as meat, arrriving in quick sporadic bursts because somewhere a bulb was loose—he could see into the twisted sputtering sign of its filament, understood it was his special task to tighten the threads before the circuits blew, and somehow managed to free a leg and topple his rider and insert a knee and jerk sharply upward until Dash screeched like his daughter and fell away to roll about in the clotted earth, arms plunged to the elbow in the shadows of his groin as if seeking there the promised alembic on the map at journey's end. Dallas jumped to his feet and ran, and the road ran with him, curling off into the night where all is born and still aborning and a fire without heat or light consumes in an instant the apparitions of this world and the folly that waxes fruitlessly in the vain benedictions of its hectic star.

FATHERHOOD IS A CRUCIFIXION.
You die by degrees with outstretched arms.

It had been raining steadily since he left, a violent late summer downpour, loud torrents lashing at the pavement, drumming on the roof inches above his tensed head straining to keep the road in front of him, the wipers useless, guiding on the blurred running lights of a recklessly weaving van with a GOD RULES sticker plastered to its rear door. White veins of lightning stood up stark as winter trees on the far sky where he half expected to spot a grim black finger or two reaching down through the low racing clouds. The rain, this hard precipitate of polluted American lunacy, was, he knew, a shower of lead. When the country took a piss it came down out here and if you were wise to the facts you stayed in your car, under cover, let the others fend for themselves, let it come down on their Judas heads back there in the mud of their failed Calvary.

On May 15, 1973, Joseph and Rebecca Saunderson of Findlay, Ohio, hurrying home from a family reunion in Pennsylvania just ahead of a threatening squall line, observed an egg-shaped luminous ball hovering motionless over the Pymatuning Reservoir. The frightened couple watched in stunned disbelief as a tube descended from the belly of an obviously manned craft to touch the surface of the water.

They described this tube to local police as resembling a giant drinking straw. Of course. The Occupants grow strong on the fermentation of our decay.

Probably it was late. He wore no watch, never had, never would, it was a device that tended to tease one down the wrong road.

The gun lay gleaming, a child's toy, in the shadows on the passenger's seat beside him. He picked it up, pointed it straight ahead through the windshield at the round target of a spare tire mounted on the back of the bouncing van. He pointed the barrel to his left at a passing Mitsubishi and squeezed the trigger. He had no son. He tossed the empty weapon back onto the seat.

On Etheria the main occupations were war and hunting, spiritual combat in accord with the rules of creation.

Once when he was young he drove all night in the rollicking company of Les "The Best" Squires, ex–Brandenburg High first string tackle and future County General lab tech, on the rumor of a party worth losing sleep over. Festivities were well into the third day the morning they arrived. There were unconscious bodies sprawled all over the yard. There was a pig in a fire. There were naked people up in the trees. A contingent of Hells Angels dropped by, friends of a friend. All the Angels had seen UFOs at one time or another, singly or in clusters, and when they caught him smiling, they stomped on his fingers and whipped his back with car antennas. He had never before seriously considered the subject.

In his personal kit he packed two small vinyl brushes, one for his teeth, one to scrub away the dirt, the "collections," from beneath his nails. He chain-sucked rolls of Pep-O-Mint Life Savers. He drove in his stockinged feet, though he wasn't tired, his eyeballs sat like marbles of pure receiving crystal in the bony box of his face. He was amazed how calm, how light, he felt flying eastward through the rain. He was not angry. Except for the child in soiled clothes draped unconscious across the backseat, he might be absolutely anyone out on a casual trip to almost anywhere.

[182]

Families were bunk, temporary and uneasy alliances of strangers who would hate each other less without the coercion of blood, the spiraling bonds of genetic ivy holding its victims fast to a blasted tree.

Women loved him. Other women. At the conventions they thronged about, seeking autographs, pictures, the big answers, the urgency in their faces that pleads, Beam me up.

On Etheria there were no women, each being an integrated bioset of the basic three.

A cold November morning in 1980. Arthur Klein, an insurance salesman out of Rochester, New York, was driving alone on the road to Albany. The sky clear, the highway empty. He had just checked the time (4:41 A.M.) when a large bell-shaped object zoomed up over the trees ahead, stopped abruptly right above his car, which had just lost all power. The night turned white. Then the car was working again, he was a mile down the road, brain reeling from the aftereffects of what felt like at least two double martinis, and a radio DJ was clocking the A.M. at 5:28. Forty-seven minutes removed from the life of Arthur Klein without a trace. He had been spliced by the chronosurgeons of Etheria. Painful months of hypnotic regression therapy helped reclaim this sequence of events: mysteriously levitated from the interior of his car, he was drawn upward, helpless as a baby, into a glowing room, unceremoniously stripped, arranged on a cold slab of blue stone, penetrated by a black wandlike device, and serviced by a naked Occupant with barren eyes who sat patiently atop his shuddering groin, waiting for him to finish. In a confidential memo to the ICU (International Clearinghouse on UFOs), Klein reported that the texture of an alien vagina was similar to that of "oily emery cloth."

Our lives were bits of tape that could be altered at will by these masters of psychotronic technology, and at the Zero Time, if he had a choice, there were certain sequences he wished edited permanently from the Dash memory loop: an old black house turning on a platter of vegetable green, a gutted unfinished saucer gleaming in the morning sun, a goat

[183]

at the window, a cat on the stove, a vampire wife, a ghoul son, a demon daughter, a scrawny-assed witch—snip, snip, and burn it up.

He drove with offensive relish, concentrating on the game in which you were docked for each vehicle that managed successfully to pass your own. He crossed one entire state without losing a point.

In space even the darkness possesses the clarity of light, a chunk of black quartz veined with starshine, a kid's notion of a robot brain.

At The Hunting Lodge in Bedford Falls he left Zoe locked in the VW while he went in to negotiate with the desk clerk. When he returned, dangling room key in hand, an amazingly blond family in white shorts was gathered about the car, which was rocking furiously on its struts, the filthy opaque windows vibrating with the scary cries of an undomesticated and certainly illegal beast. "Stand away from there," Dash commanded, "circus property," and hastily got inside, backed away through a scattering of tanned limbs, and gunned the blue Bug around to a parking space directly in front of their room, where he could hustle his jungle daughter inside like a smuggler slipping a load of contraband through customs.

The long odyssey to M31 is also, of necessity, a calibrated passage through a series of rooms on the mother ship, each room a cube of different-colored light—blue to purple to green to orange and so on—a seven-chambered decompression lock of bone-deep wavelengths of energy that gradually reconditioned the human body for the home it had lost: Etheria.

He turned on the shower, yanked Zoe out of her raggedy dress, shoved her into the stall. As she splashed happily beneath the warm, pacifying spray, he stretched out on the bed and closed his eyes. Immediately the mattress began moving under him, bumpy as the car, rolling down a motel corridor of curtained windows and creamy mango paintings of a pseudoVenice expiring in a pseudosunset. It is the heart that winds the springs of time. It is the head that forges the hands.

He had no family, never did, never would. A white divider line skipped across the imagined ceiling in a broken current of metronomic beats, each speaking his name in a clear familiar voice quite close to his ear . . . Dash . . . Dash . . . Dash. . . . His eyes flicked open and for a moment he didn't know where he was or where he was supposed to be. Clouds of vapor were floating eerily into the room, all the mirrors were fogged. He rolled off the bed, rushed into the bathroom. Zoe, naturally, had fiddled with the faucets, turning up the hot, but she was standing docile as a drenched cow in the heat and steam, munching contentedly on a candy-sized bar of crimson motel soap. He toweled her off, opened the drapes, and positioned her naked in front of the window. The sky was a bloated gray, the bulging undersides of the clouds tinged with a dull yellow as though something with a lantern were struggling to work its way out. "C'mon, sweetie, talk to them." He seized her head, aimed it up. She wriggled under his grip, made protesting squirrellike noises. "Do what I tell you, damnit." She spun away from him, knocking the phony brass nautical lamp off the fiberboard table, a sharp explosive puff as the bulb shattered. "Fucking Christ!" She crawled under the bed just out of reach.

There is no money on Etheria. Everyone gets what they need. For nothing.

When she got hungry, he brought back a greasy bag of powdered jelly doughnuts they consumed sitting side by side on the floor. He gave her a piece of tektite to fondle. He watched television without really being aware of what was on. The ends of her nerves were miniature plugs that connected directly to the mainframe. Why couldn't we all do that? Suddenly down on his knees, chest unexpectedly full, he hugged his daughter's tense whippetlike body, ghost bugs of her energy skittering through his flesh. He kissed her cheek and nuzzled her ear. "I love you," he whispered. When he let go, she tried to scratch at his eyes. Through the plaster partition he thought he could actually hear the sound of breathing in the next room. Of course. The next room is always occupied.

[185]

There was a term, a dry bone of legalese, that had been rattling inside his head, amusing, pertinent: alienation of affection. Our sin, our chain. Curse of the clan.

"I have something to say to you," said Dot. That was all she ever said. In his mind her face was always her first face. It didn't change.

He had no family.

The television tube eyeing him so intently picked up just one channel, an independent station broadcasting nonstop reruns of sixties sitcoms he'd never seen any humor in the first time around despite the nagging laugh track, the sets as identical as the families inhabiting them, so what was young Dot doing bustling about the antiseptic spaciousness of one of these dummy kitchens illuminated so cleverly even the pastel cupboards cast no shadows and each chintz-framed window opened out on the exact same view? She was dressed apparently for the prom, the features of her face exaggerated into acute and revealing detail he'd never noticed before. Her hands, always just maddeningly out of view, were engaged in an obviously complex food task as a squad of black-and-white emperor penguins milled around at her feet. Then he was there, too, walking into forgotten doors, banging against strange furniture he didn't even know he had, trying unsuccessfully to knot a tie of some slithery trick material while the potted plants on the sill laughed at him and the cooking timer went bing and Dot shoved a warm cookie into his objecting mouth. Then he stepped on a webbed foot. But the plates shone like mirrors and the spoons sparkled and the tollhouse cookies were piling up in fragrant mounds on the gleaming countertops and the suds in the sink swelled like eggs of a certain reptilian nature and the crowding penguins made movement difficult, but the cookies were good, the shelves stacked with colorful cans, it was always summer outside, as a bill nipped his hand and the heat from the oven began to build and the bubbles were spilling onto the waxed linoleum, breaking, oozing, releasing a—but the cookies . . . He woke with flushed cheeks and a hollow thudding in his sinuses and

[186]

a clear sense of crucial knowledge imparted that was fading now quick as he tried to embrace it. He staggered to the john to find Zoe swishing her hands deliriously about in the toilet bowl. "Stop that!" he shrieked. Her hands beat faster against the porcelain, so he was forced to pull down her panties and discipline her there right on the wet tile, crying, "You little bastard!" until she screamed and bit his thumb. It was time to check out.

Jellyfish over Jericho, pie tins over Poughkeepsie, aluminum bathtubs over Alabama. The wonders to behold if we simply lifted our heads.

It was a grim industrial dawn, the morning carnival in full revelry, interstate traffic steadily thickening, arterial movement narrowing down to a sputtering stream, a gooey trickle, closing toward complete cessation and final seizure. His eyes in the rearview mirror looked back at themselves without recognition. His head ached terribly. Some joker during the night had ripped off the antenna, leaving a radio capable of providing only the desolate distraction of static. He opened the glove compartment, checked that the gun was still there hidden among the cracked sunglasses and wrinkled maps. Cars inched along for miles like prisoners on a chain, then abruptly darted forward for a couple dozen yards, changing lanes with abandon, stealing into sudden pockets of space just large enough to squeeze bumper to bumper. And he helpless before such commuter idiocies, punching in futile rage on the silent horn as Zoe, having quickly forgotten the recent bathroom scene, bounced energetically about the backseat, emitting a run of gutturals, her song, private as blood and the tangled skein of her unique wiring.

Sometimes, in small towns on moonless nights so dark you might as well be underground, there would be visible, if you stared long enough in the right direction, a play of mild light out in the graveyards, soft fuzzy dots moving around among the trees and the stones like lazy croquet balls for up to an hour or more, occasionally hopping over one another in a tranquil game of leapfrog, then, without warning, rocketing straight into the air, high, higher, directly up into that huge circular thing with revolving spheres of red and blue you never noticed until now. It's gone before you can even comprehend what you've seen. A fact little remarked upon in the literature, but true: they like to linger over our cemeteries. Why?

He left I-80 and drifted along a local road until the inevitable 7-Eleven showed up. The layouts of these places were all the same, so he could find what he wanted and get out in a hurry. He bought a bag of prepackaged snack foods, a couple six-packs, and a child's nonbreakable, nonspillable drinking cup that even as he drove he kept constantly filled with warm Bud and by early afternoon Zoe was thoroughly wasted, a skinny cherub posed in a careless slump against the dark blue leatherette, a bit of spittle pasted to the corner of her mouth, scarred face in numb repose at last, glowing with false health in the gold light of a newly minted sun.

"The most interesting skull. Such depth of character. Look at this extraordinary protuberance in back. May I touch it, please?" Her plump wrinkled hands, festooned with metals and glittering rocks not of this realm, reached out avidly to palpate the phrenological wonders of Zoe's head. Queen Lividia, monarch of all Magnetron and its Moons to the Third Sphere, exerted a pull of almost three hundred pounds on this planet and swathed in great purple robes rarely moved from the silver painted throne set within the shuttered living room of her Escondido bungalow, the odor of Balkan Sobranie still clinging to the faded furnishings though Al had transcended this level many many years before. "Oh!" she exclaimed, hands drawing back with a start. "This child, she's on fire!" Her eyes bulged like pink gumballs from her overpowdered face and Edsel hid behind Mr. Al's brown armchair and wouldn't come out, not even to sample the Queen's cosmic rhubarb pie. And on the way back to the motel Dot discovered he had wet his pants and Dash spanked him so hard he bruised a muscle in his pen hand and next morning explained to the California delegation at the UFOFEST the soreness was due to a lab accident on Etheria. And even though he couldn't sign any books they made almost two grand that day, a new record.

Everywhere the open road was breaking down. Sweaty work crews, coated from hair to boots in concrete dust, nibbled away at the brittle pavement with picks and jackhammers, trucks carting away the chunks like loads of valuable ore, traffic in single file crawling past a shirtless black man in goggles, bandanna tied across his mouth and nose, red flag drooping from his fist, the bored face looking back a dead ringer for Barney Hill's, famous 1961 abductee.

Then a brief acceleration ahead to the next bottleneck some twenty miles farther on: a caravan of gawking drivers creeping through a clot of patrol cars, ambulances, pulsing lights, and a Chrysler LeBaron, its windshield splintered into silvery lacework, hood buckled, front tires gone, sitting sideways in a litter of glass, metal fragments, and clumps of rubber, and down in the median gulley a broken Nissan upside down, white sheet draped discreetly over left door and window, the type of ordinary roadside scene Dallas, even as a small child, wanted the family to regard, to stop and photograph. Instinctively, Dash looked to the sky. All clear.

Thirty bodies the Air Force has locked in a hangar at Wright-Pat. Sliced, diced, and on ice. Mongoloid heads, no digestive systems, their blood was transparent.

He stopped for lunch at a joint called Danny's, a brick-and-glass bunker squatting behind a thick hedge. He parked in the shade in back, freshening Zoe's cup before he went in. He watched himself approaching the wide glass doors of the restaurant, and he liked what he saw—here was someone definitely from out of state. Inside, the air-conditioned aroma of fried food and the clatter of hungry humans at lunch—adult noises, the sounds of his kind? A waitress brushed by with barely a glance, "Sit wherever you like." He chose a corner table, back to the wall, senses aimed outward in a radial shotgun pattern. The couple across the room had just had sex but were contemplating divorce. The man in the Izod shirt had stomach cancer. The lonely girl by the door was pregnant. Grandma Blue Hair thought she was in Cleveland on V-J Day. The chubby boy in jeans was a secret rapist. Faces were flowers of flesh, some got pollinated, some did not. From a slot in the opposite wall a disembodied pair of hairy arms fantastic as lobster claws shoved a platter of yellow chicken under a sickly pink light. "Of course no one suspected that he'd be there," remarked a woman at an adjoining table, and her companions laughed, exposing their false teeth. The coffee machine shone with the boldness of hard surreptitious things. The minute hand on the wall clock was moving too fast. All the eyes in this room were dead.

The menu was decorated with drawings of curlicue anchors and leering whales. He ordered, chewed what was brought him dutifully as a child, tasting nothing. When the girl returned with the check he understood perfectly what her expression meant.

"Yes," he said, trying to match verbal affability with the smile centered on her eyes, brown and bovine. "I am exactly who you think I am."

Her ringed hand, sliding the bill facedown across the table, paused, her eyes shrinking slightly, the habitual wariness of the long-term service employee. "Excuse me, sir?"

"Quite all right. I'm used to it by now. Happens wherever I go." The smile fixed at the same width and intensity.

"I'm sorry, sir. What happens?"

"Perfectly natural. I'm startled, too, whenever I encounter anyone famous."

"You're famous?"

"Yes, I'm Dash."

"You are."

"Yes, I thought you recognized me."

She leaned forward, peering. "Sure," she said. "Dash. It's just that we get so many famous people dropping in here. And the sunglasses and everything. Nice to meet you, Dash." She formally extended her hand. "Have a nice day."

"You, too," he replied. "Make your own reality."

Because there *are* other universes next door. Vast systems turning in dimensions beyond the reach of intellects constructed out of home-grown materials. The systems orbit around and through one another and where they touch, within the undetectable ellipse of their intersection, there is slippage in the gears: whirlpools, singularities, premonition, coincidence, accident.

It was amusing to see himself encased in a blue bubble rolling merrily over bleached cement. The passing countryside was not his. The people in the surrounding cars were all strangers. Even the weather was odd: in a disturbing reversal of the seasons the days, as they declined on toward fall, were growing progressively hotter, the land withering in drought. Southerly winds and bad energy prevailed.

Zoe sat up cranky and hung over, creased face slick with sweat. She immediately began to wail and tried to dislodge the ball bearing of pain from her head by knocking it repeatedly against the back of her father's seat. He tossed a handful of M&Ms over his shoulder, calming her down.

It must have been hanging out there for some time, bright as a pocket watch against the blank expanse of unadorned sky, spinning as if on a fob, and spinning, he knew, was a form of watching. He pulled the Bug off the road and waited. It was about a mile off to the right, revolving on its axis a couple hundred feet above some high tension lines, a file of huge stick figures marching away over the beanfield. It twinkled and sparked as if to burn a hole through the screen while blind tourists roared by oblivious. He had no idea how long he watched. "Zoe!" He reached back over the seat, shook her roughly by the shoulder. "Zoe, Zoe honey, wake up!" She groaned. "Zoe, c'mon now, quit faking." She didn't move. "You little bitch!" He threw open his door, got out, and pulled her from the car by her ankles. She lay facedown in the white gravel, whimpering. "Now look," he said in his most pleasing abject manner, "look, look, look," lifting her up by the waist and carrying this life-sized marionette around to the front of the ticking car, where he braced himself against the hot fender, she propped more or less upright between his tight legs. "Now looky up there." Cupping the exemplary shape of her head in his hand, he directed her gaze to the proper quadrant. "See, see that." He jerked an arm about in feeble mimicry of her grand ballet. "They want to talk to you. They've been searching for a long time. Now talk." She sagged against him, knees buckling. "C'mon now, sweetie, this might be important." He raised her own arms in his and waved them strenuously about. The wash from passing cars shuddered into them, hot and damp as dinosaur breath. They stood together like that for some moments, swaying unsteadily like sailors on dry land. Her arms were like rubber batons, and while it lasted it was he who stood upon the podium, he who conducted the music of the spheres, but there was no response. Then a rosy nipple of light atop the blazing object winked back at him, an encyclopedia of feeling communicated totally in an instant, and the thing was gone, it was there and then it wasn't.

Charles Fort: "I think we're property . . . something owns this earth—all others warned off."

Einstein communed regularly with agents from beyond our solar system, meeting the muddy-faced entities over strudel in his Princeton, N.J., home. He had been a contactee from the age of five.

Jonathan Swift was an alien.

That afternoon he spotted the first dero team, the usual trio in a black Mercedes with tinted windows, trailing him right behind the Hyundai. He saw himself smiling in the mirror, remembering the two policemen blinded by cosmic rays in Zacatecas; Captain Mantell's last words over Godman: "It's metallic and tremendous in size!"; the besieged family in Hopkinsville, Kentucky, bouncing bullets off the goblins at their windows; the firefight between a training squad out of Ft. Hood and men in cerulean suits with glass heads; Grover's Mill, N.J., 1938; and Dr. Reich himself, who downed several over Orgonon in 1955. He was about to enlist in the shooting war.

[192]

At dusk he noticed a second Mercedes approaching from behind in the passing lane. He peeled away off the interstate, one of the black cars still pacing him. He pulled into the first gas station on the right and sat quietly by the pumps under the harsh yellow light, watching in the mirror. The traffic came at him in colors: blue, green, brown, blue, red, blue, blue, gray . . . no black, no black at all. The greasy guy in the glass booth was giving him the eye, so he got out of the car, gathered Zoe in his arms, and headed for the john, just a respectable father here, tending to the lavatory needs of his youngest. He set her down on the pot like a doll. "Pee, damnit!" he barked. She yanked the toilet paper roll off the wall. Her clothes stank, and his brusque attempts at cleaning her limbs and face with a wet paper towel only succeeded in rearranging the grime into charcoal streaks across her skin. She yelped when he touched the scabs on her cheeks, a nice infection brewing there. He carried her back to the car, filled up the tank—one eye on the road—and bought her a couple bags of chips and pretzels and a can of grape soda—she needed the vitamin C. From under the scratched and dimpled hood fringed still with bits of leaf and twig he removed a hefty elongated contraption of bound metal pipe and rubber tubing—it resembled an old nineteenth-century Gatling gun —and laid it carefully inside the car, balancing it across the tops of the seats. He checked his money, the gun in the glove compartment, and one of his tattered maps, plotting out a deviously complicated route along the jagged blue capillaries of secondary roads. "Wave good-bye to the nice man," he said, and rumbled off into the night.

He didn't have long to wait. Thirty minutes later on a deserted stretch of rolling two-lane blacktop—the glow of an occasional farmhouse drifting by on either side comforting as a harbor buoy—a set of piercing high beams popped up into the mirror. He accelerated for a mile, then slowed to well below the speed limit. The lights stayed where they were, pacing him precisely. "Okay." One hand on the wheel, he reached back, settling the pipes out straight and level. "No, honey," he cautioned Zoe, who had come alive at this novel activity beside her, "no, don't touch." A spacebuster's rule of thumb: always aim *between* the lights. Now. He pressed a red button at the base of the device. There was no flash, no sound, the dero machine simply vanished forever from the mirror. The war had begun.

Now he drove like a professional, attacking the paved surface, pedal to the floor on the straightaway, downshifting the curves, hysterical trees leaping out of his path, disintegrating clouds of gnats, barreling through towns so small the only sign of life was the traffic light blinking a slow forlorn yellow at the single intersection, vacant early morning hours, the country deep into REMs, the troubled territory under the covers, and he alone the solitary soul awake to the menace stalking the land across these four postwar decades of pap and pop. The signal had gone out from the steeple, and the rider bounded through the night with the message. The message was in the child. A child shall save you.

He bounced over potholes, he rattled over "gatorbacks," wheel jumping in his hands, "crickets" chirping in the engine, oil splattering from the crankcase a quart every hundred miles, eyes tunneled out ahead on the road stripes sliding and weaving across the dark like white snakes desperate to mate, their frustration hypnotic in its anxious beauty, mind and body locked together on automatic pilot, an entranced state of exhilarating movement, pure flight without destination, the truest flight of all. . . . The arrow flew at him and away before there was time to respond. He jammed both feet onto the brake pedal, sending the VW into a crazy sideways skid down the center of the road to stop several hundred feet past the sign pointing in reflective bubbles straight toward WASHINGTON, D.C. The headlight burned weakly through a haze of rubber smoke, the engine was dead. When he tried to restart it, he flooded the carburetor and had to sit there like a fool astraddle the divider line, exposed, impotent, hoping the antique battery wouldn't give out altogether before he got going again and that Zoe, who had been catapulted to the floor, would stop screaming for Christ's sake before a patrol car happened by and hauled them both in as public nuisances. He waited a couple minutes, spoke aloud a word given to him through Zoe by The Occupants, twisted the key, and the plugs fired and an hour later he was cruising along the beltway through the dead air of a D.C. dawn.

The sugary confections of government sprang up about him, the aggressive spike of the Washington Monument, the rounded and ribbed lid of the U.S. Capitol, the Jefferson Memorial's planetarium dome, all fashioned of the same creamy edible substance, images so familiar their three-dimensional actuality was preposterous, objects dreamt into being on a whim. Low in the pink breaking sky a couple of rogue lights cavorted, gathering and dispersing in exquisitely timed coordination, a company of supremely intelligent fireflies rehearsing an extraordinary dance. And despite his pleas, his urgent gestures, Zoe, perversely stubborn, ignored completely this astonishing air show. When her cup was empty, he refilled it with flat brew.

Ten days in July. When saucers were strung like Christmas lights over the city and the radar at both National and Edwards registered anomalous blips buzzing Congress, the White House, violating restricted air corridors, making a mockery of national security, and interceptors were scrambled from Wilmington, Delaware, and as one of the jets was surrounded by clusters of blue and white the pilot radioed the ground, "They're closing in on me. What should I do?" This was in 1952. No one had an answer then. No one has an answer now.

As if on cue, morning congestion closed rapidly around, boxing him in, sleek black cars patrolling every lane, guided one and all by button shark eyes. Caught in this current of chrome and glass, he was across the Potomac and touring through Alexandria before he had a chance to exit and turn around. A cup came flying over the seat, narrowly missing his head. If he could have stopped, he'd have whipped her with his belt. She'd wet her pants again, too; he'd been inhaling the fumes for the last hour.

Back in the District he cruised the alphabet streets, searching for the hotel (name forgotten, of course) he and Dot had enjoyed a memorable stay in during the famous International Saucerology Forum commemorating the twenty-fifth anniversary of Kenneth Arnold's epochal Mount Rainier sightings. A deputy from the UN Secretary General's office had attended, along with half a dozen frequent flyers to the backside of the planet Venus, the man whose lunar potatoes (a breakfast gift from congenial Star Persons) had been mysteriously confiscated by the federal government, a wall-eyed grandmother who sold cloud portraits she'd done in needlepoint, a cast member of the television series *Star Trek*, a dog who'd been to Pluto (do you know even know where you are?), and the usual assortment of CIA, dero, and disguised Occupants. Edsel had been conceived there in a room somewhere among the upper stories, but it wasn't nostalgic sentimentality that sent him cursing up and down and around and around—the place, as he remembered it, was cheap and clean.

Here in this part of town black cars were replaced by black faces and the wedding-cake columns and frosted facades of the country's monuments to itself were glimpsed down shadowed back streets from unfamiliar, unphotographed angles. In the middle of the sidewalk on an old kitchen chair sat an emaciated woman in a winter coat, nylons rolled down about her sagging ankles, a rotting fish in a metal pan laid across her lap like a sleeping child, blue-and-green bottle flies swarming over the fish, her hands, her face. Two elderly men in a dirt yard were trying to kick one another without losing a drop from the brown-bagged wine quarts clutched in each right hand. A pack of mongrel dogs chased some quick-limbed furry creature over the moon rubble of a vacant lot. A sweating adolescent with muscled arms strode across an intersection, a belt of live M-6o rounds draped about his neck.

On Etheria the snow is warm and there are violet moons

and each inhabitant is cradled in the velvet webbing of the others' minds. Everyone can fly. Everyone is free.

He passed the nondescript yellow brick building twice in his impatient circling before he even noticed the sign: MOUNTJOY INN. It looked like the kind of residential hotel people grew old and died in, waiting for something else to happen. Forty-five minutes later he finally found a parking space a minor march away. Carefully, he locked the car, then struggled down the street with bag and money box in one hand, Zoe in the other, pulling at him like a stubborn dog.

On the corner outside the hotel was a big man in small ill-fitting clothes hunched over a lusterless battered saxophone. The instrument case lying open on the pavement in front of him contained a few scattered coins bright as the eyes that peered surreptitiously through a snarled curtain of gray unwashed hair. Out of the bell of the horn erupted a cacophony of sour notes whose disorienting progression seemed to have something to do with the periodic switchings of the WALK-DON'T WALK sign suspended from the pole above his head. At their approach he peeled his lips off the mouthpiece and chuckled, "Heh, heh, heh, you two sure do look like hell." Then he closed his eyes and blew his way back to whatever world these discordant squawks sounded sweet on.

Dash fumbled about in his pockets. Zoe was rocking back and forth from her waist in a blind spastic boogie. The Occupants were clever, and this bum had all the marks of a genuine Ditto man. He folded a five-dollar bill twice and tossed it into the magenta-lined case.

The musician nodded, pausing in his solo to say, "A blessing for you," and producing from somewhere among the diverse layering of jackets, vests, sweaters, and shirts a small object he pressed solemnly into Dash's open hand: a used sax reed. Dash gaped as if he'd just been presented with a wad of fresh snot. "What the hell am I supposed to do with this?"

The man shrugged. "You got a horn?"

Dash looked him up and down, openly contemptuous. "Go wash yourself."

[197]

"Thank you, sir." The sax man bowed. "Thank you, thank you, thank you." His smile simple and lucent, untainted by the slightest edge of guile or sarcasm.

Dash had to drag his backward-glancing daughter up the stone steps of the hotel and into a lobby the size and decor of a cabdriver's lounge: fake rubber plants listing from the dusty corners, rattling floor fan, cardboard table, tired furniture, pink bald head cresting the top of a shabby brown armchair, a waiting room for interminable waits. The senior citizen behind the desk had wiry unkempt hair colored the flat black of cheap dye and eyebrows drawn on her forehead in high, questioning arcs. The portable television at her elbow was tuned to a professional wrestling match she monitored intently while folding and cutting strips of tissue into clever pastel roses. The counter was a mess of bright paper petals. She handed Dash a registration card and a pen and returned to her scissors. While Dash concocted a recent past, Zoe squatted at his feet, trying to pry the pretty tiles off the floor. Visit A Civil War Battlefield, urged a rack of brochures near the door. In the corner beside the mailboxes was an emerald parrot in a soiled cage. "What's the word?" said the bird. "Checking out, checking out." The woman read the address off the card. "Tourist?" The eyebrows resembled croquet wickets.

"Business." There was something unsettling and vaguely familiar about her, a face in the crowd at some long-ago symposium. He paid a week in advance, and she handed him the key to a room on the third floor.

"No hot plates, no fans, no smoking in bed," she intoned, then, spying Zoe attempting to scale the counter, "My, what a lovely child, Mister Klaatu."

"A gift from above," he replied, seizing Zoe firmly by the hand and turning to go.

"Elevator's broke," the woman called after him. "Stairs is over there to your right."

Zoe's legs gave out after one flight, so he had to carry her shrieking up this cinder-block echo chamber to a hallway reeking of stale bodies, smoke, and harsh disinfectant, where peculiar faces peeked out furtively at them, half-cracked doors closing silently as they passed. Their own door was warped into its frame, and after wiggling the key repeatedly in the stiff lock, Dash had to lean his shoulder into the wood to get it open. Inside was a room just like all the other rooms he had put time into on all the other trips of his life. Everything was used, including the air. He went to the window. It was painted shut. On the opposite side of the gray mottled glass, gleaming perfectly even in the dampened light of an overcast sky, the iconic structures of the nation, saintly domes and fairy towers, and above them a clear triangle of light holding steady over the green rectangle of the Mall, each separate disk bouncing playfully within this configuration from one angled point to the next. He watched for a few minutes, too mesmerized to even think of forcing Zoe, who was busy licking out the inside of her cup, to the window. Then he noticed a dark-suited man in a window of the office building directly across the street, staring back at him through a pair of big binoculars. Quickly, he stepped behind the wall, dropped the blinds with a clatter. He looked with spreading horror at this room he now occupied, its cage of space, its useless miserable objects. Zoe was in the upright fetal position on the bed, rocking, rocking over the creaking springs.

When they put the silence on you, there is no recovery. You are turned into a media buffoon or worse. Roswell, New Mexico, 1947. A bright object falls out of the blue, killing all four aboard. A weather balloon, the press is told. But Edgar Moseley, who witnessed the crash, the pear-headed remains, spoke freely of what he had seen until a visit from the dark suits and the facts vanished into the labyrinth of a stroke. Since 1953 the CIA has managed all news concerning UFOs. The films and tapes made of Zoe's "seizures" at the Institute they conveniently "mislaid." Reality is a place you can access only with the proper clearances. Everything genuine disappears. What's left, the cardboard maze we're *free* to scurry about in, is pure Dittoland.

He riffled through the pages of the phone book and dialed the number of *The Washington Post*. "I want to speak with one of the Watergate guys." In the world of hold he was entertained for several endless minutes by a stringed deluge of "Raindrops Keep Falling On My Head." According to Zoe, the Zero Time will come when 70% of the American people accept in mind and body the fact of an alien presence in our sky. The last Gallup poll put the percentage of believers at 57. We're just a mere 13% from our goal, people, please help us, help yourselves now and come forward, open your arms and accept the craft into your heart. Please. A male voice with the curt tone of the young and ambitious came on the line to take his story, see that it got to the right people. "What I have to say is too important to entrust to underpaid functionaries." He yanked the cord out of the wall, tossed the phone crashing to the floor. "Let's go, kid." And he lifted her into his arms and hurried down the stairs and into the street where two new formations were demonstrating their skills for all to see, one in the shape of a large red diamond, the other a flashing blue circle that rotated in silent grandeur over the White House.

Zoe started clawing at his arm the moment they entered the Senate Office Building. Gleaming corridor vistas, unnatural odors, insolent individuals on the march, it must have seemed to her a replica of the Institute. She shrank back toward the door, mewling. Dash waved a fresh packet of M&Ms in front of her nose and led her down the hall, one M&M at a time, checking the plaques posted outside each door until he recognized a name and walked in. The receptionist was young, blonde, too little that was organic in her smile. The Senator was away in Japan. "I'm a registered voter and a tax-paying resident of Buchanan County." The Senator had been in Japan since last Monday and would not return until late next week. "And I'm the Speaker of the House. He was on television only last night discussing Star Wars from this very office." The Senator often gave interviews that were broadcast later by tape delay. "Can I go in and see if he's at his desk? Maybe the Senator caught an early flight." The Senator appreciated hearing from his constituents, and perhaps if you would care to write him at this address . . . Could your little girl get her hands out of the jelly bean bowl?

The television station, at least the part of it he was permitted to see, looked just like a real estate office. No one there knew his name, either. The talent coordinator was at lunch. "It's important," he said. "Thirteen percent." Neither the bewildered secretary nor several affable fellows from building security seemed to disagree. But unattended for far too many empty minutes, Zoe had managed to overturn a large chrome ashtray, wriggle out of her panties, and was just assuming her preparatory crouch over the beige mound of spilled sand, butts, and ash, when someone grabbed his arm—rude, machinelike fingers tight on his flesh—and an extended moment of consummate physicality ended out on the sidewalk, father and daughter raging together for once at a common enemy without Unit affiliation. The sky seemed exceptionally large and open here, and when he looked up he could feel the magic light falling down around him, the tickling pressure of it, steady as a wind against the translucent fabric of his face.

Out on the Mall a gang of scruffy kids was tossing around a yellow Frisbee, the athletic contortions of their bodies oddly reminiscent of little Zoe at her window. Their dog, an untethered menace, came bounding instantly over, fangs bared. Zoe screamed, hung cringing to Dash's leg. "Sarah!" called one of the boys, and the dog swung around. "Sorry!"

"Keep your creature off us," yelled Dash, stroking his daughter's head. "I'll mess him up good, I'll break his back, I'll tear out his balls."

June 3, 1981. Betsy Strickland's cocker spaniel is run over by a furniture van on the street outside her home. The dog's skull is cracked open, revealing that one-half of the animal's brain had been replaced at one time by a smooth silver lobe of unknown origin and construction. The object is handed over to local police for further examination and is never seen again. The dog had liked to sit by the picture window for hours on end, staring out at absolutely nothing.

When they arrived at the Reflecting Pool, Zoe broke loose and jumped in fully clothed, splashed in a frenzy among the reflections, glossy fragments of blue and white, the way things are. Then a cop with a shellacked exterior ordered Dash to pull her out. Up in the air lights gathered and wheeled in mute chorus.

There was a crowd in front of the White House, an angry eruption of the populace outfitted in grotesque masks and black armbands, a parade of red placards jostling along between the wooden barricades, the uneasy teams of helmeted police stationed at ten-yard intervals, chanting something unintelligible about abortion in a performance designed as much for the network lenses as that curious figure who maybe even now might be lurking behind the curtains across the deep green lawn. There were unmarked cars lining the curb, manned, engines idling; a row of uniforms behind the iron gate; much nervous coming and going in the guard booths—the dero machinery in high activation all around the block. Dash took in the scene at a glance and decided this was not the day to petition his leader. Turning away with Zoe in tow, he shouted back at the demonstrators, "Fuck the monsters, fuck all of 'em!"

Every president since Truman has known exactly what you suspected they knew. Details are presented in the initial briefing right after the oath. In 1954 Eisenhower himself met secretly at Edwards Air Force Base with a delegation from Alpha Centauri. It changes a man. The millstone of such knowledge dragged through life like a curse and on down into a marble crypt.

Funny, but he couldn't for the moment recall the name of the hotel or how to get there. He wandered around with the tourists, feeding Zoe Eskimo pies and orange soda. At a shady fenced-in playground he sat on a green bench beside his fellow parents and watched his daughter ignoring the other children. The sky had grown so busy with intricate movement he dared not look up for fear of vertigo. The kids on the swings were cutting neat parabolas into the blue afternoon humidity. A small boy with a round outsized head kept going up and down the circular slide; up, around, and down; up, around, and down. In a child the fundamental affinity for the delights of that shape were clear and undisguised, easy access at that age to the helical truth of our nature. Up, around, and down. It's the shape that is the key: you can find it prominently incised on the shimmering walls of the mother ship.

He must have rested his eyes for a moment because when he opened them it was dark out there, too, and all the children had flown away home. He walked the streets, aimlessly, through inexplicably deserted neighborhoods, hoping for the appearance of a familiar sign. Light spun without cease in the darkness above, and there were glittering deposits of devil's jelly all along Pennsylvania Avenue, clumps of angel hair dense as Spanish moss glowing momentarily in the leafy branches of the trees and evaporating without a trace. He was exhausted—there is no surcease for the prophet—but sleep, he recognized, was at this point a fluctuating region lying well beyond the rim of plausibility. So he walked, the sound of honey bees swarming in the hollows of his ears and somewhere the faintest suggestion of many voices reaching out together toward real melody. . . .

The convoluted eye of the plastic rose in the clear plastic vase on the nightstand had obviously been focused on him for quite some time. When he got up off the bed, there were hairs left behind on the pillowcase, an alarming number of them. In the bathroom mirror he saw fallen lashes on his cheeks. He checked his teeth and gums. Still firm. The bombardment was probably coming from that office across the street.

It was daytime, so stores must be open. He went out and bought several rolls of aluminum foil to tape over the window. Later, he sat at the rickety desk, a cap of foil molded to his head, writing in his notebook: In the space of mind there is universe. This is factual. They seek to intervene. Violation is the goal of the terminal entities. Cosmic consequences that you read as comic. Ssssss. And heed. Don't let the Egg Man touch you there. The inside is all down from when you fell out of the clouds. Don't worry. The pain of reentry can be endured without loss. Remember the great Doktor Reich. Listen to your organ.

When he peeked out the window again, it was night. Bewildered, he looked around the room. Zoe. Where was she?

He slid his bag out from under the bed, removed an army field cap, and secured it firmly on his head over the foil shield. He tucked the revolver into his belt. The notebook he hid in the desk behind the top drawer. He took some bills out of his cash box and left the hotel.

Stuff that has fallen out of the sky, documentation available upon request: rocks, metal plating, chunks of green ice, pellets of fire, baby snakes, toads, hairy spiders, black goo, fresh blood, flakes of meat, pieces of tooth.

This was the landscape you could never lose. The capital of Dittoland. Pay no attention to the "people." Avoid the pink street lamps—bad radiation of the worst quality. Actually, the city was rather pleasant at night, the daytime crush of visitors and bureaucrats dissolved completely, the air cooler, the monuments seemed lit from within, constructed out of stone quarried from mines of light in "the land beyond the Pole," as Admiral Byrd wrote, the hole Adolph Hitler squandered a fortune in reichsmarks attempting to locate.

He crossed and recrossed the Mall as though weaving an invisible string between the sentinel trees. He walked briskly with upright posture, an important man in an important town on a special mission. He paused in the soft shadow of a large oak, staring up at the white helmet of the Capitol dome looming inscrutably there over all. He could feel the potent thoughts radiating outward from the ornamental tip.

At the Lincoln Memorial the Old Railsplitter's gaze was impossible to evade no matter where you stood, discomfort-

ing eyes with the pupils scooped out like granite olives without any pimento. Clearly, it was not a human face. The naive
folk of that century had dubbed the flying objects "airships."
Mysterious ropes hung down from the heavens.

He was finding it increasingly difficult to concentrate on
the solids and shapes that made up the city, the once persua-
sive data of his tellurian senses was losing its authority. He
felt slightly dizzy, and the expected nausea had arrived, taking his stomach for a ride. It was important to keep moving.
He let his feet guide him through areas most tourists never
see, where even down in the hole of a night as bad as this one
there were still crannies of activity, illumination, and a living
presence, even if it was an angry bandit face lunging from the
shadows to demand, "What are you doing here?"

"Do you know me?" inquired Dash. "Don't I know you?"
He removed the gun from his belt. It felt good in his hand,
out in the air. "Do you know this?"

"Hey," said the man, backing off, "I didn't mean nothing."

"I don't, either." He wiggled the weapon impatiently.
"Where's the other two?" he asked, quickly checking his
flanks.

"What two?" said the man. "What're you gonna do?" There
was a barrel and a set of eyes on him that all looked alike.

"I tasted electricity at Allendale," said Dash. He paused, as
if expecting a reply. "My hands were fired in the furnaces of
Andromeda. I know what happens to light when you ride past
it. I've wrestled the angel. I've seen the stars of paradise. Do
you think I can be stopped? I've got antibodies. I've been
inoculated with the truth."

"Please," the man begged, "don't kill me."

"You're already dead." He pulled the trigger. "Bang," he
said, amused by the ludicrousness of the situation. He was
still smiling when he whipped the barrel into the side of the
man's face. It went crack like a nut. It went down like a sack
of sand. These dero—so pathetically constructed, yet so dangerous, their powerful mimetic abilities alone enabling them

to infiltrate all too easily, to pass as human, friend, wife, son. He knelt down, employed the gun like a hammer. When he was finished, he wiped his hands on the dero's shirt.

He walked.

He tossed the sticky gun under a bush outside the Department of Justice. Go figure, G-men.

He walked.

A radiance beckoned to him, a breaching of the darkness where mellow neon spelled RAINBOW CUTRATE LIQUORS. A rowdy band of dispossessed were gathered outside the door around the makeshift hearth of a beat box booming out sounds only his son could have appreciated: "My name is Adam Ace, No words do I waste, Jam my piece up in your face, It's your bitch I want to taste." Squadrons in the sky wheeled right, then left, then right again. A stellar wind bore down upon him cold and severe and it was as if his skin wore no clothes and his bones no flesh and when he looked up there were unaccountable tears in his eyes and a splendid white Cadillac drawn up to the bus stop, a fancy painted dragon curled over the trunk, several women crouching at the open windows. He passed a derelict urinating against a wall, stepped through the stream of warm piss dark as blood in the light of the sign. He glanced to his right and discovered a woman there beside him. "Hi," she said. She had on a white halter top, a pair of red leather pants, and an olive drab baseball cap just like his. "Need a date?" she asked. He inspected her face. Human eyes looked back. "Yes," he said, and she took his arm possessively in hers. She smelled of flowers and auto exhaust.

"What's your name?"

"Beanie."

He looked at her.

"No, really." She directed a long filed nail at her head. "My hat. Used to have this silly yellow propeller on top." She laughed and squeezed his arm. "Like it?"

"I can't call you Beanie."

"No problem. What do you want to call me?"

"The name your mother knows you by."

She sighed like an exasperated child. "You're weird, mister." Then, as if they'd just spent a difficult time haggling over price and she'd had to settle for less, she said, "Trish."

"Yes. That's a name."

He led her confidently around the next corner and was pleasantly startled by the apparition of his own lost hotel lurking in feigned gentility behind a couple of shedding sycamores. He escorted Trish boldly through the dim lobby, the nosy clerk dozing unaware amid a heap of ageless blossoms. Queried the parrot, "Checking out?"

After the usual struggle he forced open the door to his room and she sauntered in as if she'd only left it an hour before. "Cozy," she said.

He was scanning table surfaces to make sure he hadn't left notebook or money in view. "This place is so worn out."

"Listen, honey, compared to some of the cribs I see, it's the Hyatt Regency."

"No, I mean all of it, inside, outside, the whole place, it's a storage locker for bad meat."

She stared at him. "You straight arrows are definitely the freakiest."

In the fluorescent glare of the overhead the cosmetically enhanced lineaments of her face revealed aspects unforeseen, inestimable. "You look like somebody."

"Yeah, I know. Your mother." She went to the window, the click of stiletto heels loud and menacing in such a tiny space. She fingered a corner of the foil screen, edges of her mouth in a sarcastic curl.

"Don't touch that," he ordered in his most paternal command voice.

Her mouth shifted into full obscene smile. "Oh, I get it. You're one of those Pentagon guys, right?" She came over to where he stood, pressed her groin and breasts up against him. "Well, don't worry about me. I'm in the business of keeping secrets, too."

"The Pentagon is a blind den of gibbering idiots."

Her hand, delicately thin and ruby-clawed, went to rubbing insistently at his crotch. "CIA?" He stared down into her face, the features so fluid, metamorphic, there'd be no easy way out once you were in.

"FBI?" She had the other hand now around in back, working his ass.

"I've never been a member of a paramilitary organization of any kind."

"Okay, then, let's just see what we do have here." She went to her knees and unzipped his pants. "Uh-oh, here's something that's bursting with classified information." She held the gaping mouth of his erect penis to her ear and pretended to listen. "What's that?" she asked in mock concern. "It's hot and cramped and you're being held against your will. You want out?" She paused and looked up, hand still gripping him tightly. "Your rubber or mine? You gotta be so careful these days."

"I'm not afraid."

"Sure, mister, try it from my point of view." She got up off the floor and went to her purse. She tossed him a packaged condom. "Price of admission." She sat on a corner of the still undisturbed bed and lit a cigarette. "Listen, what's *your* name, anyway?"

He stepped out of his pants and walked into the bathroom. "Dash," he answered, studying the image of himself in the mirror. There were a few more black eyelashes on his cheek. There were round rosy sores on his chest.

"Dash?" She let out a short, nasty laugh. "So tell me about funny names. What is it, some kind of code?"

With his fingernail he could scrape skin snowflakes off the wings of his nose. He opened his mouth. There were fuzzy patches of mold on his tongue. Have you ever looked into the eyes of a goat? he asked.

"Okay, don't tell me. I know you military guys, and don't try to tell me you're not. I know military from across town."

They have my daughter, he wanted to say. Was the bottle of chloral hydrate still in his bag under the bed, or had he left it back in the country in the ashes of a junked life? We can do anything we want in here, and what would it matter finally? he said. He stood above a large turd twisting in the waters of a porcelain bowl. The spiral *is* the form of thought.

When he came out of the bathroom, Trish was reclining naked across the turned-down bed, drawing curlicues in the air with the ember of her cigarette. Her long, angular body was a precise duplicate of Trinity's. And the sons of God saw that the daughters of men were beautiful, so they took for themselves such women as they chose.

"Okay, Dash," she announced, rolling over to stab out the cigarette, "let's see just how fast you really are."

She grunted and groaned on cue for him, whispering furiously into his ear, and when it was over, she sat up cross-legged against the peeling wall and smoked another cigarette, as if on break from unloading heavy crates off a truck. "You liked the dirty talk, didn't you? You officer types always do."

There were yellow bruises on her legs and thin ugly scars down her arms.

"I want to do it like dogs," he said.

She shrugged. "Bow-wow."

There was a place he had to get to, the urging of the car over the final hill, past the last peaking into a true end, clarity of an alternate order, stationary, whole, unimaginable. He looked up at the specter of himself doubled in the dim bureau mirror against the far wall, stripped, flushed, kneeling as if in prayer, and plugged securely into the soft socket of a trusting ass upraised just for him. "I love you," he said. His blood gathered into a fist, punched through the bounds of his body.

He opened his eyes, though he had not yet been asleep, converging on the parallel tubes beaming down from a yellowy ceiling, the once white impasto shattered like a windshield into a black-veined web that seemed to pulsate with the rhythms of human breath. Little cigar-shaped apricot objects darted about just ahead of his glance, afterimages of the fluorescents overhead. He felt as if his insides had been scraped clean of residue, an odd tepid sensation neither sweet nor sad, simply different. His hand went out, encountered the momentary surprise of adjacent flesh, nerves measuring, remembering. He turned onto his side to look, to fill all that new inner space with the splendor of light descending in gentle sheets, fabricating a pair of flawless buttocks in layer upon layer of gold leaf.

He opened his eyes, though he no longer slept, to discover the tubes off, the room in total darkness, and this Trish perched like a bird on the end of the bed, the penlight from his bag stuck in her mouth. All he could see were radiant teeth, a disembodied grin of phosphorescent bone.

He opened his eyes on hands of orange, hands of yellow, climbing agile as monkeys up the flowered drapes. A black mist swept dramatically across the ceiling. He could smell the wood laughing as it went up. He rolled over. She was gone. The empty cashbox lay upside down on the already warm floor. Pulling on his pants, he ran to the door. The wall behind him cackled and blazed. Out in the corridor a gray-bearded bald man hobbled up, clutching a foam fire extinguisher. He was wearing a strikingly immaculate white terrycloth robe, and his small blue eyes were dancing with either the luster of alcohol or the tenacious vigilance of the mad. The man held a crooked forefinger to pursed lips, signaling hush, then with a conspiratorial hunch of the shoulders, mouth trembling in an expression of suppressed glee, he pointed crazily upward. Dash raced down the hallway and on up the murky stairwell, two steps at a time, flight after flight, and crashed on through a battered metal door onto the roof of the hotel and the manifestation of a dawn for the end of time.

His bare feet padded unfeeling over the droppings, the nails, the cinders, the nasty rosettes of glass from smashed wine bottles. He could neither speak nor call to mind the simplest word. The sky was on fire, a gyrating compass of flame. The big blue lid had popped open, and all the treasure denied us for so long was raining down, an incarnation of perfect benevolence, an outpouring of M31. It was what he expected, it wasn't what he expected. Packets of radiant energy rippled in ticklish waves over his face, burnishing the skin, playing nerves like guitar strings. He was aware of the changes in pressure, the subtle variation in weight of each distinct color, and the not unpleasant sensation of heat building on the receptive surface of his body. It was the day the stars came out, it was fireworks forever, it was the Fourth of July on Labor Day, it was special effects for everyone. A shower of illuminated disks, haloes, coronas, blotted out the sun, and against a searing expanse of unbearable red a storm of silver flakes, glittering like mica, fell over the stunned marble of the entombed city. As susceptible as any primate to the seductions of flashing and blinking, he stood transfixed to the melting roof, a charged antenna of hair and skin. Hundreds of incandescent ships in all the known shapes and sizes went shuddering diligent as electric bugs, a harmonized proficiency, spinning the air into beams and girders of pure color, condensing majestically, inevitably—beauty as revelation—into an overreaching lattice of burning crystal. And the sound of their passage was the sound of massed voices lifted in ecstatic song. And all around there were winged creatures with peeled heads and lidless eyes and chattering tongues. And the rivers of light cascaded down, flooding the floor of the earth. He looked up and high above his craning head was an immense crown of red and blue and green and yellow winking in unison like a ring of painted mouths opening and closing, a slip away from the discovery of speech, and he saw lowering through a wide funnel of light the platinum hull of the mother ship and he could see outside and inside simultaneously and wherever he looked was a whiteness of such intensity as to scorch the eye though vision persisted, miraculously, beyond pain and the loss of line and tint, deep into the nova furnace at the heart of matter where, amid the rush and roil of eternal fission, a form was assembling, moving toward him out of a cloud, the resplendent triangular head of a giant being with great obsidian eyes in which his own insignificant reflection was sucked instantly away into the infinite.

Then he realized this head was speaking to him in a telepathic language based on units of intuition rather than words and into the private honeycombed spaces of his body always just out of reach of booze or food or sex there came a thick welling of sweet oil, of goodness. The light grew on him until it pierced his eyes and he held up a hand and could see right through it. Other figures approached then out of the flux, smaller, more human shapes with faces he could recognize and yes, Trish was indeed here and behind her Dot and Trinity and Dallas and Edsel and little Zoe and Maryse and her Mignon and Gwen and her Beetle and others, too, the music of a vast intelligence enveloping all like a warm fluid. Then a hatch dropped open in this illuminated egg overhead and he couldn't help it but tears fell onto his cheeks and buoyant with rapture he stepped out to greet the beginning of his real life and the big silken ship started getting bigger and bigger but without moving because he was moving, weightless at last, going up and up and up. Hey, he could fly. It was amazing. He was light.

ALWAYS ALONE, SHE'D COME IN her clumsy waddle down to the beach late in the day when fun seeking was ebbing with the light and all the surfers and sun worshippers, most of them kids not much older than herself, were already packing up their sandy towels and wrinkled tubes of cream for tomorrow's party, a few minutes less for each outing now, Fall's paring knife well into its work. The regulars, of course, knew her by sight, that small pale face appearing vampirishly at dusk, but they found her as easy to ignore as an abandoned lifeguard's chair or the half-buried antlers of weathered driftwood, aware in an elemental way that even if one bothered to approach her, there would be no response.

She took her place on one of the tall dunes, her dune, land at her back, and gazed steadily westward, drawing tufts of long grass between her fingers, a little girl atop a toadstool of sand. The sea on these vigil evenings was gentle and gray, the shade of the darker gulls, and the touch of salt air a modest rush on her cheeks, a brushing of down. She liked to sit quietly and watch the sun flame out, the great ball growing ever larger, ever redder, as it was delivered with satisfying punctuality to the briny absolution of the Pacific and the waves foamed like milk on the shore and the birds swooped and cried. There was a special clarity to these moments she absorbed gratefully as a plant takes on light, her mind so stripped, so clean, scraps of the past blew through it like litter down an empty street. She had wept for Beale, but no more. And as for the others, recall what the sheriff said: they just up and disappeared. Up: that was the word. The world was a place of shadow and mystery which time, one poor sputtering bulb, could only darken and distort. But she wasn't supposed to brood. There was a certain look she'd carry back to the house her mother recognized at once and would make her sit on the living room floor, shades drawn, pressing a crystal to her forehead, rechanneling, endlessly rechanneling.

On the beach her restless fingers, never far from her belly, slipped furtively up under one of these ugly tentlike blouses she would always hate, to stroke in widening wonder this extraordinary swelling that shifted, she swore, in secret sympathy with the tide. And sometimes as the sky contracted, primaries washing to pastels, and bled away into space, she'd find herself smiling goofily for no apparent reason. The faces, of course, were always there, out at the edge, a lingering gallery of faces in variously detailed states of composition, the putative fathers, so many, some not even human, but what did that matter now? She rubbed at her hard belly with a mystic's innocent faith, utterly certain after all that even as the planet tilted into darkness there was ripening beneath the caresses of her gypsy fingers a globe of skin swimming with colors of astonishing beauty never quite seen before in these particular combinations, colors the future would need to fill in between the lines, whether on this world or on out to the stars.